SANCTUARY

Branwell Brontë – unexhibited artist, unacknowledged writer, sacked railwayman, disgraced tutor and spurned lover – finds himself unhappily back at Haworth Parsonage. There he must face the disappointment of his father and his three sisters, whose own pseudonymous successes – allegedly kept secret from him – are only just becoming apparent. With his health failing rapidly, his literary aspirations abandoned and his once loyal circle of friends shrinking fast, Branwell lives in a world of secrets, conspiracies and seemingly endless betrayals.

SANCTUARY

SANCTUARY

by

Robert Edric

Magna Large Print Books
Long Preston, North Yorkshire,
BD23 4ND, England.

British Library Cataloguing in Publication Data.

Edric, R
Sanctuary.

A catalogue record of this book is
available from the British Library

ISBN 978-0-7505-4254-8

First published in Great Britain in 2014 by Doubleday
an imprint of Transworld Publishers

Copyright © Robert Edric 2014

Cover illustration by arrangement with Transworld Publishers

Robert Edric has asserted his right under the Copyright,
Designs and Patents Act, 1988 to be identified as the author of
this work.

Published in Large Print 2016 by arrangement with
Transworld Publishers

Magna Large Print is an imprint of Library Magna Books Ltd.

Printed and bound in Great Britain by
T.J. (International) Ltd., Cornwall, PL28 8RW

For

Beverley Forrest
Steeton, Keighley

and

Lynn Knowles
Hipperholme, Halifax

Guard your good name. My own given names imprison me with their history, and are serpent and lamb to me. Some would say my very nature is born of them – I am betrayed by my instincts and damned by my desires. It was ever thus.

Patrick Branwell Brontë
Letter to Joseph Leyland, February, 1848

Haworth, West Yorkshire, 1848

1

I met a pack man on Sober Hill, leading a string of Galloways and carrying half a load himself. I watched him come towards me over the brow of the high slope, following the line of blocks at his feet. I could hear his panting at a distance, the wet rasping sound mixed with the clatter of his ponies' hooves. Seeing me ahead of him, the man raised his hand to his eyes and studied me before coming on.

He stopped a few yards short of me and let his pack fall to the ground. He took out a cloth and wiped his face. He was a short man, sturdy and with broad shoulders and a curved back. It seemed an effort for him to stand straight and face ahead. I had seen him often enough before, but had never spoken to him or learned his name.

I commented on the day to him, but he only shrugged, as though the day and its weather, its distances and hardships were of no concern to him. He clucked to his animals and they too stopped walking, lowering their heads to pull at the rough sedge all around us. The man watched them for a moment and then spat heavily at his feet.

'Where are you coming from?' I asked him.

He nodded over his shoulder. 'Colne way. And before that, Burnley and Nelson.'

'And headed for Leeds?' I said.

'"Headed"?' he said, amused by the word. 'It's one of the places I'm going to.'

'Cloth?' I said, indicating the ponies, and already regretting all this effort of conversation.

'Unmade kersey,' he said. 'For finishing in the mills. Leeds. Some to Bradford.'

The dozen or so animals moved slowly around us as they foraged, and again the man watched them.

'I had near to sixty at one time,' he said absently. 'No call now.' And as though on this cue, we both turned at the whistle of a train passing in the far distance.

I looked beyond him and saw the faint ribbon of smoke rising above the horizon. I alone followed the course of the invisible engine.

It was a common enough complaint of the local pack men that the railways had killed their trade.

'My father before me had a hundred animals,' he said. '*His* father a hundred more.'

'Why do you persist?' I asked him. I did nothing now to conceal my lack of interest in what he was saying.

He shrugged and said, 'Because I know

nothing else,' and then, 'And because I have three sons.' He looked back in the direction he had come, as though expecting to see these three following him along the same hard path.

I guessed him to be forty, but it was difficult to tell because of the way he had been moulded by his loads. I had seen the same in the local miners – old men who had washed themselves back to pale, clean boys of thirteen.

He dug with his foot at the block upon which he stood. 'Buried,' he said. 'They get half the use they once did.'

'Less, I should imagine.'

'If you say so.'

Disused, the stones either became overgrown or sank into the ground and disappeared for ever. Around us, pale paths crossed the hillside and moor in all directions.

'They should pull them back up and keep them in order,' he said. 'They have an obligation.'

'"They"?' I said to him.

'The Authorities. Bye-laws. The men responsible.' It was a vapour of reasoning. First the canal through the bottom, and now the railways spreading faster than the planners could plot their lines and the navvies swing their picks.

One of the ponies came close to us and

pushed its head into the man's side. He rapped it with his knuckles, causing it to snort and shy away from him.

'There's no need for–' I began to say.

'No need for what?' he said angrily. 'In six months it'll get more than a slap on its head. And not just this one.'

'I see,' I said.

'I very much doubt that. Your sort never do. Or if you do, then you're careful to see only what you want to see.'

I was alarmed by this sudden hostility and took a step away from him.

'My sort?' I said.

He grinned at me. 'Your sort. You're the parson's son. Over in Haworth. That suffering man.'

'Then you know me?' I said.

He smiled again at the clumsy remark. 'Oh, everybody knows *you*,' he said. He wiped a hand across his mouth.

Neither of us spoke for a moment. The perishing east wind rose around us.

'Do you ever wonder at it?' he said eventually.

'At what?'

'All this newness and change, all this...' He tailed off, suddenly uncertain of himself – though whether at what he wanted to say or his reason for saying it to me in particular, I could not be sure.

'Sometimes,' I said.

'Everyone talks forever of "progress",' he said.

'Meaning they speak of it most when they profit from it most?'

He nodded. 'And people like you and me, we are the men pushed aside and left only to watch and then made to applaud all these other men's successes.'

I wanted to tell him to speak for himself, to leave me out of his tightening bundle of despair. But nothing I might have said – none of my denials – would have convinced him, and so I stayed silent.

'What do you do?' he said. 'Your work. You were never educated, so you cannot sit on your father's easy cushion.'

My father's easy cushion?

'No,' I said. 'Besides, it was never my calling.'

'So?'

'I used to work on the railway,' I said. 'I have been a tutor to private households.' *I was once an artist.*

'I meant what do you do *now?*' he said. The words were their own answer, a buffer to my slowing engine of a life.

'Now I merely persist and endure,' I said grandly.

'And what's that, then – "endure"?'

'At present, my prospects appear–'

'To be exactly what they are,' he said, grinning again. 'Pointed downwards and running fast.'

'If you say so,' I said. It seemed to me now that he believed I had come up on to that cold hillside with the sole purpose of confronting him there, and of providing him with an outlet for his own scorn and disappointment in the world.

'If *I* were your father...' he began to say.

'Believe me, the man has no comfortable life.'

'I heard he was blinded by work and worry.'

'A cataract,' I said. 'Long since remedied.'

'All that close Bible reading and such.'

'He works tirelessly for the good of his parishioners,' I said, feeling suddenly weary.

'No one doubts that. Not like Colshaw over at Bacup, who should be hanged for the men he's killed.'

'Killed? I'm certain he's done no such thing.' I had seen Caleb Colshaw three months previously, delayed in Haworth by bad weather, sitting in our parlour, blocking the fire and licking his lips at the sight of my sisters.

'I meant all the men, women and children he's turned away from his door, all those he's denied the Church's charity,' he said.

'These are hard times for everyone.'

'Not for the likes of Caleb Colshaw they're not.'

Nor, presumably, for my father or for me.

A second whistle sounded and he again raised his head. 'The word in Colne is that you stole their money,' he said. 'The railway.'

'An accounting discrepancy for which I was held responsible, and for which I bore full responsibility,' I said.

'They say that, too.'

'And believe what they choose?'

'You know Colne.'

'And you?' I asked him. 'What do you believe?'

'I daresay it hardly matters one way or the other,' he said. 'You take to or against a man for no good reason whatsoever. Besides, it seems to me that you've taken against yourself hard enough these past few years not to care overmuch for the opinions of other men, and especially not the likes of me.'

'My name is on the Railway List awaiting a suitable availability,' I said. 'Surely that must tell you something.'

'And until that appointment's made, I daresay it tells *me* exactly what it tells you,' he said. Then he made the clucking sound again and his ponies formed their walking line. He watched them settle into their stride ahead of him. 'They could come and go on these paths without me to lead them,' he said.

And with that he finally left me and followed his animals. He walked along my own path home, but it was beyond me to accompany him, and so I waited where I stood and watched him go. In the distance, the fading trails of smoke and steam hung in the cold air like the smudged lines of a chalk drawing.

2

A week later, when the snow had finally gone from the lower roads, I went to find Leyland in his new studio. Swan Coppice was a much smaller place than his old works, and cramped – filled with old furniture from a previous tenant – its floor crowded with Leyland's own unfinished and unsold work. I had spent the previous night in Halifax, chiefly at the Talbot and later at the Cock, where I had fallen asleep and been left undisturbed until two hours previously. Nicholson had woken me and told me how much I owed him – how much I *still* owed him. It was a debt, he insisted, that had risen by a considerable amount the previous evening. I searched my pockets for what little I still possessed and handed this over to him. He spread the coins in his palm and said they didn't amount to the smallest part of what I owed. When I contested this, he said flatly that he would send his bill direct to my father, silencing me in an instant and forcing me to make yet another of my empty promises.

In truth, I had gone to find Joseph so that when my absence from home was later raised, I might tell my father – or, more likely, Charlotte, my true gaoler – that I had spent the night with him and his family.

It was a month since our last encounter, and upon my arrival Leyland was surprised to see me, and wary too. I made a joke of the early hour, knowing that whatever I told him was belied by my dishevelled appearance. I began to explain myself, but he held up his hand to me.

'Where?' he said.

'The usual haunts.'

'And in the company of?'

I listed those few I could remember.

'They take advantage of you,' he said. 'Of your good nature and generosity.' It was a kindness on his part; these days, the opposite was more likely true.

'What little remains of either,' I said. 'Besides, I was a wealthy man at the start of the evening. Beresford still employs the maid from Oxenhope.'

He laughed and cupped his hands to his

23

chest. 'Dancing around you all night, diverting your senses and shortchanging you.'

'All part of what we are,' I said.

He came to me then and put his arms around me like the steadfast friend he was.

'I should have contacted you sooner,' I said.

'I heard you were overtaken by events,' he said, and held me firmer for a moment.

'I should still have come. Or at least have sent word, something of an apology.'

'No need,' he said.

There was every need – even though in my own mind the cause and course of our parting disagreement was forgotten – but we were both happy in this understanding, in this slate wiped clean.

He released me and went back to the work on which he had been engaged upon my arrival.

'You're busy,' I said. I tried to sound more hopeful than I felt, looking at the room around me.

'A returned commission.' He picked a piece of shattered stone from the straw of a case. 'A mantel for Bradley Hall. William Morley, lately appointed far above his capabilities to the Circuit. He wanted marble, but I persuaded him to consider something cheaper. I had no money for what he wanted. A mantel and door mouldings. It would have been more than I'd earned in the past quarter.' He held the stone up to the light, felt its shattered edge and then let it drop back into the straw.

'Is nothing retrievable?'

'Morley cancelled the commission and then cursed himself for having listened to me in the first place.'

'This wouldn't happen if—'

'If what? If I were still in London?'

I nodded, wondering how many times I had said the same thing to him, and to what diminishing effect. A decade ago, he had been young and successful, the 'coming man'. And now he looked and behaved as though he had been stripped of everything he had once possessed. I knew well enough to say no more on the subject.

'You were seventeen,' he said unexpectedly.

'As were we all. Once,' I said, waiting for him to explain.

'When you first saw my bust of Satan. You told me at our first encounter. In the Leeds Exhibition.'

'And you yourself were only twenty-three.'

'As were we all. Once.'

'It is still the most remarkable piece of sculpture I have ever seen,' I said.

'So you forever tell me. I remember asking you how you measured the likeness when so many of my other admirers denied the existence of the man himself.'

'Perhaps I saw its inner truths and realities,' I said.

'You wondered aloud how I had achieved so much by such an age.'

'I envied you,' I said. 'It was only natural. I *still* envy you.'

He reached out and briefly held my dirty sleeve.

'You instantly became – and remain – my dearest friend,' I told him. I put my hand on his to convince him of the sincerity of this.

'And you mine. We've come through the thick and thin, the two of us, we wanderers of the borderlands.'

And again, I didn't completely understand him.

'You and I,' he said. He tapped his forehead. 'Our reason, our sanity, assaulted by ambition and promise.'

'Our bonds are our bonds,' I told him. 'However they were forged.' I went to the far side of the room and picked up a plaster hand.

'Keep it,' he said. 'I'd forgotten all about it until I came across it a few days ago.' Painted like flesh and put at a short distance, the hand would have looked severed and real. I told him I couldn't take it.

'Then Illingworth might,' he said.

I smiled at the name – another of our shared landlord creditors.

'You, too?' he said. 'How much?'

I shrugged. 'Would he take it?' I had offered the man books and other bits and pieces, all of which he had refused to tally against my own rising debt.

'I doubt it. We live in an age of money. Everything is cash. Cash, bonds, bank notes, deeds of promise.'

'You sound like Emily,' I said, causing him to laugh. He held all my sisters and especially my father in great esteem.

'Besides,' he said, suddenly brightening, 'we have triumphed over these same men before.'

Meaning that others, unable to bear our shame, had settled our debts on our behalf.

'But only because others—'

'It was still a triumph,' he insisted. 'Of sorts.'

'Of sorts,' I conceded. I scratched my nose with the finger of the plaster hand and put it back down on the bench. I watched him closely for a moment. The smile fell from his face. 'Do you honestly fear for your own sanity?' I asked him.

He sat on another case, brushing sawdust from his sleeves. 'Sometimes. It's my – our – nature. We are the men we are.'

'And you believe we would lead happier, more settled lives—'

'If we possessed more ordinary or common longings, yes. But then, of course, we would

27

be different men entirely. It's a circle of an argument, no beginning or end.'

'And if we were different men, then it wouldn't even enter our heads to consider it?'

'You see why we remain such friends,' he said. 'Is Nicholson pressing you hard for his money?'

'He thinks he is,' I said. 'The usual threats pointed in the direction of my father.'

'He does the same with me and my brother.' He searched a mound of papers, pulled out a sheet and gave it to me.

It was a print of his *Hounds*, the source of his fleeting fame.

'Geller gave it to me. He saw it in a shop in Bradford and thought it might bring me pleasure to see the piece again.'

I looked fondly at the print. 'And does it?'

'My first instinct was to tear it into small pieces and throw them in his face.'

'He will have acted with every good intention,' I said.

'I know. And it is all those small kindnesses and considerations that pierce me the deepest. Everything these days is a reminder, a loss made visible.'

'I sometimes feel the same,' I said. 'My sisters, especially.'

'They, too, mean well,' he said.

'I know. Paving the way to Hell.' I expected him to laugh, at least to smile.

'They imagine they're protecting you,' he said.

'From what, from whom?'

'You know that perfectly,' he said. He drew a bottle from the case in which the broken mouldings lay. 'I bought it yesterday. To console myself.' He blew a fine dust from the glass and I felt my throat constrict at the sight of this. 'What shall we toast?' he asked me.

'Our proud names,' I told him.

'To us, then,' he said – it was our commonest toast – and he raised the bottle to his lips, drinking several mouthfuls before passing it to me.

As I took it from him, he held my arm again and said, 'I never forget your praise for my work.'

'And I shall never forget seeing it, knowing that a man from this same place had achieved something so – so lasting.' It seemed a weak compliment and I regretted it.

'Most of it shall certainly last longer than I shall,' he said. He took back the bottle.

'Men will look at your work in the centuries to come and know you for the artist you are,' I insisted.

'I wish I shared your confidence,' he said.

And in that moment I wanted nothing more than for *him* to say the same of *me* – to say that one day, however distant and unknowable, men would look back at some lasting achievement of my own and know *me* for the man I, too, had once been.

'When will you pay Nicholson?' he said, wiping his lips on his cuff.

'When I meet him in Hell,' I said.

'At the tail end of a long queue, then,' he said. He laughed and passed the bottle back to me.

3

I came upon Charlotte in the churchyard, reading a newspaper, her face close to the print. She was startled by my arrival and looked around us before speaking to me.

'Patrick Reid has been hanged in York,' she said. She held up the drawing of the hanged Mirfield murderer. It was clear to me that she was remembering her happy time at Roe Head with the Wooler sisters. 'He looks very like you,' she said.

I looked more closely at the dead man's face.

'Nothing like,' I said, though there was some resemblance. 'Besides, good riddance to him.'

'I once dreamed that *you* were hanged,' she said.

'On what grounds? Something truly

heinous and memorable, I hope.'

'Don't joke about it. You were hanged and only I saw you there. That's all I can remember.'

'You sound as though you believe it's a prophecy I might one day fulfil,' I said.

Taking back the paper, she folded it small and pushed it into her apron pocket.

'He drew large crowds,' she said. 'Reid. Even his friends and associates said he was ever a fast man, always chased for his debts and surviving day to day on tit-bits.'

I told her she was making herself plain enough to me and she bowed her head in a kind of apology.

'Look,' she said, pointing to the bank across the lane.

I looked and saw the first snowdrops there, early this year.

'Mary's tapers,' she said. It was what our father called them when his parishioners brought them into the church for him. Aunt B said she had seen the flowers in bloom before Christmas in Cornwall's warm zephyrs.

A man and woman passed us by and greeted us. The woman seemed unwilling to acknowledge me, and the man, having spoken to me, was reluctant to say any more while in her company. The woman's skirts trailed on the wet ground and were stained to her knees.

31

When they had passed, Charlotte said, 'The crowd in York declared the day a holiday. Forty arrests were made for disorderly behaviour.'

'And did the condemned man declare his repentance?' I asked her.

'At the very end.'

'Then he is saved and now he wanders freely and happily in a well-provisioned Heaven where he will never again consider murdering his fellow man.'

She shook her head at the remark.

I watched the man and woman descend the hill and turn into Lodge Street. Only a day earlier, John Brown had prompted me to return to the Fellowship there, but I had resisted his every persuasion.

'He was half an hour on the gallows,' Charlotte said. 'The crowd was filled with tray- and barrel-men.'

'They have a nose for money, that crew.'

'I suppose so. The Sheriff is calling for an end to the public audiences.'

'They say it every time,' I said.

She sat without speaking for a moment, and then said, 'I woke with a fright and soaked with sweat.'

'Earlier?'

'No – when I dreamed you hanged. It was all too real to me, and beyond bearing.'

I saw then that what she was telling me was that I was not hanged by the law in her dream, but by my own hand. I again wanted to make light of this, but could think of nothing to say. I wanted to reach out to her and to hold her, but so completely were we now sundered after the events of the past months that this, too, was beyond me. I pointed to the snowdrops, vividly white against the mud of the bank. 'You should pick some for the house,' I suggested. In spring, the bank would be all nettle and dock.

'I will,' she said, and left me to cross the lane.

Mary's tapers. Just as marigolds were Mary's gold, foxgloves Mary's thimbles, and buttercups Mary's sweat. I had learned the names as a boy, walking beside my father in those years when I was his obedient and worshipful shadow. There were others, but try as I might, I could no longer bring them to mind, and I was saddened by this – another small happiness forever denied to me.

4

The following morning I was sleeping in the kitchen when I was woken by a sudden knocking at the door and by the urgent shouting of a man calling in for my father. Before I could rise and respond to this, Emily appeared beside me and unlatched the door.

A man came directly into the room and grabbed her roughly by the arm.

'Your father, your father, we must have the parson as fast as he can come,' he shouted at her. He looked all around him as he spoke, clearly hoping to see my father already there.

Emily tried to calm him. She closed the door behind him, shutting out the sleet that blew into the kitchen. She told the man to sit down and then asked him what was so urgent. But he refused to sit. He remained agitated and insistent, and I saw then that he was barefoot, and that he wore only his trousers and a sleeveless vest, both of which were soaked and clinging to his body.

'I'm Arundel Booth,' he said. 'Arundel Booth.' As though this might explain all.

'I know who you are,' Emily told him. 'Now stand for a moment and compose yourself. I shall send for my father when I know what it is you want of him.' They all three of them protected him like this.

It always surprised me to see this side of Emily's nature, this sudden authority and rigour – like a vein of quartz running through soft rock.

The distraught man let her lead him to the chair beside me.

'Father is sleeping,' she told him. 'He was out much of the evening on Church business.'

'My daughter is close to passing beyond,' Booth said. 'Maria. Parson Brontë came two days ago. We thought she might go then. We thought she might pass beyond while in his presence and thus ease her journey into His waiting Kingdom.' He clasped his hands at the words and raised his face to the ceiling.

'I remember,' Emily said. 'I remember.'

Then the man looked at me. 'You were asleep?' he said. 'At this hour?'

I could think of nothing to say to him.

'Will he come?' he said to Emily. 'He said he would. Tell him Maria.'

'I'll fetch him,' Emily said, glancing at me, the name of our own dear lost sister hanging between us. 'Water,' she said to me, indicating the man.

There was no kettle sitting on the stove and so as she left us I poured the man a cup of water from a jug.

He took it and sat with it in his hands without raising it to his lips. I finally recognized him from the Bull and the Lion and other places.

'Haven't seen you in a while,' he said to me when we were alone, his voice now calm and low.

'I've been busy,' I told him. 'Away. Business.'

'Of course,' he said. 'Business.' He turned to the door, listening to Emily's footsteps through the house. Another door opened and closed, and afterwards there was only silence, adding to our shared discomfort.

Finally, he seemed to sag where he sat. 'We know she will die,' he said. 'It would have been best all round if it had happened while the parson was last there.'

Another of my father's solitary burdens.

I was framing my response to this when Emily came back in to us, followed by my father, buttoning up his coat.

'Maria,' Booth said immediately.

Avoiding my eyes, my father said, 'I know.' He then looked directly at me and told me to accompany him.

Booth started to protest at this, and my father held up his hand to silence him. 'I'm not well,' he said. 'My son will be of some practical assistance.' It seemed his greatest concession to me. 'Stir yourself,' he said to me, indicating my unlaced boots and my own coat on the floor beside me. It was clear to me that he would brook no protest whatsoever in front of the man.

Booth, prompted back to urgency, put down his cup and went to the door, pulling it open and letting the sleet back into the room.

Emily suggested to my father that perhaps I alone should accompany the man and then report back to him, but this too he dismissed. She gave him his gloves and fastened his scarf for him, taking off his hat and tying the scarf over his head. She told him that his hat would only blow off in the strong wind and then busied herself fastening his buttons while my father complained of how ridiculous he would look.

'Then look ridiculous,' she told him. There was both humour and affection in the words.

Booth was by then already outside and rushing home.

'Stubbing Lane,' my father said to me, waiting as I pulled on my own coat. And then he left without me. It was a journey of a few hundred yards.

I waited for Emily to help me as she had helped him, but she kept her distance from me. She told me to hurry.

'I'll only get in the way,' I told her. 'Besides, how am *I* ever going to speed anyone's ascent into *His* waiting Kingdom?'

'Perhaps by swallowing your own disbelief and cultivated cruelty,' she said.

I was taken aback at the words.

'Go,' she said. 'Not for the man or his daughter, but for Father.'

I needed no further urging and ran out after him.

I caught up with him at the boundary wall. I put my hand on his arm and supported him, slowing his pace. The wind and sleet took my breath away.

'I didn't realize you were home,' he said to me, barely audible above the wind.

'I was told not to disturb you,' I said.

'My guardians. We are both fortunate.'

'I know,' I said.

After that, neither of us spoke until we reached the cottage on Stubbing Lane. A lamp was lit at the door, Booth beside it, beckoning us forward. All he wanted was the absolving consolation of my father's presence.

Entering the room, my father whispered to me, 'Low fever.'

'Typhus?'

'He's lost three other children over the past' – he stopped to make a calculation – 'eighteen months.' He was saddened by the realization and shook his head.

The dying girl lay on a pallet in front of a poor fire. She can have been no more than four or five. Smoke hung in a pall across the small room; I could feel it in my eyes and taste it on my lips. The girl's mother sat beside her, with four other children gathered around her, all of them moving closer to her at our appearance.

My father went to the dying girl and lowered himself beside her. He took out his small Bible – his 'visiting' Bible – opened it and began murmuring to himself.

The mother wiped the girl's wet face with her fingers.

Still at the doorway, Booth said, 'Are we in time?' and waited for the woman to nod. 'I ran all the way there and back,' he said, letting everyone know that he had played his part in the day's drama.

The low fire added scarcely any heat to the room. Its ashes lay scattered in the hearth and on the bare boards.

The mother leaned back from her dying daughter and put her arms around her other children. I thought they might cry, but none of them did – nor the woman herself – all of them watching closely as my father continued his praying.

'Is she being called?' Booth asked him.

My father raised a hand to him.

'Only, you must be able to tell these things better than most,' the man said.

My father lowered his hand and then beckoned me to him. 'Wipe her face,' he told me. He took a cloth from the woman's lap and gave it to me. He saw me hesitate. 'Wipe it.'

I did as I was told. The girl's pale flesh was slick and shining with the sweat of her brow and cheeks. The shift she wore was sodden, and her blanket too. I was careful not to lean too close to her, but I could hear clearly her dry, laboured breathing.

'Is she...' I whispered to my father, and he nodded once. To the mother, he said, 'She will soon be at peace and at her rest.' He smiled at her and the woman responded with a smile of her own. She held a hand over her mouth.

'And in His Kingdom?' she said.

'Better than that,' my father told her. 'In His *arms*, in His Kingdom.'

'Then we shall see her ascend,' Booth announced grandly.

'Whatever you see or don't see, you will *know*,' my father said. He leaned even closer to the girl and touched his fingers to her brow. She stirred beneath him and then grew calm. She breathed more evenly for a few moments and then fell silent. Her final breath emerged as a long sigh, and when it was finished and as her lips parted slightly, my father laid his whole hand over her small face.

'Has she gone?' Booth asked him.

My father began to recite the Lord's Prayer. When he'd finished, I rose from where I knelt and stood behind him.

The woman explained to her other children what had just happened. She thanked my father and said she was grateful to him for having arrived so quickly.

'No,' my father told her. 'It is I who should be thanking *you*.'

'An innocent soul safely delivered into His care,' Booth said. 'She needed no time to repent even a solitary sin.' He seemed almost proud of his daughter's achievement.

'Quite,' my father said. He rose stiffly to his feet, holding out his hand for my assistance.

The smallest of the three children, a boy, started to cry, and Booth told him to stop, and then to come and kiss his dead sister while she was still in a state of grace.

My father indicated to me that we should leave, and as we went the woman again called her thanks to us.

At the door, Booth held my arm briefly and whispered that he would thank me properly when we next met. I was only grateful that my father was already outside and ahead of me and that he did not hear the man's sorry promise.

5

The next day I entered the parlour to find Charlotte and Anne standing by the hearth, the pair of them holding a letter, from which Charlotte was reading. She fell silent at my appearance, and quickly folded the letter and held it to her side.

'*Another* private communication?' I said.

Neither of them answered me. The dull ticking of the mantel clock filled the room. It was three in the afternoon and already dark. The sky, though dry and windless now, had not brightened all day.

'It is addressed to me,' Charlotte said eventually.

'And thereby denied to me,' I said. I regretted the words the instant I'd spoken them.

Charlotte looked hard at me. 'Perhaps you imagined it was a letter for you,' she said. 'Another letter from that woman, perhaps?'

At this, Anne flicked Charlotte's arm and said, 'Don't.'

I regretted my remark more than ever at seeing this, at seeing again in that sudden instant and in that solitary gesture how we

42

all now stood.

I expected Charlotte to apologize – if not to me, then at least to Anne – but instead she was set on her usual course.

'No,' she said firmly to Anne. 'Let him know it. How long must we indulge him in his fantasy? How many times does a grown man have to be told, to be warned of the delusion in which he lives, of the destruction upon which he is set?' Her voice was raised and she stopped suddenly, panting slightly.

'I only meant...' I began, uncertain of what I might say to her.

'You only meant that you continue to crave her need of you, that you hang on the woman's every breath, however weary of you and your pathetic attentions she herself has now grown.'

Again Anne touched her sister's arm in an effort to temper her, and this time Charlotte responded to the gesture.

'I know what she thinks of me,' I said.

'No,' Charlotte said, her voice lower. 'You *don't* know. That's my exact point. How many times does it need to be said to you? The woman *used* you. She used you to her own ends solely to give herself a romantic thrill. A love affair with a much younger man. A thing nurtured in the dark, and which died the instant it was exposed to the light of public scrutiny.'

43

'She–'

'And most of all to the scrutiny of her wealthy, failing husband.'

'Who is now dead almost two years,' I said, knowing this was only an echo of the argument I had once believed it to be.

'And who still governs her life to the last penny. *Her* life and the lives of her – *his* – children. You are *nothing* compared to any of that. Nothing. You can give her nothing she desires that her wealth cannot provide.'

'I gave her everything once,' I said, but more to myself than to her.

'Precisely,' Charlotte said. *'Once.'*

Anne, who had worked at Thorp Green beside me, and who knew my situation better than most, cast me a sympathetic look.

'We do understand,' she said to me.

I imagined for a moment that she was about to come to me – two paces, three – across that dim room and embrace me; that they might even both come to me and enclose me completely. There had been a lightning-struck oak at Thorp Green, held upright within an iron girdle. Now *I* was that oak and they perhaps my supports.

But neither of them moved, and I saw that, as usual, Anne followed Charlotte's lead. Anne, too, had retreated hurt from the place, and it still grieved me to know that the blame was wholly my own.

I resisted the urge to shout at Charlotte that

at least I had loved and been loved by another, and that my own current fantasy was nothing compared with her own hopeless longing. But whatever I said would have wounded her too deeply and so was beyond me. Besides, she already read my thoughts on the Belgian, and this was enough for both of us.

'I'm sorry,' I said eventually. 'I didn't mean to appear so ... so...'

Anne came to me finally and held me for a moment. I looked at Charlotte over her shoulder. She, too, signalled her apology to me. We were all so closely bound by our smallest hurts and pleasures.

Anne stepped back from me. My coat was damp.

'I was outside,' I told her. 'Earlier.'

'It stopped raining before dawn,' Charlotte said.

My lie signified nothing.

'I sometimes feel as if I am an intruder in my own home,' I said to her. 'I go out into the world and then I seem forever to return with my tail between my legs and licking my wounds.'

Charlotte smiled at the words, some distant memory perhaps fanned, like embers, unexpectedly back to life.

'You return because this is the only place you can truly recover yourself,' she said. 'It's the same for all of us. The world and all its countless watching eyes and pointing fingers and gossiping mouths is held at bay by these walls. None of us feels any different. We *all* know why we return. It is the same cold wind that forever blows us all back here.'

'And the same ever-welcoming father who forever awaits our return,' Anne said.

'And that,' Charlotte said.

'And I imagine he rejoices more at the sight of some being blown back to him than others,' I said.

'You were never the Prodigal Son,' Anne said.

'Once,' I said. 'Perhaps. But that was a mould long since broken.'

'Besides,' Charlotte said, 'where else would we go?'

The clock on the mantel chimed the quarter.

'We all of us once imagined life might be different,' Anne said hesitantly in the following silence. It seemed a sad and unanswerable admission.

But Charlotte replied to it by saying, 'But that is all life is – a succession of imaginings. Imagined opportunities, paths taken, paths not taken, plans, preparations and longings, some of which come to fruition, many of which do not.'

'And in my case, all of which crumble and turn to dust in the instant I attempt to close my grasp on them,' I said. I had intended the remark to release the room's tensions, but was not successful.

'Father says that, whatever our circumstances, we are all still bound for Redemption,' Anne said, unable to suppress a smile.

'A light in the dark,' Charlotte said absently.

I remembered her tales of the lighthouse she had visited with Ellen Nussey at Flamborough Head. Hidden somewhere between the pages of a book in her room were her sketches of the structure and of the rocky shore over which it stood watch. There was always talk of summer holidays in those short days, most of which, we all knew, would come to nothing. For myself, I could only remember Scarborough and the scandal there.

'Will it be made clear to us, do you think?' Anne said, her voice changed. 'Our Redemption?'

'Of course it will,' Charlotte told her.

'Not to me,' I said. 'I am already too far beyond salvation.'

Charlotte shook her head at this. 'No,' she said sharply. 'That is just something you say, not something you truly believe. You say it to protect yourself. We will all, in our own separate ways, be saved.'

I wish she had not added this qualification. I thought frequently of my own salvation, of what it might entail – of what, surely, it would one day demand of me.

In the hallway, Keeper began barking at someone passing by outside. We waited for a knock at the door, but none came.

'Counting the child yesterday, there have been nine deaths in the past week,' Anne said. 'Nine.'

'And all souls saved?' I said.

'Oh, undoubtedly – every single one.'

'So you see,' Charlotte said to me. She tucked the folded letter between the buttons of her blouse.

'I love you all,' I said brightly.

'Of course you do,' Anne told me. 'We are your sisters; of course you love us.'

'And I your brother.'

'And you our brother.'

Despite all adversity, we were still clothed and nurtured by our lives, still made upright and whole and steadfast by them.

6

'Louis Philippe is dethroned,' Emily said to me later that same afternoon. She was excited by the news, which she had just heard from someone in the street, and she stood for a moment with her hands on her knees to catch her breath.

'Believe what the newspapers say,' I said, 'and the whole of Europe is in flames and turmoil. What, do you imagine for an instant that the same rioting and overthrowing will some day happen here?'

'There is forever unrest,' she said. 'The factory workers are constantly–'

'"Unrest",' I said dismissively. 'Precisely. Unrest. Where does *that* come on the scale of uprising, overthrowing and revolution?'

'It *could* happen,' she insisted, annoyed by my dampening of her enthusiasm.

'I daresay,' I said. 'But it will be a light shower or two compared with the thunderstorms endlessly raging over there. The French never settle. One thing always leads to another. They imagine they can go on and on with all these alterations until everyone is happy and that they can all then settle back into their lives and afterwards pile up unremembered in their graveyards.'

A month ago, my father had preached against elaborate burials. Charlotte had copied out his sermon for the printer.

'Besides,' I said to Emily, 'there is no real contagion in these things. Fires that burn on the horizon, and all that.'

She took off her cape and boots and then pushed past me into the kitchen. She took a parcel from her pocket and unwrapped it to reveal bones and scraps of gristle.

'For Keeper,' she said.

'I hope you aren't encouraging the man,' I said, meaning the butcher. I fixed a serious look on my face.

She reddened at the suggestion. 'I say "Good morning" to him, that's all.'

'There are others here who would make a meal of that.' I pointed to the scraps of gristle.

'Very amusing,' she said, and then held her fist to me.

I wanted to ask her a thousand questions. I wanted to ask her about her writing, and whatever else she did secretly now. I wanted to ask her if it was true what I had recently overheard Charlotte telling Anne – that Emily had not written a single line of poetry since she had seen her earlier efforts published and then completely ignored. I wanted to ask her if it was why she now turned her back so fiercely on the world.

Keeper came into the kitchen and, smelling the bones, leaped up on to the table. Emily quickly pulled him down and scolded him. The dog stood in the doorway, growled softly at her for a moment, and then turned and walked away.

'Perhaps that's why the Queen has so many homes,' I said. 'To hide from all the home-grown revolutionaries.'

She rewrapped the small parcel.

50

'It must be a great burden to you, to believe yourself so all-knowing,' she said to me.

Her words sucked the air from the small room.

Then she followed her dog back out into the hallway, singing as she went.

7

A year and a half has passed since the day I encountered my father in his study and he looked up from his book, considered me where I stood, closed the book, laid his hand upon it, beckoned me in to him and then took the volume up again and gave it to me.

'Your sisters' work,' he said, taking off his spectacles and rubbing his eyes. 'Poetry. They have seen fit to publish their own poems.' His voice was low and he averted his gaze from me as he said all this.

It surprises me still to see how minutely some events remain etched on my mind, while others have gone completely from my memory over that same time. I remember every painful detail of those few minutes in my father's company – his awkward revelation – and yet whole weeks, months even, continue to elude me, regardless of my efforts to recall them.

I wish I could say that I felt the burn of that small book in my palm, but instead I felt only a chill of shock, and an emptiness, and for a moment I struggled with my response to his words. It was a small volume, thin, poor-quality paper, duodecimo, and with long primer type. It was bound in bottle-green cloth with a geometrical design of no significance, and with its price of four shillings printed boldly on the cover. I remember that I considered this last a common and unnecessary detail. The word 'Poems' was spelled in gold, adding a lustre, whatever their true worth. I read the names my sisters had chosen for themselves, and saw immediately the secrets and the disguise they contained.

I felt a numbness in my fingers.

'At their own expense?' I asked my father.

'A London publisher. They have supported the venture, yes. Charlotte tells me it is the usual way.'

'Of course,' I said.

'Did you know of their enterprise?' He looked up at me for the first time since I had taken the book from him.

'Of the poems,' I said.

'But not of their collection into a volume and its publication?'

The word 'No' dried in my mouth.

'Perhaps...' my father said, but then he too

fell silent.

'I hope what little they have invested they will see returned,' I said. I opened the book and looked more closely at its small print.

'It is a difficult thing to read,' my father said. 'My eyes tire more and more easily. I'm afraid I can make no estimation whatsoever of the quality or value of the poems themselves.'

I wanted to tell him to stop making these painful excuses to spare my feelings.

My translation of Ovid had been coming and going from various unresponsive publishers for the previous five years. It had once been my greatest hope.

'You knew nothing of it at all?' my father said.

A month earlier, Searle Phillips had asked me if I knew of the Bells and I had told him that I did not. He had been sent a copy of the book for review in the *Leeds Times*, but said he did not consider it worthy of the effort or space. Three brothers, he said. It had become a guessing game in our small world with its endless quest for diversion. He, too, continued to praise my own published work, and I had wondered only afterwards if he had intended *me* to take the book to appraise for him. And after that I had wondered if he had *known*, and if he too was sparing my feelings by feigning ignorance.

'I would value your opinion,' my father said to me. 'Especially if you are already familiar with the contents. Perhaps you might even mark your own influence over the individual poems. You see, of course, that they have not used their own names. We are spared *that* particular attention, at least.'

I shook my head at this.

'What? You think it a secret soon revealed?'

'Searle Phillips already suspects,' I said.

'Surely not. He would have written. Surely?'

'I was with him last month.'

'And what was his opinion of the work?'

'That it was of little consequence and would fade swiftly from sight.' It was more than he had said. I pretended to read further from the book.

'And do you concur?' my father asked me.

They were my sisters, his daughters.

'It's such a difficult thing,' I said. 'Such a thing of personal taste. One man sees greatness, another only trash.' At that moment I imagined my sisters in the corridor outside, their ears pressed to the door.

'Charlotte did not ask for my blessing,' he said.

'Perhaps she believed...' I faltered, uncertain of what I wanted to say to him.

'When she told me what they had done and then gave me the actual volume, I thought at first she meant that she herself had stitched the book together, as you all once did when you were children. But then she showed me the thing more closely and said they had chosen to take their chances in the literary world.'

I almost laughed at hearing this.

'I hope they haven't brought more upon their heads than they are able to bear,' he said. 'Public scrutiny can be such a hurtful and unforgiving creature. Charlotte, perhaps, possesses the strength to withstand it – but Emily and Anne?'

'I imagine Phillips is right,' I said, 'and the whole affair and its puzzle will disappear fast enough. The bookcases of the world are already filled to bursting with poor, unread and long-forgotten poetry.'

I held the volume back to him, but he waved it away. 'Perhaps you might still read it and make a report to me,' he said.

I knew how much this would displease my sisters, Charlotte especially.

My father cleared his throat. 'I confess that it surprises me to discover it is the work of the three of them alone,' he said. 'But upon reflection I see that you might be better served by working independently of them.'

'Their anonymity...' I said, again uncertain how to proceed.

'Of course. A common enough practice, I imagine, but one of which I cannot wholly approve. Why should a man – woman – insist on presenting something of this nature to the world and then deny themselves its creator?'

'*I* should do no such thing,' I said firmly.

'Of course. A man must stand by his reputation and his word.' He glanced at the drawer in which his own printed pamphlets lay carefully collected and hidden, a respectable dust covering them all. 'And *is* there a prospect?' he said.

'Of what?' I understood perfectly what he was asking me, but needed a moment to compose my answer. 'Of my own work being finally gathered together and presented?' I said.

He nodded.

'It may all be a matter of quality to be off-set against quantity,' I said. 'Publishers work to numbered pages, financial dictates, a wayward and capricious market.'

'Hence each of *them* providing only a third of the work?'

'Precisely that,' I said. And no single one of them exposed alone and in her entirety to the world.

'Do you believe they have rushed into print where patience might have been more advisable?' he said.

'I can't say,' I told him. But my feelings were clear to him.

Of my own work, over a dozen poems had

already seen the light of day – in the *Guardian, The Times,* the *Herald,* the *Intelligencer* and the *Gazette* – and neither he nor my sisters had the first idea of my successes.

'And the volume itself?' my father said. 'The actual thing?'

I sniffed at it. 'They might have negotiated for something more handsome,' I said.

'Is the paper cheap?'

'Perhaps they were constrained,' I said. 'Everything is a gamble these days.'

'And they do all three of them come and go from their reliable employment.'

And they alone had Aunt B's legacy to squander as they saw fit.

'I must frame an honest response to them,' he said. 'Charlotte imagines I am reading the thing now. What do I know of such modern stuff? You know better than anywhere my own preferences lie.'

'It is still an achievement,' I said. 'Finding a publisher to share in the gamble.' I read the name and address on the title page.

'You think the man might one day come knocking for the balance?' he said.

'All the way from London?' I said, causing him to smile.

'I suppose not.'

'Tell them your eyes are tired,' I said. The dimly lit room was its own permanent dusk in those months. I finally handed the book back to him and he pulled open the drawer of his desk and laid it carefully inside. I saw how the tips of his fingers rested upon it before he closed the drawer and sat back in his chair.

'You notice the forenames,' he said. 'Would anyone know immediately if they were the names of men or women?'

'That, presumably, was their intention,' I said.

'A disguise within a disguise? It, too, seems ill-considered.'

Or perhaps this was Charlotte's way of pushing the other two even further behind her skirts. Her own sexless pseudonym was the first of the three, and to my mind this cannot have been a coincidence.

'Would you have dissuaded them?' I asked him. 'If you'd known beforehand what they were plotting?'

'"Plotting"? Would you put it as strongly as that?'

'Preparing, then,' I said.

'I might have advised greater caution,' he said.

'In the poems themselves?'

'Possibly. But mostly in exposing themselves to the public glare and to the sharp tongues of the critics. And worse still – to the scorn and ridicule of people they might actually know.'

Which, to my mind, was precisely what they had *not* exposed themselves to.

'And who can tell?' he said. 'Perhaps now you yourself might feel sufficiently encouraged to continue with your own efforts in that direction.' He looked at me fondly as he said this.

Efforts. In that direction.

'Perhaps,' I said. And again, the word dried in my mouth.

8

The miners are being evicted today from the small diggings above Green Holes. There are close on thirty of the men, many of whom were put out of the Hepworth and Arran mills last year. The bailiffs and land agents are set for midday. My father has petitioned the Parish Council for something to be done for the evictees – at least for them to be allowed to carry on their work until the land is finally turned to something else. The landowners, however – a bundle of the usual men, mostly far beyond shouting distance of the place – have represented themselves to the Church Commissioners in Bradford through their lawyers, pointing out that the matter is no business whatsoever of my father or the Parish Council.

Of late, all my father's sermons are built

upon the hour and the troubled times through which we are living. It is not Emily's revolution, but it is discord and trouble and hardship enough.

There is also talk of the same men facing eviction from their allotments at Lumb Foot when the new intakes there are turned to improved grazing.

Once again, the landowners point out that this is what they are – owners of the land – but my father, as usual, takes the view that a man might also possess a 'moral' right to ownership. A blind man can see the course of this argument through the courts, should it ever unwisely reach so far.

In the past, I might have argued with my father, tempered his increasingly feeble blows and wasted energy; but not now.

I was reading in the parlour when he arrived to ask me to join him on his mission to Green Holes. It was a rare morning of lucidity and clear-headedness for me, and because of this I agreed to go with him.

We were joined a moment later by Charlotte, who said she was thankful I was accompanying him. She instructed me to temper his exertions and to bring him safely home. If there was violence, she said, *he* was to be my only consideration.

'They are men of the land,' he said to me, already rehearsing his speech. 'Toilers. Men with families who will now go hungry.'

'And the landowners have the force of the Law on their side,' I said. It was what their lawyers would call an open-and-shut case.

Charlotte cast me a cold look, but said nothing.

When I was a boy, and my sisters girls, my father would repeat over and over the tales of his military drilling under Palmerston, ready to repel the French invasion which never came. This was still a great and worthy thing to him – proof, perhaps, of his having risen above the alehouse-keepers and road-builders of his forebears.

'Man is bound by so many ties,' he said now, allowing Charlotte to fasten his boots.

'They must look for work elsewhere,' I suggested. 'Like–'

'Like who?' Charlotte said sharply. She meant me.

My father, too, understood her meaning, and he silently rebuked her with a shake of his head.

'He's right,' he told her. 'The landowners *do* have the Law on their side.'

In truth, I wished he'd said nothing; his support undermined me.

'And *you* have a much higher authority,' Charlotte said.

The Lumb Foot intakes spread the full length of the bottom, and as high as Clough Hey. Even neighbouring Oakworth Moor was being enclosed and parcelled off with pasture rights already sold. The last of the common land beyond Stanbury was being divided into grass lots, and much of the standing woodland at the valley top was already under contract to the burners. Sometimes it seemed that wherever change was possible, it came.

'These are hard times hereabouts,' my father said. 'And these men are reduced to little more than slaves.'

'The diggers on Hartshead Moor were evicted last month,' Charlotte said to me. She and my father had gone to them, too. A long journey, and all on foot.

'Where the Luddites and the military once clashed,' I said, remembering another of my father's tales.

'Clashed indeed,' he said, smiling at the memory. 'But mostly those men just stood and shouted at each other and shook their fists. Today everything is different. Today there is a great failure in the land – of the factories, of the crops and the seasons, and of waged labour. And there is a failure too of faith and hope in the future.' It was a solemn, heartfelt speech and it silenced both Charlotte and me.

Eventually, I said, 'It's a hard path. To Green Holes. And a long one – almost three miles.' Neither of which was a deterrent to my father. Hartshead Moor had been three times the journey.

'Life,' my father said, 'is composed of one hard path after another. At least, most lives are – those lives worth the living.'

'You make everything plain to me,' I said, but with affection.

'And you to us,' Charlotte added, equally fondly.

It was not yet ten in the morning, and the day showed no sign of sun. The bailiffs – 'busies' as most here called them – would come with at least one constable, and the miners would be read to from a Court Order. Leeds or Bradford or Halifax would be mentioned, the courts and punishments, and the men would be intimidated into defeat before they had even begun to fight. This was not the Hartshead of thirty years ago; it was the working of the modern world, and if my father did not see it, then at least Charlotte understood it all as clearly as I did.

I had been three years old when my father told me that our already altered name was derived from the Greek word for thunder and called me his 'Thundering Boy'. This had caused my sisters great amusement, but it had caused me only pride. It had bolstered my confidence and marked my own early path ahead of me.

And only a year later he had told me that he had once been offered – and had turned down – the position of chaplain to the

Governor of Martinique. He would have lived with the man surrounded by all his suffering slaves. What might he have achieved there and in *that* society? What ills might he not have remedied there? But, in truth, my father would not have truly challenged the Governor's authority – he was far too young and unformed for all that – and would anyway have returned swiftly home. 'Martinique or Yorkshire?' he used to ask of us as children – which should he have chosen? – as though this were the greatest joke – the heathens there or the heathens here – one and the same to him and all of them crying out for his rescue and his balm.

We left soon after to go to Green Holes and the suffering miners.

Upon our return six hours later, Charlotte immediately sought me out to ask me how the day had gone, what my father had achieved amid the men.

'You can well imagine,' I told her. It had rained most of the day and the cold was in my bones. My father had stood before the fire for a few minutes and had then gone to his bed for the night, too exhausted by the excursion even to eat.

'So, a wasted journey,' she said.

'I doubt they are ever that where Father is concerned,' I said.

She thanked me for having accompanied him and for bringing him safely home. Both

Emily and Anne had gone upstairs to help him prepare for bed.

Charlotte helped me out of my own wet clothes and dried my head and chest with a warm towel. I felt like that small boy again, and she again seemed a mother to me. More balm.

9

Despite my exertions, I spent another restless night. I dreamed of my secret lost daughter. I dreamed she survived beyond the few short weeks of her hidden, precarious infancy, that she had grown, and that she and I were living together still in Broughton. There was no place in my dream for the child's mother – I shan't name her – as absent in my dreaming happiness as she has since remained in my life.

I spent long, empty and blissful days in Broughton, along the Duddon, and walking amid the fells there. I was close to men I admired, and was employed in a position that for the first time in my adult life offered me what I was starting to crave.

In my dream, my daughter was eight – the age she would have been today had she lived – and she and I were playing beside the river. She gathered flowers and brought them to me where I sat on a fallen bough. There was food and drink, and the air was charged with excitement and pleasure. She was my equal, that imaginary child, and the bond between us unseverable.

I woke in darkness from that lingering dream, and immediately regretted its passing, struggling as I came to my waking senses to retrieve something of its immediacy and joy. But this, naturally enough, was in vain, and the dream and its pleasures slipped from my mind as easily as that river drained daily from its estuary.

And instead of my child and the banks of the Duddon, I could think only of her mother and of my first visit to meet her parents at Sunny Bank. The girl herself could scarcely read. She could sign her own name, and this was a great achievement for her. Her father was a labourer, and suspicious of me and my intentions. He warned me bluntly about those intentions, and in the next breath asked me if I took a drink. I did my best to reassure him on the former.

The family and their other children were of little consequence to me, but I learned from them, and from the small society of Broughton itself, how a gentleman and a professional man might make a true place for himself in the world, how he might develop the regard of his peers and equals. I learned also what talents I truly possessed. My ad hoc education might have been a thing of no value in Leeds or Bradford, but there in Broughton, with a little dressing up, it was something of true worth.

My return from the place was a cause of great consternation. I came back under a cloud. It had altered me. *Everything* altered me in those days. It was another sharp turning on my road through life.

Once, in my private imaginings, I had called my daughter Mary, as close as I dare come without disturbing the memory of my lost sister.

I never knew the name her mother attached to that short-lived existence. Her own, probably, another of God's precious lambs, or perhaps that of *her* mother. She spoke often enough of the woman, and seemed intent on making her own life a copy of her mother's. Even now I do not know the true cause of my child's death, or even where she might be buried, were she ever considered worthy of such a thing. I can easily imagine that she was never baptized for shame, and that she was laid in unconsecrated ground as a consequence.

Another of my lessons learned at Broughton was how to turn my back completely on a gathering predicament – to turn my back and then to walk swiftly away. If only I had had some other destination in all the back-turning and walking away I have done in the years since.

For weeks following my return, my sisters quizzed me on what had happened at the Postlethwaites'. I told them everything I could remember, but avoided all mention of the girl and our involvement. I laid a false trail to the landlord's daughter, a girl called Margaret Fish. The name amused my sisters and they made a long joke of all the little fishes that might have one day been swimming around me. I laughed with them better to mislead them and to drape some comedy over the tragedy of the episode.

My father, of course, kept his disappointment to himself. I knew he felt it, that it ate at him to know, but he remained silent as my sisters' mocking inquisition ran its course.

I finally told Charlotte that I was dismissed through neglect of duty, that I had grown too fond of my other attachments. By then it was an easy enough thing for her to believe and to accept.

My questioning lasted a month, and after that they lost their interest in the matter. While it lasted, I consoled myself with the knowledge of what an explosion would roar through the house and its foundations were I ever to reveal the truth to them. And when it was finished, and my secret still intact, I saw how much would have been destroyed and lost for ever by that explosion.

In my dream, we had walked hand in hand, my growing daughter and I, past a congregation of Baptists gathered at the river's edge, and I had pulled the child swiftly away from them. Her mother's parents were of that ilk. She had asked me about the small, noisy congregation and I had told her to ignore them. I told her to look instead to the fells and the high mountains which filled the horizon ahead of us. I told her to look to these places and to find the true wonder and awe and terror of the world there. I know she did not understand me, but I said it anyway in the hope that it might at least plant a seed of appreciation in her soul. I knew her mother's parents attended a chapel overlooking the estuary, but that was all. I knew in my heart what an unsuitable match the pair of us would have made. I knew it even before that first visit to meet her family. 'Do you take a drink?' her father had asked me, and I had told him that I took it only when it was offered, when it was close at hand or when I was in funds. He laughed with me and announced that he and I were going to be great friends. I waited for him to ask me about my prospects, my lies and exaggerations well practised. I was not a virgin before Broughton, but at Broughton I felt myself for the first time to be something other than a participant in the momentary pleasure of the thing.

I see now – too late – how my time at Broughton led to a great deal of what has happened to me since. I see what delusions I began to construct, what evasions and deceits I drew around myself. I see what losses I am able to accept, and what excesses I might easily and happily indulge.

I saw by my watch angled to the moonlight that it was not yet three in the morning. One more night amid all those months of lesser nights.

There were times following my return when I would wake in this same darkness and weep for myself in uncontrollable self-pity. 'Too near pleasure for repentance and too near death for hope.' Fine words, but not a sentiment to be too closely considered first hand. I wept and I turned my back on Broughton and the lost, as-yet-unborn child I had abandoned there.

Two months later, when I was alone in the churchyard, my father came out to me, put his arm around my shoulders and told me he would do for me whatever I asked of him. He told me I could deny my troubles to everyone else, but not to him. He told me he shared my anguish. He said nothing of his own lost family or wife or small daughters, simply that he understood whatever I might be suffering. I tried to imagine how he had borne his own great losses. He told me that he felt a great sorrow for me because I could not share his belief in the Kingdom of Heaven and in every man's eventual arrival there. It surprised me to hear him say this so simply and forthrightly. My immediate concern then was that Postlethwaite might have written to him and repeated every breath of gossip and scandal that had attached to me in Broughton.

He told me there was no matter he would not discuss honestly with me, no subject upon which he would hesitate to offer good advice. I told him I knew all this already, and that I appreciated his kindness. My remark surprised him. 'Kindness?' he said. 'I am your father.' I asked him to forgive me if I had offended him, and this too was a surprise to him. His hand tightened on my shoulder and then he released me. Above us, I remember, the rooks made their usual clamour in the gusty air and the high trees, and he watched them for a moment before leaving me and returning indoors.

10

The charcoal workers have returned to the woods beyond Ponden. Some men have also come into Sladen Bottom for what little remains there. It is the first time in four years that the burners have thought the work at Ponden worth their while. I had heard in Haworth that, against all expectation, the combing trade had picked up of late, so perhaps this is what has brought the men back to us.

I went with Anne to see the men along the Sladen. I recognized some of them from years past, as did Anne, and they welcomed us to their kilns. Their arms and faces were black with their labour, and their eyes and teeth shone vividly white where they wiped themselves. Each time one of the men spat to clear his throat, he excused himself to Anne.

Having damped their kilns, several of the men came to us. It was my father's custom to go to them between Sunday services and to hold a service out in the open for the men and their families. They asked after his health now, and all of them spoke of him kindly.

One man, occupied in raking slag from a small furnace, came to us and greeted us the most warmly of them all. His name was Sam Pierce, and at his last visit my father had prayed for a full day beside the man's young, dying wife. He shook my hand and held Anne's in both his own. He told us he would send my father whatever he needed by way of wood, charcoal or cinders. Then he told us of the baby girl that had been born to his new wife.

I struggled to remember the dead woman's name.

'Melissa,' Anne said.

'The same as the girl now,' Pierce said proudly. The other men arranged themselves around him. One of them took out a pinch-beck flask, wiped his lips and drank from it before offering it to me. Anne cast me a glance, but I took a mouthful to be sociable, burning my mouth and throat on the raw spirit.

Pierce laughed at my discomfort. 'We have clean water,' he said to Anne, who insisted she wasn't thirsty. 'Charcoal,' he said. 'Pour the water through and wait for it to settle and come clear again. The most healthful drink on God's earth.'

He told us that his brother had also recently died, and that whatever it was that had killed him had run its vicious course through the man like colic through an exhausted horse.

Anne told him she was sorry for his sad loss.

'No need,' Pierce told her. 'He died ready and waiting for his Maker. You can tell your father that.' He said the funeral had lasted a week and that people had come from a hundred miles distant to attend it.

Smoke from the kilns drifted over us, but none of the men moved to avoid it, merely closing their eyes until the wind shifted again and drew the smoke away from us. Elsewhere, it lay like old snow along the lower banks.

'And you?' Pierce said to me. 'Are you bearing up?'

'The usual trials and tribulations,' I told him, making light.

He asked me about the navvies and boatmen at Luddenden Foot, and we reminisced briefly about the men we had both known. It saddened me to hear how many of those men had died or been injured in the six years since I had left the place. One man – a bargeman called Oliver Eade – had had both his legs crushed in a tunnel collapse and had died from unstoppable bleeding less than an hour later. Another man we knew had been caught between uncoupled carriages in the Leeds shunting yard and been killed. Pierce said the man's wife and children had been fetched to see him while he still lived and that he had died during a final kiss. Afterwards, Pierce said, the whole yard had stopped work and then sung a hymn. He told me I could tell my father that, too.

'How long are you here for?' Anne asked him; it unsettled her to hear these tales so plainly told.

'A good while,' he told her. 'There's going to be a lot more felling hereabouts in the coming months.'

I looked at the already sparse woodland around us.

'And not just here,' Pierce said. 'Sleepers and props fetch twice what you'd ever believe.'

Anne said that if he was in the district for some time, then he and his new wife and child were welcome to attend the church. It was her signal to me that it was time for us to leave. I watched the flask still being passed from hand to hand and regretted that it was not returned to me.

'Here,' one of the men said to Anne, and gave her a piece of folded buff cloth.

Anne unfolded this. 'Nankeen,' she said. She held it to the light and then against her face.

'It'll come in for something,' the man said, embarrassed now by his kind gesture.

Anne went to him and kissed him on his cheek. She told him she knew the exact use for the piece of cloth and that she had been intending buying a piece for some time now. It made the gift greater than it was; it was one of her skills.

When we left them, the burners all waved and told us to return. Sam Pierce told us to remember him to my father. He repeated his offer of cinders to us.

I knew my father would insist on visiting the burners now that they were here. Besides, there was always the need of a bag of cinders in that wet place.

Leaving the trees and returning to the open ground, Anne looked back over the thin columns of smoke rising through the naked crowns and said, 'I envy them.'

The remark surprised me.

'Their freedom,' she said. 'Their lives.'

'They live under the sky and in the rain and the wind and the cold,' I told her. 'The smallest contagion and they die like rabbits at harvest.'

'I still envy them,' she said.

We followed the path to the Three Stones trough and then back down to Haworth. I saw the church in the distance, and I saw Charlotte too, standing at the gate and watching us come towards her. When she was satisfied it was her brother and her sister who approached, she turned and went into the house long before our arrival there. It was a common habit of hers these days, to keep this casual watch over us and to mark all our departures, absences and returns.

11

I remain convinced that Pottage the gardener told Edmund Robinson of his wife's affection for me. And I am just as certain that he embellished that account to his own advantage. I told all this to both Leyland and John Brown upon my return. Leyland had come to Haworth at John's urging, fearing for my sanity, and the pair of them had locked arms in consoling me. I was more circumspect in front of John, but only because of his position as my father's sexton.

The following week, in Halifax, I gave Leyland a much fuller account of what had happened at Thorp Green. There was no accuracy lost in the first tale – I would lie to neither man – but it was Leyland who was put in possession of the greater abundance of fact. It was to Leyland I wrote and signed my name Jacob, Son of Joseph – Jacob the Supplanter – certain that he alone would understand me. Everything I continued to hear of Lydia following Robinson's death convinced me further that she herself was tethered to her husband's memory only by the chains of his settlements and conditions, and not by the slightest degree of genuine affection for the man.

I wish now – I confessed as much to Leyland then – that I had gathered together my poems written in praise of Lydia and offered them to some editor as a whole. Leyland, ever observant, told me that the poems might have played some part in my severance from Lydia – on the one hand creating suspicion in Edmund Robinson's mind, and on the other providing him with all the proof he would later need to fasten those binding chains around his unhappy wife.

It was always Emily's belief, in her own blunt way, that I brought all my misfortunes upon myself. She laughed at the so-called 'mystery' of my dismissal, telling me that she knew me well enough to see through any mystery that attached itself to me. She had lost count, she told me, of all her warnings to me.

Charlotte, I knew, felt the same, but her own condemnation of me was manifest in this new cold silence between us and the empty spaces in which I was now left to wander alone without her once-comforting hand. We might have been a great deal to each other in those first painful months, but we each chose instead to turn our faces from the other and to suffer alone.

I also told Leyland that I had been the one seduced, that I was not the seducer. He called me a bragger and said that I had been a fool to fall for a frustrated woman's charms and play-acting. I saw only what I wanted to see, he said, and it was ever thus.

I lived then in a state of perpetual distress, and my mind remained for months a storm of unsettled emotions and raging uncertainty. I was sleepless for days on end. And on the few occasions when I did venture out into the world, I walked like a somnambulist wandering in his restless dream.

I know my father found it easiest to blame the older woman, and that he was greatly supported in this by Charlotte, who said that the slightest encouragement from *any* woman had always acted as an intoxicant to me. My father recounted that even as a small boy I had always read far more into things than they ever warranted. Every slight towards me I had treated as an insult or assault; every passing kindness as the greatest flattery or encouragement.

Charlotte told me that Lydia Robinson had played with me, and that the instant she realized she had exposed herself to me, she immediately retreated to her husband and all the comforts he provided. She accused me of behaving like one of my own juvenile creations, insisting that I had always delighted in the evil of those creations for evil's sake alone.

Anne had little to say concerning the turmoil of my immediate return, except in her usual quiet and pointed way to tell me that I indulged myself in my misery. Charlotte, she said, fought against her own unhappiness since her return from Brussels, whereas I seemed almost to enjoy my own self-torture and all the attention it drew to me. Why, she asked me, must my smallest scratch forever bleed?

Charlotte told me that there was no calm in the house since my return, that I made comfort scant there.

I swore Leyland to secrecy over much of what I told him, but he said that most of my horses were already loose and running. I wish now that I had been more attentive to his own troubles in life. I see now that I pushed away far too many helping hands which were never afterwards held back out to me.

There is little good reason to spin out this old tale again here, except to remark that it has been the backdrop to the stage upon which I have wandered and waited for these past two years. I cannot deny that I was a changed man after my return; and though my closest confidants might once have expressed their faith in my recovery, I doubt many would say the same of me now. Like that sensitive boy, my every venture into the world leaves me with yet another bruise, yet another insult to bear.

I used to insist to Leyland that I was a man more sinned against than sinning; I doubt he would even laugh with me at the joke if I repeated it now.

Charlotte told me that I needed to show more resolve. My father insisted that I needed only peace and calm in which to recover my equilibrium, and to begin anew.

The peace and calm have yet to come. There has been no new beginning, only a recurrent ending of sorts. I am a man as wary now of the calms as I once was of the storms of life.

I know I punish no one but myself with all this awful wailing at the past, but it is still my nature to do it.

12

It was one of my duties at Sowerby Bridge to walk the Summit Tunnel through Blackstone Edge to check the line for fallen bricks and loosened mortar.

I knew by their reaction to my engagement on the railway that neither my father nor my sisters approved of the work, that they considered it beneath me. Assistant Clerk in Charge. My decision was a perversity to them, but it was a perversity in which I revelled, and from which – despite all that was alleged to have happened later, and despite all my accusers – I still consider myself to have gained a great deal.

The tunnel was newly finished and the railway recently arrived. It was a new world, a world apart from Haworth and all its binds and tethers. None of them saw this. None of them saw in me the rising man ready to live his life at a tangent to their own small and close-bound existences.

My father told me that I should fret for the want of stimulation, that my energies would be wasted in complying with the dictates of lesser men.

Charlotte even went so far as to accuse me of bringing our name into disrepute.

Working on the railway was a time of great society for me, being seemingly so far from Haworth and yet so close to Halifax, where Leyland was working again, and where there was always a welcome and equal society in the public houses of the place. I met Grundy then – the time of our true friendship. I impressed no one at home with my tales of the twenty trains a day, or of my free journeys to and from Manchester and Leeds and beyond. On one occasion, known to no one, I spent an entire day travelling from Sowerby Bridge to Hull, and from Hull to Liverpool, and from there back to Sowerby Bridge. Coast to coast. The entire country was open to me.

There was much talk of the miracles of engineering along the line, and though I know the word offended my father, to me that is precisely what those graceful bridges, long, smooth tunnels and deep and perfectly lined cuttings were. I travelled over three hundred miles in a single day, in comfort, certainty, and with only a few dozen paces of my own as I crossed from one platform to another with my badge in my hand.

Everywhere I went, the engines sat at their rest like giant creatures, hissing and leaking steam and pouring smoke. And every time I saw them I wanted to touch them, to feel their heat and their bulk and their tremors. Their drivers, firemen and guards acknowledged me with shouts and waves, salutes almost.

Running out beyond Selby I was surprised by the sudden flatness of the land there, and by the silver lines which pierced it to the horizon in their gentle curves. Going in the opposite direction, my breath was sucked from my lungs when we emerged from the Summit Tunnel into the shored-up valleys beyond – hard to tell where nature and the work of man combined and then separated. My face was blackened by smoke and then washed in the cooling steam.

I worked in the beginning with a man called Abbot, who lived in Sowerby Bridge and who was frequently absent from his post. I did the work of two men in those days, and Abbot forever expressed his gratitude to me. Grundy, however, warned me against the man, saying Abbot took advantage of everyone he worked with. But I assured Grundy that I already knew this and that Abbot's idleness suited me. I told him I was finally ready to make a name for myself after all my false starts, and that at every opportunity I would bring myself to the attention of the managers and Board men with a view to promotion.

He understood the prospects I saw ahead of me and it became a kind of bond between us. I told him it was my distant ambition one day to be the overall manager of the station in Leeds, where new spur lines and platforms appeared almost monthly. The massive arches raising the line above the river and the town had recently been completed, and I could already imagine myself in the signal room there, overlooking everything that was happening. It was Grundy who told me what further qualifications and experience I might gain to bring about this ambition.

For his part, Abbot told me I was a fool, and that I ought rather to emulate his own career on the railways. He said he was the least regulated man in Sowerby Bridge and that this suited him better than anything else – and would suit me too if I were to follow his example. Sometimes I didn't see him for three or four days on end. At other times he was at his post without exhibiting the least sign of sobriety for just as long. I made my calculations and knew it benefited me to be paired with the man. Better Abbot than another ambitious man like myself.

I informed my father that I possessed this ambition, and even though he agreed that it was an admirable thing for a man to have, I knew from his tone that he remained unconvinced where *I* was concerned. It worried him above all that I spent so many nights away from home, my whereabouts unknown to him. What he meant, of course, was that I was spending so much time in the public houses of Halifax in the company of all those men I now called my companions – Leyland, Grundy, Edward Collinson, Richard Waller, Will Dearden, Wilson Anderson, Joe Drake, Teddy Sloane, the Cousen brothers, John James and John Thompson – all of them endlessly circulating in the same few places, and all of them to be relied upon for an evening's company. I doubt if my father had ever once had the happy experience of walking into a public house and of being greeted on all sides and by so many. I went with those men to galleries, exhibitions, functions and concerts. I forget how many times I attended Haydn's *Creation* or the Master's *Messiah* in the company of one or more of them.

I considered lodging permanently in Sowerby Bridge, but I made my promise to return home each weekend. However, on more than a few occasions I concocted excuses and wrote to say that I had been asked to work longer hours. It was always a relief to me not to have to make that particular journey.

It was work, true work, long hours and occasionally tiring. I used both my intellect and my brawn. If there was a problem to be solved – extra carriages to be ordered, empty ones to be removed and side-tracked, uncollected cargo to be made secure – then that was the task to which I turned my hand. I lived an independent life and I was judged by the results I achieved. It was my conviction that I made myself indispensable to my masters.

The timetable was all. Without it there was only confusion and disarray, uncertainty and disappointment. Charlotte called me a time-server, and I countered by telling her that the empty days she and her sisters enjoyed between employment were a luxury few could afford. I showed her the receipts from my pay packets and she said scornfully that it was *other* receipts upon which I ought to be keeping a closer eye. I understood her perfectly and countered again by repeating something Grundy had told me – that a man who worked hard more than earned and deserved his pleasures. I remember still the way she repeated the words back to me and then turned slowly away from me.

I showed my father the architects' drawings and the engineers' calculations for their vast schemes – drawings in which every single brick, every rivet and bolt was drawn – and I asked him how he could not appreciate them and what they represented. But the drawings and plans only convinced him further that this burgeoning world was not one with which he needed or wanted to concern himself. True miracles, he insisted, came only from within. Sometimes he seemed smug to me, too satisfied with his worn-out certainties and his own contented ignorance. I daresay that most of what I wanted to say to him, I said to Charlotte instead. Afterwards, the time was never right for apologies.

Examining the Blackstone Tunnel – frequently at night when the interval between engines was the greatest – I would pretend to myself that I was walking on a downward slope with my lantern and that I was descending into the earth itself. The vaulted walls dripped with the water running through them from above, and when it rained a stream would form between the tracks, quickly draining away in the bed of stones there. It was this water which loosened the mortar and the occasional brick, but these were easy to spot and remove, even in the darkness. I made a note in my book where any damage had been caused and then submitted my report to the overseers. The wall of the tunnel was painted with distance markers, and so I knew to the nearest yard how far I had progressed, and how far away ahead the light or the night awaited me. On occasion, I would fit myself into the hollows built into the walls and stand there like a saint in his niche as a train passed slowly by.

I offered to take my sisters into the tunnel – I know Emily at least would have appreciated the experience – but they all refused me.

Abbot seldom accompanied me on these inspections – he said they were beyond our contractual obligation – and on the rare occasion when he did deign to come with me, he invariably turned back before the entrance was lost to sight behind us. I laughed at him and told him he was a coward. I told him the darkness was nothing more than that; but secretly I was glad to be rid of the man and all his petty concerns, to be alone with my lantern and the echo of my songs running back and forth along the tracks.

There were bats in the tunnel, and foxes ran its full length, saving themselves the long journey over the hill above. I saw their eyes caught in my light and shining like emeralds in the distance as they turned to look at me and calculate my threat. I threw stones at them to keep them clear of me.

I once even encountered a poacher a few hundred yards from the western entrance and he told me it was a good place to set his wire traps, that a great many rabbits were tempted into the quiet and the darkness of the place. He asked me if I was going to prosecute him for trespass, but I settled instead on two fat bucks to take back to my stove at Sowerby Bridge.

In places there were already short stalactites hanging brightly from the roof of the tunnel. The drivers told me these shone like icicles in the lights of their engines.

13

I saw a great bird today, circling below the cloud over Rush Isles. I was with Greenwood, the stationer, and Cousin Gifford, who had brought out his tumblers to fly them in preparation for a contest. The birds were precious Jacobins, and he refused to unfasten their basket until the great bird had gone from above us.

'It's an eagle,' Greenwood announced.

'More like a buzzard,' Gifford said, shaking his head at Greenwood's folly.

'There *were* once eagles,' Greenwood insisted sadly.

'No doubt. But that's not one.' Gifford took out a bottle and offered us each a stiffener against the raw wind.

'I worked up here as a boy, starving crows,' Greenwood said. 'My father gathered stones for Parson Hale. He built a mound and called it their harvest. Educated men still come to ponder over what ancient king or prince is buried beneath it.'

We all laughed at this. We had quartered the place often enough during our shooting matches, coming from the White Horse Tavern and bringing down fewer and fewer birds as the day progressed. Gifford complained of men shooting at his pigeons. He showed us his yellow hands – the only colour, he insisted, that would not easily wash out from his work as a dyer. He told us it was a mark Saint Peter would recognize.

'What, and let you straight into your Other Home?' Greenwood asked him.

'My Long Home, yes.'

'Then I'll buy some yellow dye,' I said.

We settled ourselves into a hollow, and Gifford drew the thin stems of dead bracken over his birds. He searched the sky above us for the hawk, but it was long gone.

'Yonder,' he said, pointing to a stack of rocks, 'is where Grimshaw saw fornicators.'

'He saw them wherever he looked,' I said. 'And he seemed to spend half his life doing just that.'

'Talking of fornicators...' Greenwood said hesitantly.

Gifford and I waited.

'I was lately in Leeds,' Greenwood went on, 'visiting a wholesale bookseller. He asked me if I wanted to extend my stock. Drawings. French.'

Gifford and I exchanged a glance.

'And did you?' I asked him, winking at Gifford.

'I told him that the people here were a decent, God-fearing lot.'

'And then spent an hour examining the offered stock?' I said.

We laughed again and then all three of us lay back in silent contemplation.

'Tell me about the pictures,' I said eventually to Greenwood.

'Use your imagination,' he told me. 'Or, better still, don't.'

'He's blushing fit to burst,' Gifford said.

Beside us, the birds cooed and clucked like chickens, awaiting their release.

Gifford said he was now having second thoughts about letting them fly. I thought this a pity, especially having carried them so far. I enjoyed watching the pigeons soar up and then tumble down like broken toys at the clap of his hands – just as the pheasant and partridges and grouse had fallen at our shooting matches.

'They say Grimshaw preached people into Hell and then left them there until his next sermon, when he led them safely back out again,' Greenwood said.

'He might just as well have organized an outing to Leeds,' I told him.

He threw a sod of earth at me.

'At least Parson Brontë considers both our labours and our ease,' Gifford said.

'Grimshaw saw fornicators at the Hell Hole cliffs every Sunday afternoon between sermons,' Greenwood said. 'They say he stood and watched them at their exertions and then shouted down at them like Satan himself.'

'They say a great many things about Grimshaw,' I said. 'Too many, to my mind.'

After that, none of us spoke for a long while, happy to stay silent and to feel what little heat the sun contained on our faces and to be out of the wind in our hollow.

A few minutes later, Gifford began to snore, his birds beside him still clucking in his ear.

'The world is a vast place,' Greenwood said.

'Meaning we see too little of it?' I said.

'Perhaps.'

'Did you buy nothing whatsoever from the Leeds bookseller?' I asked him.

He waited a moment before answering me, watching Gifford where he slept. 'Well...' he said eventually, and he tapped his nose and grinned at me.

14

I returned to my senses following another seizure. I was in the parlour, stretched on the floor in front of the fire. Anne knelt beside me, a bowl of water by my face. Several minutes passed before I was able to push myself up and rest on my elbow. My jacket had been removed and the buttons of my shirt and vest unfastened. There was an unmistakeable aroma of vomit in the air. A damp patch on the rug showed where this had already been cleaned up.

'How long?' I managed to say.

Anne wrung water from a flannel and wiped my cheeks and mouth.

'You were insensible for twenty minutes,' she said. 'Father heard you call out. He and Charlotte came to you.' She motioned to a fallen chair.

I tried to remember, but little came. My life was now so fixed in its routines that the memory of any one day – hour, even – might serve for any other. Then I remembered that I had been reading a newspaper at the table. The torn and crumpled pages lay scattered around me.

'What did I call out?' I tasted the vomit in my mouth.

Anne held up the bowl to me and I spat into it. She shrugged. 'It was just a noise, that's all. The same–'

'As usual?'

She dried my face with her apron, then held her palm to my forehead.

'Father has gone to fetch Wheelhouse,' she said.

'The man has no idea.'

'He might at least have helped to revive you.'

'No need. For good or ill, I always return to my senses. And Charlotte?'

'She waited in here with me until a few moments ago, until you started to recover, and then she went in search of them.'

I wondered if this were true. 'We had words earlier,' I said, remembering more.

'I heard. The whole house heard. Father thought...' She stopped talking.

'What? That this was the cause of the seizure?'

She nodded. 'Charlotte, too.'

'It wasn't,' I said. 'I should suffer from the things almost daily on that particular understanding. It was only–' I felt suddenly airless, waiting for my spinning balance to settle. It was my third complete collapse in as many months.

Years ago, Wheelhouse had told me confidently that the fits were a thing of my childhood and that I should leave them behind me when I became a man. Elsewhere, it was the common opinion that they were born solely of my nature, and precipitated by over-excitement of any sort. I am still assaulted with sympathy, understanding and advice, but never with any single dependable remedy. Charlotte tells me that sympathy is worn thin in most people, as though it were something I had taken too freely and deliberately squandered.

Aunt B told me as a boy that the seizures

marked me, though whether for good or ill, she wouldn't say. She told me it was why my father would not send me away from home to be schooled. She said he had sworn to my mother to protect me, to keep me forever safe by his side. She said he had told her at great length of his own relatives back in Ireland who had suffered from the same thing.

'I was sick,' I said to Anne, indicating the stain. This was a new symptom. Until a year ago, there had rarely been vomiting, only a kind of thick and bitter froth at my lips.

'We were afraid you might choke,' she said. 'Charlotte cleared your mouth and held you on your side. You struck out at her.'

'I had no idea of what I did,' I said.

'We know that.'

I had been told before that I roared – growled like a beaten dog, Emily said – and that I possessed a great strength when I resisted restraint during the seizures.

'Did I harm her?' I said.

Anne soaked and wrung out the flannel again. 'Father blames your drinking,' she said. 'And your remedies. He believes you seek to suppress your feelings, but that you succeed only in stimulating something otherwise beyond reach, and that this is what brings on the fits.'

'He's been listening too long to Wheel-house,' I said. 'No one can say for certain

96

what causes them. Wheelhouse will come, examine me, put on his best expression of grave concern and then tell me to rest and avoid all stimulation. I shall be ordered like a child to lie in a darkened room and take only water and broth for a day or two. Read nothing, talk to no one, make no unnecessary exertion. Imagine how quickly a man might sink and disappear into *that* particular mire. Imagine how quickly *you* would disappear. Tell me honestly – what is *that* a cure for? What was it *ever* a cure for?'

I tried to push myself fully upright, but was unable to.

'Wait,' Anne told me.

My legs felt turned to cloth, my bowels to water, my head to air.

'Charlotte told Father you had received a letter,' Anne said hesitantly.

'And that she believed that this was what had over-excited me?'

'Over-agitated, yes.'

'It wasn't. And nor was the correspondence what all-seeing, all-knowing Charlotte took it to be.'

'She thought–'

'She thought it was a letter from Lydia.'

'None of us wants that woman's name mentioned here.'

'No,' I said. 'Of course you don't.' It was beyond me to argue the point, and especially not with Anne.

She wiped my face again and then stroked my hair back from my brow with her fingers.

'Forgive me,' I said. 'Tell Charlotte it was a note from Leyland. He misses my company. Imagine that – me, sorely missed.'

She smiled, drew a cross over my face and said, 'Then you may consider yourself forgiven.'

'Of everything?' I said. 'For ever?'

She pretended to slap my cheek.

When they were girls, both Anne and Emily would cover their ears at the sound of anything they considered disturbing. I still saw that same instinct in Emily, but I had thought that Anne had long since outgrown it.

'I *am* sorry,' I said to her. 'It was good of you to stay with me.'

'Of course I stayed with you,' she said. 'What else would I do?' It was something I was beginning to hear all too frequently these days – reassurance, rebuke and resignation all rolled into one. Men speak of being killed by kindness. I wonder if this is the same, or if it is something more practical in nature.

I tried again to stand, and this time I was able to rise from the floor with Anne's support. I returned to the table and sat there. Anne gathered up the scattered newspaper. She read the headlines, telling me that she was searching for whatever *I* might have been

98

reading when I was afflicted. I told her I still had no memory of this.

'Father believes you ought to immerse yourself again in the classics.'

'"Immerse"? Because they would calm and reassure me? Because they would help my disordered mind back to its proper place?'

'That was his belief. He himself–'

'He himself ignores anything which does not already have the judgement of at least a century – more – laid upon it.'

Even this gentle mockery of the man was too much for her and she threw down the pages she had gathered up.

I apologized again to her.

'You yourself once took great consolation and pleasure in the same works,' she said.

'I know,' I admitted. I felt suddenly nauseous and started to retch, but this time my exertions were dry.

Anne brought the bowl to me, and as she set it down I held her arm for a moment.

'Oh, Branwell,' she said, and it was almost too much for me to bear. The balance of my debt grew ever more disproportionate in whatever direction I looked.

When I was a child, my seizures started with a flashing of small lights which fractured and then obscured my vision. This was accompanied by the sound of the wind in my head, and there were perhaps five or ten seconds of this combined warning

99

before every ounce of my strength was lost on an instant and all my conscious senses ended as though at the touch of an unseen hand. I was told that I fell and thrashed on the ground, that I cried out unintelligibly, and that I often uttered profanities to those attempting to restrain me and keep me from harming myself. It remained a mystery to me that these profanities should remain while everything else was babble.

I suffered a seizure a week before my application to the Royal Academy – overwrought nerves and anticipation, my father said – and hence it was a journey made only in my imagination. I suffered another, equally severe, only two days after my return from Thorp Green.

I was about to ask Anne to help me with the buttons of my shirt when the front door was opened and we heard the voices of my father, Charlotte and Wheelhouse.

Charlotte was the first to come in to us. She stopped in the doorway and looked at me where I sat.

'He recovered a few minutes ago,' Anne told her. She took the bowl and cloth and left the room. I heard Wheelhouse call after her, asking for clean water, addressing her as though she were a servant.

Clean water – the man's opening gambit for all and any of the ailments he attended.

I saw the small bruise on Charlotte's cheek.

'Did I cause that?' I asked her.

Before she could answer me, Wheelhouse came into the room, looked quickly around him and then made his way to the fire. He told my father to stay and Charlotte to leave. He considered me where I sat and said, 'We meet again,' as though he and I were adversaries.

'And I for one wish to God that it were otherwise,' I told him.

Wheelhouse shook his head at the words.

Charlotte, who had ignored the man's command, came to me, swept the paper from the table and then buttoned my vest and shirt.

'Must I be made presentable to the old fraud?' I whispered to her, certain that neither Wheelhouse nor my father could hear me.

'I observe that your wayward son continues to take the Almighty's name in vain,' Wheelhouse said to my father.

'He is hardly recovered,' my father said, and I regretted this – both for the embarrassment caused to him and for the wasted excuse made on my behalf.

'See?' Charlotte whispered back to me, hissing the word in my face.

'"Wayward"?' I said to her. It seemed I was still that wandering sheep, forever drawing closer to the fold, forever wandering back out into the wilderness.

15

Three days later Emily came to me and told me that Charlotte wished to see me. I had seen little of Charlotte since Wheelhouse's visit, and I was in no mood for another of her sermons now.

'Are you her maid, then?' I said to Emily. 'Her errand-runner?'

But Emily merely considered me for a moment where I lay on the settle and then came to me, flattened my hair and straightened my jacket. I apologized to her.

'You clothe yourself in apologies,' she said to me. She tightened my thin scarf and kissed me on the forehead.

'What is it Charlotte wants? To tell me again that I am a man wandering in a maze of his own making and with no idea of its exit?'

She smiled at this. 'I doubt that even needs to be said any longer.'

I clutched at my heart. 'You wound me,' I said.

She took out a clean handkerchief, wet it at her lips and wiped my cheeks and chin. 'It concerns us all,' she said. 'There are people outside.'

'People?'

'At the gate. Looking in.' She glanced at the curtained windows as she spoke.

'They'll be here for Father,' I said.

Emily shook her head. 'He's out. As is Anne. Besides, Charlotte believes otherwise.'

'Then what?' And only then did I fully understand what she was telling me.

She helped me to my feet.

I went to the window and she stopped me from drawing back the curtain.

'Upstairs,' she said.

I followed her up to Charlotte, who beckoned us into the front room. There, too, the curtains were drawn and the room was in shade. What little light did enter was dappled against the back wall and ceiling like sunlight falling through trees.

'Anne is still out,' Charlotte said to me, unable to hide her concern.

'He says they may have come to see Father,' Emily said.

'I see,' Charlotte said, and she looked at me hard. So hard that after only a few seconds I lowered my own eyes. 'He knows full well why they're here,' she said. 'And worse, he indulges himself in my discomfort.'

I went to stand beside her and to look down through the inch of window she revealed.

Two men and three women stood at the gate beside the lilac there and looked up at the house. I recognized none of them. The men were older, in their fortieth years, and the women younger – the men's grown daughters, perhaps.

A month ago, Sugden had told me that a party of four men had come to the Bull asking the whereabouts of the 'old parson's daughters'. He called them 'gawpers', and when I asked him what he'd told them, he remarked that the church and its parsonage would be hard to hide from anyone. Besides, he added, they were buying his drink, and at Leeds prices. He said he knew by their accents and their conversation that they were not local people.

The last time I'd seen Phillips at the *Times* offices he'd told me that he intended printing letters from people enquiring after my sisters. We had by then spoken often of their unnoticed poems, but he told me this was something else. This, he said, was a 'stir'. To save my own face, I told him that I understood him perfectly, but that I could say no more on the matter, that I was sworn to secrecy. He had laughed at this, saying that of course I was, of course I was. He tapped his nose and spoke of the secrets I was holding up my own sleeve and what a stir they too would soon cause in the world. Oh, undoubtedly, I told him. He put his arm around my shoulders and told me I'd do well not to forget my friends and my patrons when the time arrived. Oh, undoubtedly, I told him, undoubtedly.

'They're coming in,' Charlotte said suddenly.

Emily came to stand beside me.

'Knock on the window,' I said to Charlotte. 'Shout and tell them they're trespassing.'

'And then be forced to listen to their demands? They will only shout back that they have every right to be here.'

'"Right"?'

'And that we have an obligation to fulfil.'

'Not I,' I said.

'No,' she said, the word barely mouthed. 'Not you.'

I wanted to grab her by the shoulders and shake her until a full confession fell from her lips. I could see that Emily, too, wished that her sister might now reveal more to me for all our sakes. Was there ever anything more corrosive to understanding and intimacy than a public secret?

The men and women outside came a short way into the garden, studied the house for several minutes and then retreated to the gate, where they remained standing and looking.

'Why not leave them where they are?' Emily suggested. 'They'll soon grow tired of waiting. In all likelihood, they aren't even fully convinced of their reason for being here.'

'And risk either Father or Anne returning

105

home and running their gauntlet?' Charlotte said.

'Anne would turn away at her first sight of them,' Emily said.

'And Father would walk unsuspectingly into their midst and ask them straight why they had come. What then?'

Emily stepped back from the window, away from the dappled light into the shade of the room.

We were at an impasse.

Downstairs, Keeper barked, and the men and women outside all turned at the sound.

'It's why I sent Emily to fetch you,' Charlotte said to me. '*You* must go out to them and convince them that you are alone in the house, that we three are elsewhere.'

'You, Emily and Anne?'

'Whoever they ask for.'

'The poets?'

She again looked at me sharply, and then at Emily.

Are you pleading with me? I wanted to say to her. *Are you begging me? Do I finally serve a purpose in your world of secrets? Do I finally warrant my place in your circle of deceits?*

'Tell them that the place is empty and that Father – say "the parson" – is infirm and needs his peace and quiet. Make them understand–'

'I have a much better plan,' I told her, surprising her by this bold interruption.

'Which is what?' she said suspiciously.

'I might decoy them.'

'Decoy?' Emily said.

'I might go out to them and tell them that no one is at home, but that *I* know your whereabouts. And then I could lead them away from you.'

'A wild-goose chase,' Emily said, warming to my plan.

I could see that it was starting to appeal to Charlotte, too.

'I shall turn myself into a Man of Mystery,' I said.

'A mother peewit drawing a weasel away from her fledglings,' Emily said.

'Precisely.'

Charlotte raised her eyes at this. 'Then do it,' she told me. 'Just be careful not to overplay your part. And do it on account of Father and Anne.' She turned away from me as she spoke, confirming to me that she was as aware as any of us that it was *her* the people outside were there to see – that *she* was the one who had jeopardized our privacy and opened us all up to this public scrutiny.

Sugden had told me that I ought to sell tickets to the gawpers. There was a small fortune to be made, he said – payment for all those tales yet to be told.

'I'll tell them I'm the gravedigger,' I said.

'Come to find the parson and finding the house empty except for the dog.' I said it in a rough accent, but only Emily smiled at hearing this.

Before Charlotte could object to what I was further suggesting, I left the room and went downstairs. I went to the kitchen and let myself out of the back door, walking around the house until I appeared beside the churchyard wall.

One of the young women saw me there and pointed me out to the others.

The oldest of the men beckoned me to them.

I went without a single glance at the house. I felt my sisters' eyes on my every step and gesture. I lowered one shoulder and dragged my feet slightly. In my mind I could hear Charlotte telling Emily that I was already overdoing the thing.

Upon reaching the small party, I bowed and tugged at my hair.

The women giggled at this and one of the men asked me who I was.

'My name is Boanerges Northanger,' I said, causing the women's giggles to turn to laughter.

'Such names,' one of them said.

The others hushed her to silence.

'We arrived in the hope of seeing–' the man began to say.

'No one home,' I told him. 'House is

empty. Just the dog. Burials, see? I dig the graves.' I indicated the field of stones.

'The actual gravedigger?' one of the women said. 'How wonderful.'

'It's heavy, wet soil,' I said. 'Not wonderful at all.'

I imagined Charlotte telling me to get on with my task.

'You looking for the folk here?' I said, turning and pointing directly at the house.

'Do you know them?' the same man said.

'They attend most of the burials. When not otherwise engaged, that is.' I winked at him.

This was a clear signal to him, and he said, 'And might you know where they are now?' He patted the satchel he carried.

My first thought was that he was offering me money, my second that it was filled with books.

'They'll not be far,' I told him. I motioned to the street below us. 'I could find them fast enough for you.'

'Or take us to see them?' he said. He made them sound like animals in a menagerie.

'Or that.' I pretended to hesitate. 'Except by rights I should be working. Like I said, graves need digging, and tend not to dig themselves hereabouts.'

The second man nudged the first, who shook the coins in his pocket and said, 'I shall, of course, make it worth your while.'

109

I immediately held out my hand to him – wishing it were dirtier – and he put money into it without counting it.

I had once been everything to my sisters and now I was this – a fake beggar on their behalf.

I walked away from the gate and started to descend the road. The men and women followed me. I searched ahead of me for sight of either my father or Anne, but saw neither.

Approaching the Bull, I pointed to its open door. 'We might try in here first,' I said.

'Truly?' one of the women said. 'In here? A public house?'

'First?' said another. 'You mean they may be in one of several?'

'Oh, easily,' I said. 'Easily.' I made a drinking motion with my hand.

I waited for them to catch up with me and then bowed again as they entered the low, dark room ahead of me.

16

I met Timothy – God-fearer – Finch fastening his gate nets over the holes along Cuckoo Bank. He suffered badly from arthritis and his dark hands were tight and stiff. He spoke of my father's visit to the closed drifts at Green Holes, where he himself had worked, and told me how proud I must be of an old man capable of making such a journey, in such weather, to perform such a task. I was about to remind him that I had accompanied my father to the pits, but he turned back to his nets before I could speak.

I watched him for a few minutes, seeing how little use he had of his fingers in such a delicate task.

When he came back to me I asked him if he'd had any work recently.

He untangled one of his nets, running the mesh over his forearm and checking it for tears. 'Not so as you'd notice,' he said. 'Your father came back to us, alone. He told what few of us remained that you would have been with him except that you were laid up with your own suffering.'

I had known nothing of this second visit. Perhaps there, too, I was now more of a liability than an asset.

'The men still there would have raised him up on to their shoulders and carried him back to the parsonage to save his legs,' he said. 'He's a rare good man.'

'He is that,' I said. 'Rare good.' I tried to imagine anyone in the place ever saying the same of me.

'I wanted to accompany him,' I said, 'but my–'

'We reckon never to see the like again,' he said.

I knew not to persist with my lie. 'Have you caught many rabbits?' I asked him.

He looked all around us and then nodded once. Perhaps he considered me capable of running to the land stewards or the keepers.

'Before your father came to us we had only preachers who looked down on us and who counted only our failings. It's why the place is still rife with dissenters and nonconformists. We had to find our own way again, you see? Our own way.'

'I see,' I said. My first instinct upon seeing the man at the bank had been to hide myself and then to come away from him unseen. I wished now that I'd done this.

'Your father gathered us up – those of us who hadn't strayed – and then he led us on-wards. He showed us the way and then he led us along it.' He paused, again looking around us, and then he bowed his head and sighed.

'What is it?'

'Your father. It's plain to all who see him now that he's an ailing man. And ageing. Who will come to lead us when he's gone?' He spoke as though the man had already pulled on the robes of a prophet.

'Someone, surely?' I said, hoping to strike the right note.

112

'But not you,' he said sharply. 'Not the son of the father.'

'I'm not ordained,' I said.

'Nor ever intended to be.'

'No,' I said. The ripples of my disappointing presence in the place not only continued ever wider outwards, but now it seemed flowed far into the future.

'It's not in your nature,' he said.

'No. It never was.'

'There are some here—' He stopped abruptly as two women passed us by. He acknowledged them and swiftly touched a finger to his lips. I guessed they had come to buy or collect the rabbits from him.

I wanted to tell him to do his business with them, but said nothing. The women both said 'Mister Brontë' to me, but nothing more. They followed the path away from us, turning at its junction with Brow Top and then waited there.

'Are they here for the rabbits?' I asked him.

'The young woman is Sarah Riding,' he said to me.

They had both looked old to me.

'I see,' I said, though I saw nothing.

'Seven children and her husband out of work for five months. He was a fuller at Naylor's. Put out on a day's notice.'

'I imagine—'

'You imagine nothing,' he said, again sharply. 'Least of all, you imagine nothing of

113

how she stretches a rabbit to a meal for nine for an entire day.'

'No,' I said. 'I suppose not.'

I had left the parsonage with the aroma of another of Martha's stews filling the place. My father petitioned daily for Poor Relief and Commissioner donations for the unemployed and the struggling.

'So you see,' Finch said, 'whoever comes after him, it will not be a man anywhere near the equal of your father. Some of us had hoped that Weightman might–' He stopped again and said a quick prayer.

'I think we had all hoped that William might one day...'

'The Lord had greater plans for that good man,' he said. 'Greater plans. We knew that at first your father had the strength and the will to see off most of the Baptists, Primitives and Ranters; but now... They breed like rats over in Colne and such places. An army marching ever closer to us with its filthy pamphlets and roadside pulpits. We would put our faith in your father to go on fighting the good fight, but we see what little strength he has left to him.'

'Not to mention his eyes,' I said.

'Oh? They reckoned his operation was a success and that his sight was restored.'

'It was,' I said. 'But he still exerts himself and peers through dim light for hours on end.'

Exerting himself on your behalf.

'He must sermonize and write everything down, I suppose,' he said. 'He must constantly glean the Scriptures and Texts for their grains of gold.'

'Of course.'

'And we all of us continue to be his beneficiaries,' he said. 'I remember well when the Chartists came and gathered high on Lee Moor, telling anyone who would listen to them that unemployment and famine would end only in violence by and to the working man. Your father, within clear sight of those men, told us all that there was another way. Without his quenching words, those Chartists would have set their spark to the heaped and waiting tinder.'

'And my father prevented that from happening?' It was a rare, unheard tale.

'He did that,' he said. 'He did that. There would have been bloodshed on Lee Moor but for your father. Some said the militia were already on their way.'

After that, he spent a minute clearing out and then refilling his short pipe.

'Someone new will come,' I said eventually.

'Because nothing is ever left to chance these days?'

'No – because the Church Authorities will appoint someone,' I said.

'You would have done right well to follow

115

in his footsteps,' he said.

'But, like I said–'

'I heard you the first time.'

The open rebuke made me wary, and I wished I could either answer him with one of my own, or at least finally turn my back on him and leave him where he stood, rooted in the past and all its scattered, fading glories. I wondered what it was that confounded my actions. Perhaps the figure of my father standing beside me and warning the man of his excesses, praising his smallest kindness to me. There were many now in the place who no longer gave me the time of day.

'We would not see off another as easily as we saw off Parson Hale,' he said, smiling. 'Covered in soot and on a donkey.'

'I imagine those days are long gone,' I said. I wondered if the story were even true.

'Gone and not gone,' he said.

'Of course.' *Gone and not gone.*

'They say Wesley enjoyed his visits here because the people were groaning for redemption.'

Another old story.

'See that bothy?' he said. He pointed the stem of his pipe at a distant collapsed building in the corner of a field. 'They drove out a nest of Antinomians from that place. Naked men and women crawling in the dirt in obedience. Men with two wives. Women

116

as shameless in their nakedness as the men ever were. Drove them out and then up over Stairs Hill yonder, all the way back to Lancashire, where they belonged. Men, women and children. Infants who knew no better, nor ever would.'

Ah, happy days, I wanted to say to him.

The place was as mired in this mulch of religion and tale-telling as it was saturated with water. I wanted to tell him that the Antinomian creed had always recommended itself to me. According to them, our eternal fate – our final destination of Heaven or Hell – was predestined even before our birth, so it didn't matter in the slightest how we behaved here on Earth. Every Antinomian I had ever met – though few declared themselves until pushed – had sworn to me that they all knew in their hearts who would survive the Apocalypse and ascend into Heaven, and who would be plunged screaming and pleading into Hell. It was the kind of capricious arbitrariness that I recognized and appreciated. I might also say it was a logic I embraced, and one well suited to this unsettled world of constant change and discord and struggle.

'Rain,' Finch said unexpectedly, retrieving me from my thoughts. He turned his pipe further west.

Rain from the west, fair from the east, warmth

117

from the south, this last least.

A mountain of cloud rose high above the far horizon.

'We certainly get our fair share,' I said, hoping finally to lighten the mood now that we were surely close to parting.

'We get *more* than our fair share of most things,' he said. 'I saw John Riding yesterday on his round of searching for work. He told me that all he, his wife and children had eaten for a week was poor bread and raw onion. His allotment alongside the mine was already ploughed in by the new owners. That and forty others. Oats, they reckon. Imagine that – oats instead of good vegetables and soft fruit. It said in the newspaper that we're becoming as poor as the Scots. Animal feed rotting on a sodden moor where a hundred men have been denied the right and the means to feed their families.' It was beginning to sound like another of my father's sermons, and perhaps Finch too sensed this, for he then said, 'Ask your father: he sees all this, even if you do not.'

I told him that I ought to return home before the rain. Perhaps my ailing father needed my invaluable help with something.

He shook his head at this. And then he quickly touched his forehead – a vestige of respect, if not for me, then for the invisible man still beside me, and who was now himself shaking his head at my every cruel and deceitful utterance.

He was the first to start walking, back to his hidden nets and earlier catch.

I set off in the direction of the two waiting women. I pictured in my mind nine hungry people sitting around a single small carcass, all of them imagining which nourishing, delicious part of it was to be their own.

17

The hypocrite Grundy was here today, I met Brown on Changegate and he said he'd seen Grundy in the company of Titterington. 'Talking worsted, no doubt,' he said, knowing Titterington well. The manufacture of the stuff will have been of no interest whatsoever to Grundy, who remained fixed on the railway, especially having recently been promoted to Resident Engineer at Skipton.

'Was he looking for me?' I asked John. To give me word of an opening, perhaps. To tell me that a job was waiting and that he had already written a glowing letter of recommendation on my behalf. The affair at Luddenden Foot was now six long years behind me.

'We spoke only in passing,' John said, clearly keen to avoid the matter. 'Besides, if he had news for you, it would be none of my concern.'

'I suppose not,' I said. My hopes these days are all dead leaves in a rising wind.

'Find him,' he said, wanting to sound more hopeful on my behalf – and certainly more hopeful than either of us genuinely felt. My predicament made him awkward, and I regretted this.

I call Francis Grundy a hypocrite because I am convinced he is Janus-faced – saying one thing to me and telling a different story completely to his employers. Four months ago, I took a coach to the Skipton Inn, hopeful of seeing him where he lodged, but the keeper there told me that I had just missed him, that he had been called away on urgent railway business. I had sent a note three days previously regarding my intended visit. In it I made no mention of my renewed expectations, but Grundy could surely have been in no doubt that this was my purpose in wanting to see him.

I had been in the company of Leyland, Waller and Dearden in the Old Cock when Grundy had last announced that he would put my name forward at the next opportunity. He assured me that sufficient time had now elapsed since Luddenden Foot –

and that anyway the loss there had never truly been considered my sole responsibility or failing – and that I had proved myself previously a good employee. He said the railways and all their projects and investors were going from strength to strength and that men like myself were always needed. I remember how much our conversation bored Waller and Dearden. Richard wanted only to plan our forthcoming theatrical excursions, and William to recite another of his over-long poems.

Grundy was an odd man out in that company. Leyland laughed at him behind his back because of his obsession with the stocks and shares he owned. I feigned the same scorn – indifference, at least – when I was later alone with Leyland, but in truth Grundy's passion would have been my own were I again to be in a position similar to his own. I did not make such a clear division as Leyland between artistic and industrial endeavour. In turn, Grundy chided Leyland that his own fortunes would be swiftly reversed were he to tender for some of the monumental work being contracted by the railway companies. Leyland continued to consider the work beneath his talents. Upon hearing Grundy repeat his proposition, Joseph had again been the worse for drink, and his rejection of the work had been emphatic and long.

Leaving John Brown, I went in search of Grundy and found him eventually in the Lion, sitting in the side room, not with Titterington, but with George Thompson, another of our old Luddenden Foot acquaintances. It surprised me to find the two men together so far from their usual haunts.

Seeing me enter, Thompson rose from their bench and beckoned me to them. Grundy, I saw, was considerably less enthusiastic at my arrival.

'Paddy, Paddy, Paddy,' Thompson called to me. He signalled over my shoulder for more drinks to be brought in to us.

Grundy finally rose and held out his hand to me.

'Patrick,' he said – he always called me by my first name – 'I thought we should run into you in one spot or another.'

'I saw John Brown,' I said.

'And there's little happens in this place that gets past that man,' he said. I heard the cold note in his voice.

'Quite,' I said. He knew I considered John my closest and firmest friend in the place.

Grundy sat back down and Thompson busied himself collecting and paying for our drinks.

'I came to Skipton,' I said.

'Yes. I believe I received your note. My apologies. As you might imagine, I am buried in work. The navvy towns are a constant pre-occupation.'

'I heard you were elevated to Chief Engineer,' I said.

'*Resident* Engineer,' he corrected me, perhaps sensing my intent in the deliberate error.

'Is there a difference?' I said, knowing precisely what the difference was. I took the drink Thompson gave to me.

'I suppose not,' Grundy said. 'Either way, I am busy from dawn till dusk and then often beyond.'

'He works the Irish through the night,' Thompson said. It was clear to me that he had already drunk far more than buttoned-up Grundy.

'It's tunnel and cutting work,' Grundy said. 'What does daylight or darkness matter?'

Thompson laughed.

'Quite,' I said again, causing Grundy further unease. I raised my tankard in a toast to the railway. Then I turned to Thompson and asked him about the corn business.

'Terrible,' he said. 'We're being charged at the top of the market and our poor profits fall through the holes in our pockets.'

I knew by the way he said it that he was not genuinely concerned for his losses. Besides, it was his manner – as with most of the wealthy businessmen in the place – always to answer in this way.

'And the malting?' I said.

'Oh, men always like a drink,' he said. 'In fact, that is why Francis and I are met here today.' He looked around the otherwise empty room and tapped the side of his nose.

'Oh?' I said, glancing at Grundy, who avoided my eyes.

'The navvies,' he said, the word little more than a murmur.

'You're supplying ale to them?' I said to Thompson.

'Under the auspices of good friend Francis here, yes. We have a contract. Everything legal and above board, mind.'

'And at a profit to the pair of you, I imagine,' I said, my eyes still on Grundy.

'Of course,' Thompson said. 'Business is business. Why otherwise would it exist?'

'They do like a drink, those men,' Grundy finally said, picking up his own pot.

I remembered the men I had known at Sowerby Bridge and Luddenden Foot. I remembered their company and their acceptance of me. I remembered how completely they trusted and liked me, and how they welcomed me into their homes and their society. It was a great loss to me to be banished from that world upon the loss of my employment.

'And the harder they work, the more they are inclined to drink,' Thompson said. He rubbed his thumb and forefinger together, and I guessed in an instant every detail of the arrangement between himself and Grundy.

'Then I shall drink to their labours and to your honest profits,' I said.

Grundy again raised his pot, but this time scarcely drank from it.

'And how is your father?' he asked me.

'He fails in every respect of his life except in his commitment to the Holy Writ and his belief in the Sweet Hereafter, where his every failing and weakness shall be put right and he will be surely and swiftly restored to his full health and vigour,' I said.

'I see,' Grundy said awkwardly. 'And your beloved sisters?'

'My beloved sisters come and go and wrap themselves in their secrets,' I said.

'Oh?' Thompson said. 'What sort of secrets? Suitors? Are they arranging their lives at last, then? Will you soon be that half-formed beast, the brother-in-law, and then an uncle to their crowds of squawking children?'

I laughed with him. 'God forbid,' I said. 'They all three of them have the mark of the spinster on them, and any–'

'You shouldn't talk of them like that,' Grundy said firmly. His pot shook in his hand.

'No, of course not,' Thompson said, affecting contrition and then winking at me.

'They write,' I said to Grundy, easing the moment.

'Write?'

'Poems. Novels.'

'To what end?' he said.

'To fill their days and engage their imaginations, I should think.'

'As do a million others with time lying heavy on their empty hands,' Thompson said.

'Perhaps,' I said. I did not want to discuss my sisters, and regretted having revealed even this little of them.

'Send them my best wishes,' Grundy said. 'Perhaps one day they'll accept my offer of a free journey on one of our new routes.'

'I'll remind them,' I told him.

'Perhaps the same perquisite might be extended to me and my own family,' Thompson said to Grundy.

'Of course,' Grundy said.

'Perhaps when the navvies have sobered up sufficiently to finish laying the tracks,' I said. We all three laughed in our own way.

'Sugared water of ammonia,' Thompson said. 'Always efficacious for me. To induce sobriety.' He pulled a face at the thought of the cure.

After this, there was a moment of silence. I cleared my throat.

'And me?' I said to Grundy, knowing that he understood me perfectly, and knowing too all that he was about to reveal to me by the flicker of his eyes.

'I'm afraid I have nothing to report to you,' he said.

'But you continue to put my name forward?'

'Of course, of course. At every opportunity. But you must understand, everything changes. Even *I* seem to acquire new masters with every passing month. Our boards and companies amalgamate and conglomerate faster than I can remember. Names change all the time. Besides...' He paused. 'Besides, most of our middle and senior appointments are made these days by panels and boards a long way from here.'

'Leeds, you mean?' Thompson said.

'Further, much further. London, usually.'

'That place,' Thompson said.

Everything Grundy continued to say distanced him further and further from his promises to me.

'So you see...' Grundy said.

'I see nothing,' I told him. I raised my empty tankard to the girl at the bar and Thompson did the same.

Grundy, I saw, immediately laid his hand across the top of his own drink. His little speech had taken only seconds, but it was the blackest of holes.

'I shall of course continue to press on your behalf,' he said.

'Of course he will,' Thompson told me. He put his hand on my shoulder. 'He's a friend to you, a good friend. It's how these things work. We are all three of us men of the world. We understand that much at least, surely?'

'Of course,' I told him.

'There's talk of spurs to Barnoldswick and Whitworth,' Grundy said. 'Perhaps when they are confirmed...'

We all knew the new courses stood little chance of being needed or laid.

The girl brought our drinks and again Thompson paid her, brushing aside the hand I held above my own empty pocket.

We drank a toast to prosperity. They were prosperous men – prosperous men with prospects.

'The world will turn,' Thompson said to me. 'You'll see. You've suffered setbacks, that's all. We are all made the stronger by rising to and surviving our misfortunes.'

'I seem to be more tempered by adversity than most,' I said, and he conceded the point. 'Besides, you're beginning to sound like my father.'

'Perhaps because I know what it is to *be* a father.'

It was meant as a light remark and he cannot have known how keenly I felt it.

'Of course,' I told him.

Grundy watched me closely as I raised this

second drink to my lips. I was compromised to him. It sometimes seemed as though my every weakness and failing – however inconsequential or fleeting – was endlessly displayed to the world, no matter how hard I tried to overcome or disguise it.

'Perhaps I should change direction and go into the brewing trade instead,' I said to them.

'And swallow your own profits?' Thompson said. 'I've seen it happen. Look at Gregson over at Steeton.'

We all remembered what we knew of the man.

'What is it they say?' Thompson said. '"He who suffers, hopes; and he who hopes, believes."'

He sounded even more like my father.

'I'll drink to that,' Grundy said, his hand still over his drink.

I wondered where precisely I was meant to fit into that glib and self-serving little homily.

18

Three weeks after Wheelhouse's visit to spoon-feed me his scorn and wasted cures, and now Teale has been sent for from Leeds to visit Anne, who sickened worse a week ago and has made little recovery since. Like our local so-called expert, the man is as tightly packed as an egg with his own self-importance. He talks of the journey from Leeds – at my father's expense – as though he had walked every step of the way on a hard path and against a strong wind. He looks at us all with his cold physician's eye. He said to my father that he spoke 'right earnestly' when considering his diagnoses. My father was unusually taken by the man and his airs, and he waited, hardly breathing, on his every word.

Teale spoke of Anne's nervous excitement and her alarms. Then he looked out of the window and commented on the black slabs paving the churchyard as though the two things were somehow connected. My father asked him if there were not similar churchyards in Leeds – where the slabs, hard to keep standing, had similarly been laid as paving – and Teale said that to his knowledge

130

there were none.

Upon hearing him say this, I started to speak, but a sharp look from Charlotte, who stood close behind Teale, silenced me. Every new road and passage and rail spur in the city flattened another hundred houses and not a few churches.

I had seen by the way Teale regarded Charlotte upon his arrival, and then by his manner when he approached where Anne lay, that he was almost certainly another sharer – however uncertain and uncon-firmed – of their secret. 'Sharer' is the wrong word; they have properly shared their secret with no one within two hundred miles of this place. And I saw, too, by Teale's manner that it was as far beyond him to broach the subject now as it was for him to declare a cure for Anne.

'Excitements,' the man said aloud, inter-rupting my thoughts and drawing us all back to him.

Charlotte, I saw, clasped my father's arm in both her hands, ready to support him against the worst.

'She is not ordinarily a nervous child,' my father said.

'You misunderstand me,' Teale said em-phatically.

'Oh? My apologies.'

'No need, no need. I refer to the excite-ments of her "being", her blood, her nervous system.'

'She comes and goes,' my father said. 'As do many.' He foundered in his concern for his youngest child.

'I daresay,' Teale said. 'You have clean air here.'

'And a winter just past of influenza, scarlet and enteric fever,' my father said. 'I attended many. The door was never closed some days.'

'Door?' Teale said.

'Unto Heaven,' my father said.

'Oh.' Teale looked quickly between Charlotte and myself.

I wanted to pull him away from the two of them, and to push him closer to Anne. She, I knew, would despise me for this, and was only enduring the man's inspection because it had been forced upon her by Charlotte and my father.

'And good water, too?' Teale said.

Air and water. Now I wanted to shake the man by his shoulders and ask him how he came by his expertise, how easily won it had been, how swiftly conferred upon him by his equally expert colleagues.

'There are always improvements to be made,' my father said.

I wanted to shake him, too, and tell him to insist that Teale offer us something more definite by way of diagnosis and cure. This was my *sister,* his *daughter* lying before us, and all we did was dance attendance on the man and flatter him with everything we said.

'She often appears to gain some strength, but it is usually short-lived,' Charlotte said.

'And always fails again?' Teale said. He pursed his lips and furrowed his brow. It seemed his natural demeanour. Next, like Wheelhouse, he would tap his lips in an effort of thought.

She coughs blood, I wanted to say to him. She has no breath. And when she is truly bad, it is all she can do to raise a cup to her lips. She sweats when there is ice on the windows, and she coughs and struggles for breath even when her lungs are filled with that wonderful clean air so beloved of all you experts. Perhaps a year on the shores of a warm sea, or the same in a mountainside sanatorium might be of some benefit to her?

'I wish you all to leave me,' Teale said unexpectedly.

'Of course,' my father said, and immediately did as the man ordered.

Charlotte followed him and beckoned to me from the doorway.

I went to her and she put her hand into mine. It was a rare moment. I felt the tremor of her fingers.

My father left us to walk in front of the house. It was a milder day than usual, and there were periods of warming sun amid the fast cloud. We watched him through the parlour window, his face turned to the warmth, his eyes closed, his hands clasped at his chest.

'He's praying,' Charlotte said. She watched him closely.

'It'll serve as much purpose as our expert's opinion,' I said, immediately regretting the words.

'It's as well to know these things,' she said. I had expected her rebuke, but perhaps even she was now beyond that.

'Do you believe he'll be able to do *anything* for her?' I said.

She shrugged. 'What I do know is that you object to him for no good reason.'

Outside, my father raised the ball of his hands to his mouth and then above his head.

'He rages,' Charlotte said, and then smiled.

'The most peaceful and contained rage I have ever seen,' I said.

After that, there was a minute of silence between us.

Then she said, 'The weather will improve soon enough.' She was not usually prone to such vague or hopeless reckoning.

We continued to watch my father walk in small circles on the slabs, his eyes still closed and his hands still clasped. The previous day he had spent an hour driving away the women who insisted on drying their laundry on the headstones and slabs.

'All that good air,' I said.

She smiled. 'Only warmer.'

We were both then distracted by a sudden loud coughing from Anne. The sound came muffled to us through two doors and across a hallway, but the pain it contained was still all too clear. We waited for it to finish before going on.

'Sea air might help,' Charlotte said. 'I could accompany her. We might all go.' More hopeless reckoning.

'A holiday?' I said. She was again remembering her own happy excursions.

'A return to Bridlington, perhaps,' she said. She seemed suddenly hopeful of the prospect, however unlikely it now was.

I motioned to Father. 'He could pace the clifftops and rage at the sea.'

'Or wonder at it,' she said, her own reverie intact.

'Or that.'

There was a knock at the door and Teale appeared. He came in, disappointed at not finding my father present. 'I was hoping to speak to Parson Brontë,' he said.

'He's outside,' Charlotte said, indicating where my father still walked in his small prayer- and rage-filled circle.

'He often wanders among – upon – the dead,' I said.

And again Teale looked at me with un-

135

disguised contempt in his eyes.

'Facetiousness does not become you,' he said. 'Your ailing sister lies so close and yet you still choose to put yourself and your prejudices before her.'

'He apologizes for his remark,' Charlotte said. She squeezed my arm.

'I do,' I said. 'I apologize.'

'And for his behaviour earlier,' she said.

'And for that, too,' I said.

Teale said, 'Right,' and then, 'Well,' and then, 'I see.'

'What are you able to tell us?' Charlotte asked him. 'I wished to convey my findings directly to your father,' he said. 'It was he who called me here.'

I saw what doors I had again pulled shut in our faces.

'Of course,' Charlotte said. 'Will you go out to him?'

Teale looked again into the churchyard. 'I would prefer him to come back inside,' he said. 'I have never considered a graveyard a particularly healthful place to wander for pleasure.' He watched my father for a moment. 'My predecessor in Leeds once told me that he saw Death on the faces of all the men and women who presented themselves to him.'

I wondered why he had said such a crass thing.

Charlotte went to the window and rapped

136

on it to attract my father's attention. I almost stopped her, wanting him to remain in that small world of his own making for a few moments longer.

'The graves are regulation deep,' I said to Teale. 'He and his sextons and wardens receive edicts almost weekly.'

'I'm sure they do,' Teale said. 'I'm sure everything is properly done.'

Charlotte rapped again, and this time my father stopped his pacing and turned slowly to face us.

19

Waterloo Fair day.

The bottoms and intakes in the entire neighbourhood were said to be enriched with Waterloo fertilizer, though naturally only ground-up French bone was ever brought and sold here.

Bunting hung from the shops and houses on High Street. A pedlar came to West Lane with a monkey wearing a hat and a jacket prancing on his organ. Last year, a false Turk had appeared in the same place with a small bear, which stood upright in chains and performed a shuffling dance. People had gathered in a wide circle around the creature and thrown coins. In earlier years, there had been baiting, but Old Mother Grimshaw had long since put paid to that. Besides, the bears nowadays were too uncommon and too precious to allow any lasting harm to come to them.

I met John Brown in front of the pedlar's monkey. He was with his wife Mary and his daughters, all of them pointing and laughing at the antics of the creature.

'It goes mechanically through the motions,' he said to me, 'and yet it appears to enjoy itself and welcomes our attention.' He clapped his hands as he spoke.

'But not as much as he' – I indicated the pedlar – 'welcomes our attention.' A scatter of coins lay on the ground in front of the man, and every few minutes he interrupted his playing for the monkey to jump down and scamper at his feet to gather these up. Each time the animal did this, it was rewarded with a piece of apple. At the first note from the organ, it was back up on its hind legs and dancing again.

'It looks like an imp,' John said to me, having given his youngest daughter a farthing to throw.

'Grimshaw would have declared it a demon and chased it away with a stick,' I said.

'After a day spent praying for heavy rain so that all enjoyment would have been spoiled anyway.' He looked around me. 'Is your father here?'

'I came alone. Charlotte is out some-where, and Emily is at home with Anne.'

'They were all three as wild as my own small tribe when they were girls,' he said, looking fondly at his daughters.

The music stopped again and the monkey started its gathering-up.

By then the children were eager to move on to other attractions and John was pulled away by them.

'You're welcome to walk with us,' he said to me. 'We have no plan.'

I thanked him for the offer and declined, and he made no attempt to persuade me, leaving me to catch up with his family. I waved to them and they every one of them waved back to me.

I walked towards the Bull and then turned to Bessy Hardacre's opposite. I fingered the few coins in my pocket, knowing that I possessed at least a shilling.

Bessy, as usual when the weather was fair, sat in her open doorway. She shielded her eyes against the sun and looked up at me.

'There's a man showing himself in a tent who has his two middle fingers on both hands joined like Lucifer,' she said to me. '*I won't look at him.*'

'In case it's Lucifer himself?' I said.

'That very thing. Others have already laughed at me for staying put.'

'And then gone to see him for themselves?'

'I say that if he *was* truly Lucifer, then why would he have the need of coming here, to this poor place, and making a show of himself? And why would he be gathering up pennies in the dirt when he has the wealth of Midas at his fingertips?'

'Why indeed,' I said.

'One measure or two?' she asked me, her hand already in her pocket.

'I have a shilling,' I said.

'Then buy two and spare yourself the ale to wash it down.'

'It's a warm day,' I said. 'And getting warmer.'

'Water's cold, and the Lord knows it's cheap enough.' She took the phials from her apron and held them out to me. 'Make your mind up,' she told me.

'My neuralgia is worse,' I said. 'And my facial spasms.'

'We all suffer sorely in our own separate ways,' she said.

I gave her my money and she gave me the phials.

'I told one of the girls going to see this so-called Lucifer to take an advertising board with her,' she said. 'I offered to give him a guinea an hour to stand it at his feet and point people to me.'

'Letting the Devil drum up trade for you?'

140

'Why not? Your father gets a good living off the back of the man.'

The remark made me laugh.

'Here,' she said, and gave me back two of my pennies. 'Saved from the Devil and now they're yours.'

'I'll spend them wisely,' I told her.

'I doubt that,' she said, nodding to the Bull over my shoulder.

20

If the buried Dead are set on their rising, then who among all mortal men will stop them? If the Dead shall possess the strength to push up their slabs and stone lids, then what earthly power shall keep them where they belong?

It is no argument. The Dead shall all rise. Just as they rise in my father's sermons and other men's belief just as they rise in my dreams. All my father's holy arguments are filled with the risen Dead – all men, women and children full of vigour, and all with their flesh uncorrupted, their health restored and their hope for the future – for *another* future – intact. Great marching armies of the Dead bound for Kingdom Come, where those hosts of smiling, horn-blowing angels wait only to welcome and to succour them.

Alive, the living either work themselves into their graves or are put there by illness, age, injury or disease, sometimes all four. But the newly risen and the Heaven-bound shall suffer none of these things, and instead live their new lives of plenty and ease. There will be nothing to check this great uprising, and when I ask my father, then what of the living on Judgement Day, what of *us*, he says only that we shall be afforded the same new existence. The wealthy factory owner shall walk hand in hand with the men he has killed with his unregulated labour and long hours; and even with the children of those men who have died for the want of a father.

It asks a lot, I tell my father, of the man who must suffer and struggle before he is re-born, to consider himself an equal of the man of leisure who is afforded that same reward. It does, is his only answer; it asks a great deal of that man, but he is afterwards a far better man for it.

So... I shall walk again with my mother and with Aunt B; I shall walk and play again with Elizabeth and Maria. My sorrow and grief and loss shall all fade as quick as a summer mist.

I know there is little point to my argument. I shall either die and rot and be proved right, or I shall rise when called and take my place amid the exulting marching throng and be only too happy to have been proved wrong. It profits no man to deny himself his own opportunities. What purpose is a life without hope? What does it serve a man to live his life by Christian doctrine if that life is not properly rewarded according to those same beliefs?

My father talks with the confidence of the converted – more: with the conviction of the true believer. My sisters warn me that I should not challenge him on these matters, but he himself – the old militiaman – tells *them* that he enjoys our gentle wrestling. He tires you, Charlotte tells him. And are men not expected to grow weary, he asks her. It is a circle of an argument, winding round and round and slowly consuming itself. Besides, he tells her, we might as well argue over the facts now, because when the Day of Judgement does finally arrive, there will be no argument *then* – no doubt whatsoever left in any of our minds.

21

There can be no denying that I was at my most contented and satisfied – most my own man – at Luddenden Foot. I was busy there, fully engaged, challenged and fulfilled in my work. I laboured and I wrote, exhausting myself physically and mentally. Broughton seemed an age behind me then.

I knew at Luddenden – upon assuming that mantle of easy responsibility and authority – that it was a course upon which I should have set my sights much sooner. I knew also at Luddenden that everything I had attempted before it – my efforts in Bradford especially – had all been at the urging of others.

It was seen by most as a primitive place, Luddenden – the station house and its adjuncts more resembling sheds and shacks than the stone-built structures of other halts.

My colleagues Killiner and Walton were good men, dependable, and I was close to Grundy then; I considered him hearty and vulgar, but astute. In Grundy's eyes everything existed only to be improved or made modern. His enthusiasm was infectious and we shared a great deal. It is beyond me now to account for the great change in him. Ambition, I suppose, and closing his doors behind him. Charlotte once told me that I worshipped the man, and that he was not worthy of my admiration; others said the same thing later of my friendship with Leyland. I would not deny the second, but Grundy is a different matter.

It was while we were together at Luddenden that Grundy told me he considered me a man both fond of extremes and attracted to danger. It sent a shock of excitement through me to hear him say this of me, and although I felt it incumbent upon myself to rebut both charges, I cannot deny that at the time I wore his opinions as a general might wear his medals.

Following my dismissal, it was Grundy who told me that there were rumours circulating that it was Walton who had been responsible for the shortfall in the Railway accounts. When I had insisted on representing myself to the Board to demand my reinstatement, he told me that the malpractice had taken place while I had been unofficially absent from my post, and that it would be unwise to reawaken any controversy or ill feeling in the matter. Walton, he said, would condemn me further with every word he spoke in his own defence. Besides, Grundy said, the charge of my unsanctioned absence was a far greater infringement and danger to my prospects than the few pounds unaccounted for.

By 'absence', of course, he meant that I had been in one of my usual haunts in the company of all those others. Either in Luddenden or further afield in Halifax itself. The Lord Nelson in Luddenden was my happy home in those days. A library in an ale house, convivial company and endless, educated conversation.

I have lost count of the days I sat with Sutcliffe Sawden, come from Hebden Bridge, or with William Heaton – the first and truest admirer of my poems – with Leyland, Collinson and Drake, or with James Walker, my first and most dependable patron during his tenure at the *Guardian*. The Lord Nelson, the Grape Hotel, the Anchor and Shuttle, the Old Cock, the Broad Tree at Union Cross. I could add a dozen others, all happy stations on my unknowing journey towards this present waste.

Eleven guineas, I remember shouting at Charlotte when she opened the door to me upon my dismissal. What kind of sum was that for so great an enterprise? What price was that when set against all I had given of myself to those men, my condemners?

Thankfully, my father had been absent from the house at the time of my return – I had come by way of Halifax and a week of commiseration – and so he was at least spared this much.

Charlotte told me I was feckless and lackadaisical and that she knew of no one less suited to accounting work. Looking back, I see that even then, so long ago, she was already running out of her stock of excuses for me.

I remember those months living in expectation of a prosecution being brought against me. But nothing did come. And so I continued to allow myself to be consoled by Grundy, who told me endlessly that such incidents were not uncommon, and that the Leeds–Manchester Company was notoriously over-strict in its accounting procedures anyway – that in all probability I ought to consider myself more the victim than the perpetrator in the affair. I urged him to repeat all this to Charlotte, but when he finally did so, she responded to him only with one of her looks and her silence.

After that, he began to keep his distance from me. I saw neither hide nor hair of him for the following three months, and then I ran into him in Bradford, on his way out of the George, where he had been recruiting labour for some new project. To cover his awkwardness, he told me that he had seldom been in Halifax or Haworth of late because Bradford was now the place for cheap labour. He told me he was working on commission to procure it. 'Then procure me,' I told him, and his evasions continued.

Earlier in the day, I had been with Drake and Morley, and the three of us had only recently separated. Grundy told me that he seldom drank these days, and certainly not as much as previously, and never when he was working. His warning was clear to me, and wasted. I made a point of holding my face close to his so that he might smell my breath. He told me the work he was recruiting for was in the labouring line only, and far below my standing in life. 'You mean my "station" in life,' I remember saying to him, and finding this hilarious. Grundy grew even more uncomfortable at my wit, and at my warm, stale breath still blowing on his face.

I left him soon after that and continued to wander in the town while my money lasted.

It was said that the churchyard at Luddenden Foot received no direct sunlight between November and February, but this was untrue. It is true that there were days – weeks, even – when the sky was filled with cloud and the sun seemed never to shine on the place, but there were also days when the whole place was lit and warmed by the low sun. It was of considerably greater consequence to the inhabitants of the bottom when their homes – along with the alleys and the churchyard – flooded from an excess of rain, which was a frequent occurrence in the place. Even more than Haworth, the spot seemed in perpetual thrall to excess water squeezed into tight courses and running over steep gradients.

During my year at Luddenden I was frequently visited by the Company builders and engineers, checking on the efficiency of their drains and culverts. Small landslides regularly blocked the lines as a result of all this running water, and I often walked the tracks with either Killiner or Walton, occasionally Woolven, and then communicated our findings to the Board independently of their own inspections. I cannot once remember receiving a letter of thanks – of acknowledgment, even – for this independence of thought. Later, Grundy assured me that my accounts were still somewhere secure in the Company files. But by then I had lost all faith in the man and his assurances and promises. I learned later still that Woolven himself had twice written to my old masters to complain that I was too often absent from my duty – that, apparently, I was 'long since set on some other course'.

I went three times in the length of that year to see how the churchyard at Luddenden had flooded. The verger, a man called Abraham Clough, insisted that recent embankment work had diverted the water from its usual channels and on to the graves. I was there only to deny this, to placate him, and to reveal to him his powerlessness in the face of the railways and the time he would waste in making any complaint against them. I told him on each occasion that the water would find its way into the canal, and that his own blocked gutters and drains were more likely to be the cause of his problems. I told him that I considered him negligent in having allowed them to become so blocked. He was a lazy man, a procrastinator, and I was easily able to convince him to withdraw his complaints. I told him we all lived on a great sponge of mountain and moor and that nothing he or I or the great machinery of the railway companies did would ever change that. I remember that he agreed with me in an instant – another drink put in front of him – and he told me that every hole he dug a foot deep in his own small allotment filled instantly with black water.

I learned only a month ago that Clough had been killed in an accident in a Hipperholme factory, severing his forearm in a belt-driven machine. I wish I could confess that I felt some sympathy for the man and the manner of his death. I knew nothing of his family. I wish equally that I might feel even the slightest remorse over the way I treated him and his concerns regarding the churchyard. I can see only too well what sleepless anxiety and dread those same concerns would cause my father.

22

I walked with John Brown and Greenwood to the Crow Hill hollow. I had been a boy of only seven or eight at the time of the bog burst. I remembered little of the actual event, but I listened ever afterwards to tales of the moor's saturated explosion and of the ensuing deluge.

It had been John's idea to walk to the hollow. My father was planning another of his open-air services on the anniversary of the eruption, and John wanted to see, even after all this time, if the ground was hard again, all the water gone, and if there was space enough at the rim of the grassy bowl for my father's congregation to stand and sing and pray there.

'I've seen Ranters up here praying with their hands above their heads,' Greenwood said. 'Closer to Heaven, see? It's all a contest to those men.'

'They never get closer than the muck on their feet, that crowd,' John, said, causing us to laugh. He looked all around us. 'This place is changing at a fast pace.' He pointed. 'Moor-edgers coming up the hills. Soon everything will be poor, grabbed pasture.'

'Not this high up,' Greenwood told him. 'Sour soil, see? Even the peat makes poor fuel. There was once a man – Darius Peake, he was called – who lost a son in another burst. Lost him for a year and then the body was thrown back up by the bog and as near as good as when the boy was lost. A full year – longer – and he was tanned like good leather. Brown and glossy as a horse chestnut. Even his eyes were said to be still in their sockets. The men who work the hilltop pits tell tales of others found in the bogs from antiquity.'

'I know Peake,' John said. 'It's true he lost and then found his son again. It was a momentous thing, a resurrection of sorts.'

'And then the father made a bowl of the boy's skull,' Greenwood said, surprising us both.

'What?' John said.

'A bowl. The boy's body was taken away to Leeds, cut apart and examined,' Greenwood said. 'Someone told me Peake was paid a small fortune by historians for the privilege. Some even said that the pickled corpse had afterwards been exhibited to paying customers.'

'What's this bowl?' I asked him, well aware of Greenwood's tendency to elaborate in his storytelling.

'The boy's skull was finally returned to Peake.'

'I never knew that,' John said. 'For seemly burial?'

'That might have been the intention. But Peake was persuaded otherwise by a Lancashire silversmith.'

'What does a silversmith have to do with anything?' John said.

'The man cut the top off the skull and turned it into a bowl. Then he fixed a rim of silver to the cut edge. The bone was bleached white and polished. The thing exists to this day.'

'A skull might last for all eternity,' John said. 'I've visited relic shows and seen them many thousands of years old.'

'And the bowl is still in Peake's house?' I asked Greenwood.

'It is,' he said solemnly. 'But hidden away and only brought out on special occasions. Peake said afterwards that he was haunted by what he'd done – both in handing over his son's body and then in letting it be used so badly – that he could never forgive himself.'

'Was it not against the Law?' I asked him.

'That, too,' Greenwood said. He took out a pipe and filled it, drew from it and then handed it to John, who did the same and passed it to me.

'My wife has forbidden French beans to me,' Greenwood then said unexpectedly. 'She says they incite venery.'

153

I winked at John. 'Tell us more,' I said to Greenwood.

'She says they conjure up lustful desires which she is no longer minded or fitted to accommodate,' Greenwood said sadly.

'It must grieve you,' I said, hiding my face from him. 'Do they conjure *up* anything else?'

'We have children enough,' Greenwood said.

'And the achievement saddens you?' John asked him, keeping a hand over his own laughter.

'I would never dream of turning *their* skulls to silver-rimmed bowls,' Greenwood said. 'Not even if they died naturally and were taken into God's grace, let alone sucked down all unsuspecting into a bottomless bog in a moor burst.'

'Then all the more reason to come up here and give thanks for their well-being,' John said to him. He left us briefly to pace around the shallow depression, stamping his foot into the softer ground. 'Your father is talking of having a portable pulpit constructed so that he might stand above us and be heard,' he called to me across the hollow.

'Would not a simple chair suffice?' I shouted back.

'Those Ranters stood on simple chairs,' Greenwood said. 'They were a wretched crew. I know of one set who stripped themselves naked and then rolled on the hard ground, the better to offer up their prayers. Covered in cuts and bruises, they were. Personally, I prefer going into the Lord's house in my Sunday best so that He can see what an effort I've made on His behalf.' He filled his pipe again. 'A well-dressed man likes to be seen by his neighbours ... though I doubt Parson Brontë will insist on a smart parade for this place.'

23

I came upon Charlotte in church sitting on a front pew, her head bowed. She half turned at the sound of my entry, but kept her eyes closed. I went and sat close behind her. The plaques commemorating our mother and sisters lay right beside us. The aisle at our feet was laid with their stones.

Charlotte finished her prayer and then sat with her head bowed for a moment longer, before finally unclasping her hands and turning to me.

'I thought you were Emily,' she said.

'You make me feel as though I ought to apologize,' I said. 'First for what I am, and then for what I am not.'

'Don't,' she said. 'Not today. I was praying for Anne.'

'Why do—'

'Your self-pity has no place, not here, and certainly not today.' She looked at the plaques and only then did I fully understand her.

It was Ascension Day, the anniversary of Maria's death.

'She might have lived to thirty-four,' Charlotte said.

If longing and affection alone could raise the dead, then the stones above both Maria and Elizabeth would lift and our dear, bright sisters would rise, compose themselves and sit beside us.

'Father preached for two hours this morning,' she said.

'Grimshaw's psalm?'

She smiled at me. 'Nothing so...'

'Long?'

'Punishing,' she said.

Psalm 119 had often been chosen by Grimshaw to beat his congregation into submission and then to test their endurance. It would be forever known by his name in the place. The legacy of the man hung above us like a dark cloud on even the brightest of days.

'Father called for a day of fasting and humiliation,' she said.

'I imagine many here come close to fasting

156

most days as it is.'

She considered the disorder of my clothes, my unshaved face and uncombed hair. I had been in Halifax for the past three days, with Leyland and Geller, and latterly with Heaton and Collinson. It had not been my intention to return home today except that I had expended all my companions and my money.

'To appease God's wrath,' she said.

I looked at Maria and Elizabeth's names. 'Why must we forever appease Him?' I said, my thoughts still wandering.

She shrugged at me – though whether because she did not know why the loving Lord demanded such constant appeasement or because she was again weary of my tiresome provocations, I was uncertain. I tended towards the latter.

'I remember him telling us that Maria had "fallen asleep in Jesus",' I said. 'I clung to that.' I had been a boy of eight.

'Me, too,' she said. 'Parson Ellis told me on his way out of the church today that he appreciated every word of Father's long sermon. He said that politicians and factory owners needed balconies and high gantries to address their crowds, whereas all Father needed to do was to raise himself three feet above the earth.'

I looked up at the pulpit. It still seemed an excessive thing in so spartan a place. The high dividers of the pews surrounded me on all sides. As a small boy, the place had sometimes seemed a maze to me.

'Where were you?' Charlotte asked me.

'Halifax.'

'With?'

'Several and varied. Leyland sends his regards.'

'Did you walk?'

'There and back.' Thirsty when I arrived, sober when I returned.

'We were always great walkers,' she said. She often came into the church to clear her head. She said the cold of the place emptied her mind of its concerns and confusions. Emily said the same of her walks on the moors.

'Is Leyland well?' she asked me. 'His family?'

'He has no proper commissions on his books. Pieces of municipal work, but that's all.'

'I see,' she said, meaning that the man – and all those others – still had time to wander from inn to inn with me, spending money he could ill afford, and drowning his own sorrows at the cost of alleviating those of others.

'There was a party of Evangelists on Ovenden Moor,' I said. 'As I passed them they shouted at me that the Apocalypse was imminent.'

'It always is with them,' she said. 'It's all they've got to bind together their own small congregations.'

'They shouted for me to fall to my knees and to pray with them for my salvation. I told them they were far too late for that to happen – that, in the words of Cowper, I was already fallen lower than Judas, and that the very notion of redemption was a dying breeze to me.'

She smiled again at this, and then shook her head, turned and put her hand on my arm. 'That isn't true,' she said.

We sat in silence for a few minutes, both of us lost in our thoughts.

'Father's eyes are weakening again,' she said eventually.

'Will he need another operation?'

'I was told that any deterioration after the first was to be regretted.'

She had gone to Manchester with him and had waited there while his eyes had healed and his sight had slowly returned and he was strong enough to make the longed-for journey home to return to his work.

'It was a great change in him,' I said.

'But one we cannot repeat. I was with him all day yesterday, copying out his sermon in writing he could read.'

'New spectacles?' I suggested.

'You can ever be relied on for the simplest solution,' she said, adding, 'He would appreciate you more at home.'

'Then his wish is likely granted,' I told her. 'A man needs money to roam and entertain himself.'

'That depends on where he roams and *how* he entertains himself, I suppose,' she said.

Now it was my turn to smile. She despaired of me, and yet still I felt these sunbeams of her favour.

'You might help him more in his day-to-day parish work,' she said.

'I doubt he'd thank me for my interference.'

'Then you must finally learn not to turn away at the slightest rebuff, learn to dampen your own extravagances and to better consider the needs of others.'

I bowed my head. 'I shall try my best,' I said, wondering how many times I had said the same before.

'You might start by reading to him more,' she said. 'And by accompanying him on his errands. Guide him, offer suggestions when he is in doubt.'

'Doubt?' I said. 'I wonder if he has ever truly suffered from that particular affliction since the day he was ordained.'

But again she heard only my own special pleading in this and turned away from me. My raised voice echoed in the open roof above us, and we waited for the whispers to repeat and then fade around us like the flapping wings of disturbed birds.

'He offers you every help and opportunity,' she said.

'And all *I* am capable of in return is ingratitude and disappointment?'

She refused to answer me. Instead, she rose and walked the few paces to the front of the church, where she turned and faced me. She held up her arms as though bestowing a blessing on me.

'He asked me where you were,' she said. 'He said he felt certain that you would return, today of all days. I told him you had not forgotten, that you had promised you would come to hear him talk. He told me I had no obligation to you that would make me a liar, and said that you were most likely with your friends in Halifax. He called it "that ensnaring town".'

'It's that, all right,' I said.

She lowered her arms.

I felt the cold of the damp rising from the flags into my feet. It was a warm day in a warming season, but the cold of the church was never truly dispelled. We lived in that place with degrees and variants of cold rather than with warmth and cold together. Just as we lived with those same degrees and variants of wind and rain. We were as forged and formed by these elements as the hawthorns struggling to grow upright on the moors.

Twenty yards down towards a bottom, they thrived; twenty yards higher up and they struggled even to live.

'I've spoken to Wheelhouse,' Charlotte said, distracting me from my thoughts.

'Oh?'

'He believes Father's sight will moderate with rest and warm flannels applied each evening.'

'Then he recommends rest to a man who scarcely knows the meaning of the word.'

'Which is precisely why his labours must be eased by others,' she said. Then she went to the plaques inscribed with our mother's and sisters' names and stood with her fingers pressed into the lettering. 'He said the gilding might soon need to be redone.'

'I might tell Leyland,' I said.

'It would hardly be worth his while. Besides, John will see to the work for the cost of the leaf.'

'Of course,' I said.

She left me then, pausing beside me before walking briskly to the door. Her footsteps on the hard floor seemed to sound long after she had gone.

I rose from where I sat and went to Maria's name. I put my own fingers into its letters and traced their lines and curves. And then I brought my fingers to my lips and softly kissed them.

24

Later, I met Joshua Hale on the coffin road to Bare Hills. He was sitting on one of the hollow stones there, bathing his feet in a trough.

'I hurt fierce,' he said to me without any greeting, and then pushed a finger between his dirty toes. He told me he had just walked from Trawden, where he had been to see his sister, who was lately close to death. He called it her 'calling'. 'She wanted me to stay with her, but I said to her what was the point? She was ready to go, all her affairs in order, so what was the point of me staying in that place? She has a scorbutic fever. Her skin is all dark and peeling. Her legs look like the trunks of thin trees. A Unitarian. She insists on her ordinary Jesus. I've told her for sixty years that she has things very wrong, but she never listens. Three husbands, all dead, only one ever married in a proper ceremony. Do you have a small knife?'

I took my knife from my pocket, immediately regretting this when he started to pare at his heel with it.

'I saw a West Indian,' he said. 'In Trawden.

I expected a Negro, but he was as white as you and me – whiter. A sugar farmer. He was considered good luck to everyone who touched him. My sister told me to invite him to her home, but I denied her.' He continued to scrape at his foot as he recounted all this.

I watched my knife closely.

'Where are you going?' he asked me.

'I was out walking,' I said. Remembering my lost sisters.

'But where?'

'Towards Wycoller,' I said, pointing to the path.

'That place?' He spat at his feet. 'Sam Wilson saw the Black Dog over Wycoller way.'

'Everybody claims to have seen it one place or another,' I said.

'They give it fancy names – the dog – call it a ghost of sorts, a spectre.'

I doubt there was a high, empty or lonely place in the entire county that did not possess its own elusive, wandering animal. In Pendle it was a wolf, on Manwell Moor a galloping, riderless horse.

'Have you finished with my knife?' I asked him, seeing him push his foot back into its boot.

'This foot, I have.' He raised his other to the stone bowl and started the same process there.

I used the knife to peel and slice fruit, to

sharpen pencils and to pare my own finger-
nails. It was a gift from Aunt B, something I
greatly valued.

'My sister has had her gravestone for a
hearth these past twenty years,' Hale said.
'Every year she is going to die of one thing
or another. Her children have grown weary
of their waiting. Last year she told everyone
her intestines were perforated.'

'Many people hold the prospect of their
death over others,' I said.

'Then more fool them. Some losses are
greater than others, and some losses are not
losses at all.' He strained to look at the sole
of this second foot, holding it up for me to
inspect. 'Can you see a callous?' he asked
me.

His sole and heel were also as rough as
bark, and I wondered if his sister's complaint wasn't a family ailment.

'No, nothing,' I said, unwilling to look any
closer.

'Phariseeism,' he said unexpectedly.

'What?'

'My sister. Well, not her so much as her
last husband. He changed his mind like a
weathercock changes its direction, that
man.'

'But Phariseeism isn't–' I began to say.

'Don't tell me what it *isn't*,' he said.
'What's the point in that?'

I stayed silent.

He seemed satisfied with the condition of his second foot and put it back into the water.

I held out my hand for my knife, and then watched as he closed it and put it into his pocket.

'You have my knife,' I said, indicating the pocket.

'Ah,' he said. 'You're probably right. I'm no thief.' He took it out and gave it to me. 'And shall I tell you what killed her first husband?'

If you must, I thought. I felt the first few drops of light rain on my hand.

'He was a sailor. Loved his home, and loved that suffering woman, but he was a sailor all the same. Always off somewhere else.'

'I can imagine,' I said.

'Home to beget his children and then off again. Wanderlust, they call it.'

More rain fell. I saw it in the stone bowl of water, then pitting the dry path.

'It's coming on to rain,' I said, hoping to cut him short and release myself from his grip.

'So? I was telling you what killed a man.'

'My apologies,' I said.

'He loved his home and his wife and his family so much that one time, after an absence of nearly four years, he came home, docked in Liverpool, caught the train to Bradford, and then walked the rest of the way to Trawden. And the first sight he caught of the house and his wife and children standing in the doorway with their arms out to greet him, it broke his heart. He never left the place again. Broke his heart, and he died of that broken heart less than a month later.'

'A sad tale,' I said, glad only that it had also been a short tale.

'My sister was remarried within the next six months,' he said. 'A weaver. A loose piece of work, never worth his due.'

I rose from where I sat and put on my hat. 'Getting heavier,' I said.

'Hardly,' he said, barely glancing at the sky.

I walked a few paces away from him.

'Do you have an appointment elsewhere?' he said.

'I do,' I said, wanting only to get away from him.

'Wycoller is the other path.'

'I've changed my mind,' I said.

'A luxury not many men can afford these days.'

'No,' I said, and then turned and carried on walking away from him. When I reached home, I would sterilize my knife in the kettle.

25

It is Haworth Fair Day. My father insists on calling it a 'Feast'. And after a fortnight of rain and dark skies, the summer sun has at last shown itself. The fields are sodden, more mud than grass, and the drains and the gutters run like leats. But at least our heads are dry. I have known fairs in the past when the Heavens have opened continuously, but when the people have still arrived in their thousands for their entertainment.

Leyland came for me at midday. Charlotte tried to persuade him that I was not well enough to accompany him, but Leyland understood the true nature of this gentle restraint as well as I did, and he promised her that he would take good care of me. 'Like the blind take good care of the blind,' Charlotte said to us, causing us both to leave her on good terms. I knew how highly Leyland regarded my father and sisters and I would do nothing to jeopardize that regard.

Steam rose off the verges and the road as we walked down towards the fair. Crowds were already gathering, and excited children raced back and forth on the slope.

We paused twice for refreshments. Men told us everything was cheaper in the tents, but Leyland said that he was flush – an old debt recently paid – and that I was to consider him my banker for the day.

Emerging from the Bull, we encountered Searle Phillips, who bemoaned his loss of the *Times*. He asked me about my work, my writing, what works of mine had been published by others and missed by him. I answered him as honestly as I could, but this was hard for me within the hearing of Leyland, who knew the truth of the matter better than I did.

The three of us walked together towards the centre of the fair, but soon after, Phillips was lost to us, and neither Leyland nor I made any effort to find him in the crowd. It was Leyland's opinion that none of the man's enquiries had been sincere, and worse, that there had been a measure of mockery in them.

The fair itself was a great turning lake of people. The smell of roasting meat filled the air, and queues were already forming at the rides. Tents filled all three of Whittaker's paddocks, where boxing and wrestling rings had also been erected.

We watched a fire-eater and a man who drove nails into his own hands. The latter advertised both the nails and the hammer he used on a board hung over his chest. At his back was the manufacturer of the ointment he applied to his scarcely bleeding wounds. Someone shouted out to him that he cheated by drawing the nails in and out of the same few holes. Why not? he shouted back. What else would a sensible man do who put on a performance every quarter of the hour? I'm certain that if my father had been with us, he would have said something more profound on the matter.

In the mid-afternoon, I saw Anne wandering alone by the handicraft stalls. She carried a basket in which there was some rolled material. It was a rare excursion for her. Leyland saw her too and studied her from our distance.

'Is she unwell?' he asked me.

I denied this, making light of the fact that this was how she always looked these days. In truth, she had recovered somewhat since Teale's visit. Leyland was surprised and upset by my levity and he told me that I ought to show more consideration. I could only agree with him.

Vapour rose from the ground where Anne stood and looked around her, and she seemed to me in that setting, and at that distance, more like a vision than a living woman. Some would have said it was a portent. She looked small as a child, and fragile. She acknowledged the people who spoke to her, but did nothing to encourage or prolong their conversation.

Eventually, she made up her mind about something and walked off in the direction of the Old Hall.

'She seems...' Leyland said, his concern for her still evident.

'She is the daughter of their parson,' I told him. 'It's the cross we all four of us must bear.'

'I can see that,' he said, but I could tell that he was unconvinced by my dismissal.

We saw Phillips again, briefly, standing with Elias Saunders, descendant of Moses Saunders, and we guessed by their actions that the two men were arguing. Elias Saunders was known for his arguing. Moses had long been a figure of fun among the Methodist flock, and now his burden had fallen on Elias's shoulders.

'Should we rescue him?' Leyland asked me.

'Elias will draw us in,' I said. 'An argument isn't an argument to that man unless he has at least a dozen to convince or convert.'

'I see,' Leyland said.

The moist, warming air was causing me to sweat profusely and I constantly wiped my face and neck.

After an hour of walking among the attractions and visiting several of the ale tents there, we left the great body of people and returned to the Bull. Turning out of Back

Lane, I saw ahead of me a caravan I recognized from Luddenden Foot. It belonged to a man called Roman Sharp, who had both navvied and worked for the bargees. I saw him emerge and empty a pot on to the verge. He saw me approaching him and called to me. At first, Leyland was reluctant to come with me, but he was fast enough persuaded by the appearance of three of Sharp's eight daughters beside him in the caravan doorway, all of them barefoot and with their brown arms uncovered. They, too, saw me and called out to me. Sharp had lost his wife to the bearing of the last of these girls – now a child of four – and he had raised them alone. I had seldom seen so intense or honest a love in a man for his children. All eight girls were strong and healthy, and every one of them seemed to possess a uniqueness of character when set against the remaining seven. It had been a miracle to me at Luddenden Foot that the man had been able to devote so much of himself and his time to their raising and well-being.

As we arrived at the caravan steps, Roman Sharp came down and embraced me. I introduced him to Leyland and they shook hands. The girls – five of their number, from the youngest to the eldest, who I guessed to be eighteen or nineteen – grinned down at us from above. The caravan or tent or barge in Luddenden Foot had always been a lively and a happy place, bulging at the edges and seams with life, but always with room for visitors.

'Are you here to rob the poor, innocent people of Haworth with your worthless gew-gaws?' I said to Sharp. When not at his other work, the man made kitchen- and pewter-ware. His daughters made braided straw and willow decorations.

Sharp laughed. 'That I am,' he said. He rattled the coins in both his pockets. 'Nothing better than the God-fearing when a gypsy's curse might be evoked.' He beckoned us up the steps and into his crowded home.

Inside were another two of his daughters.

'One missing,' I said, regretting immediately all the offhand remark might imply.

Sharp grinned at me. 'Rose Amelia Catherine Anne,' he said. They all had these same long names. 'Married to a man in Nelson. Moleskin stitcher. I warned her against him, but you know that one.'

I knew her well and remembered a great deal.

'Besides, you had your chance,' Sharp said to me, winking at Leyland. 'She had her eyes on you from her very first reading lesson.'

'I helped to teach her to read,' I said to Leyland. It sounded much more than the few happy hours it had actually been.

'We called it his "missionizing",' Sharp said. 'Paddy Brunty down among the heathens.'

The girls arranged themselves around us and asked us their excited questions. Two of them sat on either side of Leyland and put their arms through his, tugging him from side to side. Their father told them to put the poor man down, and when they released their grip on him, I saw the disappointment in Leyland's face.

'He has his own dependants,' I said to Sharp.

The girls laughed again and tugged at his sleeves, though whether they were testing the man or the cloth I couldn't tell.

Sharp poured out three large cups of spirit. He had done the same each time I'd visited him in Luddenden Foot. Each time I had asked him what the spirit was, and each time he had tapped his nose and told me it was better not to know. 'The Excise?' I had said. 'The very same,' he had said. It was the same drink now, and I could not contain my laughter when Leyland, choking at its rawness, asked him the same question. My reading lessons with the older girls had quickly faltered in the face of their father's generosity.

'I saw John Brown earlier,' Sharp said. He, too, was a friend to the man. 'He said he was concerned for you now that you

174

were back home.'

'He's concerned for everybody he meets,' I said, though not unkindly. 'I've had a summer cold and other small ailments, that's all. Nothing serious. The damp is driving out my blood.'

'Then you should drink up and have another. I know for a fact that this will cure a man of most of his ills.'

We drank a toast to days past. It did me good to be in the man's company again.

'These are hard times,' Sharp said. 'Twenty dead last week in Mytholmroyd alone. Influenza and a common grave. I showed my respects. Ben Corrigan among them.'

'Not Ben Corrigan,' I said. I remembered the man. Not even a man – eighteen, perhaps.

'Him and both his twin babies. His wife lives alone in their tent. The overseers will have her out soon enough.'

There was a moment's silence after this; it was a common enough story in those places.

Leyland and Sharp spoke together for a while, and I abandoned myself to the fussing of the girls.

When Sharp tried again to get them away from me, Leyland told him that I was well used to this kind of attention from the fair sex on account of my sisters. Sharp laughed at this and signalled his defeat to his daughters. But little could have been further from the truth. The attention I received from my sisters remained a cold and changing wind compared with the gentle and caressing warmth in which I was now basking. The older girls told me they were looking for suitable husbands. One of them said she wanted to leave the caravan and live in Halifax. Or perhaps Leeds. Or possibly Manchester. Or perhaps even Sheffield.

Sharp asked me if I'd heard of the riots in Bradford and Keighley a month earlier. I told him I had – my father had insisted on reading the reports to me – but I had remembered little of their causes or outcomes.

There was a further bout of choking from Leyland as he drained his cup. Another bottle was brought out and uncorked. I had often seen Sharp drunk at Luddenden Foot, but even then I had never seen violence or even anger in the man.

An hour later, when it was time for us to leave, neither Leyland nor I could stand easily upright. I banged my head on the caravan's curved roof and Leyland stood up and then immediately sat back down again. He told me he had promised to marry one of the girls, but that he could not remember which. Three of them insisted to him that it was her. He told me he couldn't wait to see our Halifax friends again so that he could tell them what an enjoyable time we had had.

'What you'll remember of it,' Sharp said

to him.

'Every minute, every second,' Leyland insisted.

We left the company, and less than a minute later he was sick over a wall at the Back Lane junction, throwing up into a swathe of ragwort and loosestrife there. Other men did the same further along.

'Feel free to join me,' he said to me during a moment of lucidity, when he was neither gasping for air nor retching.

'I hold on to mine longer these days,' I told him.

We parted when Leyland's stomach was empty. He drank cold water from a trough and doused his face and hair. It had been his intention to walk to the Halifax coach, but he said now that the long walk home would revive him. Besides, he would pass the White Horse Inn, and if he could walk no further then he might spend the night there.

Only after we had parted, and when the day had started late into dusk, did it occur to me that he might have been suggesting that he stayed the night at the parsonage.

Approaching the church, I saw the late sun on the moor tops beyond, scorching them with its golden flame and in places making them look more like the dunes of the driest African desert than the thick, sodden cloth upon which we all lived.

26

Charlotte and Anne have just returned from their mysterious errand. Mysterious only to me, I daresay. The air is charged with the news of their return, and with their ill-kept secret; charged, too, with the tales they are telling to all who wait to hear. London. I only wonder that they should consider me so blind or so ignorant, or so easily disregarded and fooled.

I went out to my father, who stood by the gate, but before I could speak to him, he said, 'Charlotte tells me I need not concern myself with their business, their errand, that it is of little consequence to me. You might likewise benefit from minding your own concerns and leaving them to theirs.'

He knew as well as I did why my sisters had been away from home, but once again we were all made complicit in our subterfuges and manoeuvres. My only surprise upon learning of their venture was that Anne had considered herself sufficiently recovered to make the journey. No doubt Charlotte had been at her persuading again.

Emily had mostly avoided me during their

absence, convinced perhaps that I would press her into telling me all. Of the three of them, it seemed it was Emily who now harboured the greatest doubts about the path they were following. She and Anne had once been much closer, but of late I sensed that they had drawn apart from each other.

There was no longer any talk among them of creating a school at the parsonage or elsewhere in Haworth.

'Ask them,' my father said to me unexpectedly, distracting me from my thoughts. 'If you must, if you insist.'

'They would only lie to me, make excuses,' I said.

Just as they did to him?

'We must depend on Charlotte to do what is best,' he said. 'For *all* our sakes.'

'To earn money, you mean?' His point was clear enough to me.

He looked back at the house, and then at the church beyond. 'Were I to lose the living here, then we all five would find ourselves without a home.'

'Surely, the Commissioners—'

'Might find a place for me? Yes, I daresay. But for my four grown dependants? All four of you remain without independent support. As usual, Branwell, you see only what you choose to see.'

'Our lives were ever precarious,' I said.

He shook his head at the remark. 'Perhaps

you might throw yourself on the mercy and consolation of your friends, but where would *they* go, what kind of home could *they* provide for themselves on the little they possess? We already live on the charity of others. What might an outsider say of us? That I have a son and three unmarried daughters, all of whom remain, one way or another, dependent on me and my scant living? My apologies if these sound harsh words, but they are the facts of the matter.'

'And do you believe that the recent "errand"' – the word made the visit considerably less than it was – 'will improve these prospects?'

He was reluctant to answer me, knowing what this might reveal, what knot might be tied upon a knot. 'Charlotte assures me so, yes.'

'On the understanding that you leave her – them – to their own devices and plotting?'

'She did not phrase it so bluntly, nor so critically. And you, of course, remain a beneficiary of any profit they acquire. I doubt any of them begrudges you a single penny of that.'

There was no answer to this.

'We overlook much that is close to us,' he said. 'Our minds and hearts should be more tempered by our needs and not our passions.' His hands gripped the low wall like they gripped the brass rail of his pulpit.

'You think I harbour a grievance against them?' I said.

'It would be only natural. You have yet to make your own true mark on the world.'

'Then I shall bide my time,' I said.

'You were never a patient child,' he said, as though this might explain everything about me. 'Nor temperamentally suited to the rigours and adversities of the world.'

My whole life in a single breath.

'I do my best,' I said. 'I bear up.'

'Perhaps. But mostly against the rigours and adversities of your own making.' He watched me closely as he said all this. 'Your sisters detach themselves and exclude you from their business because they understand what a liability you might become to them.'

And I *am the one accused of harsh words and bluntness.*

He went on. 'A man cannot live his life the way you live your own and remain a dependable proposition in such transactions.'

'"Liability"?' I said. 'You make me sound as though ... as though...' My argument sank deeper into the mire of its own clumsy making.

'See?' my father said, putting his hand on my arm. 'You rise so swiftly to these excitements. It was always in your nature to do so. A liability is just that, and any man or woman who does not include liability in their reckoning will only regret the omission later.'

'And so by excluding me – by making me their *liability* – Charlotte is doing me a favour and not a disservice?'

He remained silent for a moment, and then said, 'You were always quick to anger and slow to forgive.'

'Spare me,' I said.

'Spare you from the truth, you mean?'

The truth? In truth, I could argue with nothing he had said. Leyland had told me time and time again that when I was so minded, I would argue with myself in an empty room on any subject I chose.

'See?' my father said, indicating a group of people below us. 'Mourners go about the streets everywhere you look.'

I watched the black-clad men and women cross the street.

'It was ever thus,' I said.

'More of late.'

'The railway would have helped, brought them freedom, taken them to the sea.' The plan to bring a branch line to Haworth had failed to find backers and had collapsed. I had tried to persuade my sisters to invest their remaining inheritance in the scheme.

'Only those with the price of travel,' he said. 'I believe Charlotte and Anne walked to the Leeds coach and then walked back again upon their return. Everything these days is a cost to all and a profit only to a few.'

'The train from Leeds to London is a morning's travel,' I said. I remembered the timetable to the minute.

'Perhaps, but I imagine London and its business sees the greater advantage of that.' He raised his hand to a man amid the passing mourners, who paused to look at us. I didn't recognize him, but my father surely did – just as he would also know what relation he was to whoever had died, and what part the loss would now play in his life. He would know all of these details and many more. It was the difference between us, and it was an unbridgeable distance; and it, too, was ever thus.

'They are foretelling more rain,' he said. 'Another poor harvest.'

'After the last one?'

'So they say. I was talking to Zillah Seward. She told me they were coming soon to fell most of Oxenhope Wood. Contractors. It will be a sore loss to the place.'

I remembered the Seward woman. 'Does she still pray to Saint Fiacre?' I asked him.

He smiled at this. 'The Patron Saint of Haemorrhoid Sufferers? I imagine she does. She certainly still cages larks for sale and competition.'

'You once bought a bird for Emily,' I remembered. Despite our conflicts, we swiftly returned to these gentler courses.

'So I did. And Emily being Emily, she sent my money straight back to the skies above. She told me it was what God would have wanted her to do.'

'She'd do the same a hundred times over,' I said.

'That man,' my father said, indicating the figure that still stood and watched us, 'is Martha Cloake's husband.'

'Can you tell? At that distance?'

'He's leaning against the wall – see? – to rest his bent back.' The man was a miner and his spine was curved.

'Has *she* died?'

'Not to my knowledge. A child, perhaps. They went to the Keighley Tenters and never came back to the church. A child is an unformed soul, a difficult judgement. I shall say a private prayer for the family.'

'Even though–'

'Yes, even though they might not wish it.'

When I was a boy and Emily a girl, I once saw her clench her fists so tightly at the sight of a song bird in a cage that her nails dug into her palms and made them bleed.

27

The next day I came upon Charlotte standing before Martin's *Apocalypse*. The engraving had hung in the place for as long as I could remember. It had been my intention to confront her, but as I approached her, the two of us alone in the room, I remembered what my father had said and my resolve failed me.

'Is that how it will be, do you think?' I asked her. 'Earthquakes and fire and the Earth demolished, and all of God's people forsaken and naked and screaming in terror amid the flames and the falling rocks before being plunged into a bottomless abyss?'

I saw how she braced herself before turning to me.

'Why must you always strive so hard?' she said. 'Wherever you go in this house – in this whole place – there is a want of harmony. Your own vanity and self-esteem are wounded and so we are all made to suffer for it. Why must it always be the same with you?'

'I ask because–'

'You ask because provoking *me* seems to give you the greatest pleasure of all.' She turned back to the picture. 'It is one man's

185

vision, that's all.' She paused in thought. 'In fact, I'm surprised you don't recognize in Martin a man after your own sore heart.'

'Meaning what?' I said. 'That my own visions are–'

'Your what?' she said. 'Your visions? What visions do *you* have that might be expressed as his are? Visions? Tell me.'

It had been an unwise thing to say, especially to her, and especially then, so soon after her return.

'My nightmares, then,' I said. 'My dreams.'

'You suffer nightmares because you over-stimulate yourself, and because you settle yourself to nothing solid. You should work, tire your brain.'

'I *do* work,' I insisted.

She shook her head at this. 'You merely go over and over the same old ground. You gather up ancient papers and turn them into new piles, that's all. Past glories. I mean work, true work – something that challenges you, and which might again sustain you from day to day.'

'My plans are forever deranged,' I said, again wishing I'd remained silent.

'More excuses. You behave like a man of wealth, devoting himself to pleasure, but in reality without the means either to support or justify his actions.'

'Meaning I rest too easily on the efforts and charity of others?' I wondered if my father had said the same to her that he had said to me, or if I was reading more into the words than they warranted.

'What *else* would you call it?' she said.

A sudden, sour smell filled the room, and she screwed up her face at this.

'Martha is boiling tansy,' she said.

'For Emily?'

'For us all.' She ran her sleeve over the glass of the engraving. 'Besides,' she said, 'this is Father's favourite. I would keep it in pride of place for no other reason than that.'

I had often seen my father standing with his face only inches from the scene, raising and lowering his spectacles, looking for something either reassuringly familiar or perhaps hitherto unnoticed amid all the terror and destruction.

'Why does she do it?' I said. 'The house will stink for days. Hardacre has her remedies, and Wheelhouse remains content to diagnose and prescribe on a whim.'

'Quiet,' she said, flicking her eyes at the ceiling, where Anne again lay in her bed in the room above us. The excursion to London had exhausted her and she had not come down that morning.

'It's true,' I said.

'I daresay. But the tansy is free, and much else is not.'

I was forever reminded of my spendthrift ways.

'I once thought to fill the house with my own paintings,' I said.

'I'm sure Father would appreciate a few of them framed and hung.'

He had said the same thing to me only a few days earlier, after which I had spent the afternoon searching out what remained of my work, before then dismissing it all as either unworthy or inadequate.

'I know John Brown treasures above all else the painting you made of Tabitha,' Charlotte said to me.

'My talent never settled on its one true course,' I said. This was meant as self-mockery, but she did not hear it.

'I know,' she said, and before I could say any more, she turned and left me.

28

Leyland once remarked to me that my time at Luddenden Foot was a season of cold debauchery. But I was a free man then, and my mantle of cares had not yet been laid so heavily on my shoulders. The Lord Nelson and its library were a better home to me than any I knew in Haworth. Meeting Roman Sharp at the fair had filled my head with memories for days afterwards, and once again the past was a preferable place to me than anywhere I now inhabited.

Those labouring men and women treated me as though I had lived among them for ever. I told them of my father's forebears, and for once I felt myself blessed rather than cursed by the man's past. I made close friends and companions among those rough men. In addition to my reading lessons, I wrote their letters for them and undertook their simple accounting. I filled in their bankers' drafts so that they might keep up their payments to home.

One of my fondest memories was of the evening I spent with Joe Drake, come out to Luddenden from the Rose to gild the fancy-work on some of the boats. He was as taken with those people and their lives as I was. Wilson Anderson had recently come out to paint them. He called them nomads and said he envied their restless, wandering existence. He had lately made another small fortune by exhibiting a collection of nudes, for which some of the Luddenden tent girls had been only too keen to pose as his models. Drake told me that there was a great market for such things, and that I ought to turn my own hand to the work, especially considering my closeness to some of the girls involved. He showed me the photographic equipment he had recently acquired. He said Anderson's studies succeeded because they were not suitable subjects for the camera. He asked me to seek out some of Anderson's models, and knowing the families, I obliged him.

On his final evening before returning home, Drake and I went together to the pool under Midgley. It was a place used by the women and girls to wash their clothes and bedding, and afterwards to bathe.

By sitting on a slope above the pool, and shielded from the women below by a solitary coppice, we were able to watch them unobserved. I imagine I expressed my discomfort at what we were doing, for I remember Drake's long explanation of what separated the artist from any other man, what obligations and privileges this afforded him.

The women performed their chores and then rested on the banks with drink and pipes. The favoured bathing place was directly below where Drake and I sat and watched. He told me that some of Anderson's models had offered themselves to him – some of them as young as ten or twelve, but all of them with the bodies of women. He said that Anderson had had great difficulty in refusing these offers. I can imagine, I told him, and we were both compelled to cover our mouths to silence our laughter lest it be overheard – perhaps by those very same women below.

We watched the bathers in the summer

evening light where it lay across the slope in a shifting band. The women and girls were wholly naked for the most part, and utterly unselfconscious in their nudity as they came and went from the flowing water, swimming and washing, and then climbing out and drying themselves in the warm air.

After an hour, I told Drake that we ought to leave. Some of the younger children were venturing further from the pool, gathering firewood and picking flowers, and some of them climbed halfway up the slope on which we were hidden. But Drake persuaded me to remain. Besides, he said, according to Anderson, the young women would show no true shame even if they discovered they were being watched. He said they took pleasure in exhibiting themselves like this. They were water nymphs, and it was almost our duty – as artists – to watch and to admire them.

Later, as the light finally faded from the slope, the setting sun was revealed in a cleft of the valley to the west, after which it sank swiftly, turning the slope and water beneath us dark.

A great many of the bathers left the pool and were beckoned homewards by the washerwomen, but a few of the older girls remained and continued their splashing about.

Drake told me that one girl Anderson had

191

painted had worn nothing whatsoever beneath the simple dress in which she had arrived at his studio. Anderson swore that she possessed the most perfect female form he had ever seen, that she had perfect colour and shape, that her hair was luxurious and dark, her hands expressive, her features in good symmetry, and that her breasts supported themselves and were crowned by the most prominent and darkest nipples he had ever seen.

Anderson had made a dozen studies of the girl, who had quizzed him constantly as he'd worked. It was Drake's opinion that Anderson had recommended her to his wife as their new housemaid. Again, our hands were at our mouths.

Sunless, the slope grew quickly cold, and beneath us the final few bathers hurriedly dressed themselves. Drake complained of a cramp in his legs, and when we were finally alone I helped him upright and we went down to the water. All was now silent and still. The pale smoke of fires rose through the canopy where the huts and tents were gathered. Drake called it an evening to remember. He told me that we ought soon to visit Anderson together and congratulate him on the success of his exhibition. And who knows, he said, we might even be waited on by Anderson's gypsy beauty.

We parted at Brierley Hall and I returned

alone to the Lord Nelson and all its comforts.

Cold debauchery, indeed.

29

There had been a fire in my bedroom. The curtains burned, and part of the window frame and adjoining wall were badly scorched. The culprit was my candle, which was still alight when I fell asleep. I woke in a room filled with smoke. My father was already out of his bed and being helped down the stairs by Emily. Charlotte and Anne roused me where I lay and pulled me out of the room. When I was at the doorway, Charlotte returned to smother the burning curtains with one of my soaked bed sheets. Aunt B's precious Persian rug had already been rolled tight and dragged out on to the landing.

It was three in the morning, and the night was moonless. Emily brought a lamp into the smoky room and inspected the damage I had caused by my carelessness. Charlotte opened the window and waved out the smoke with a pillowcase. I heard my father downstairs, coughing, being attended to by Emily, who was herself coughing. Men gathered outside and shouted up to Charlotte. She answered them that the fire was out and that no one was harmed. The chief part of the men's concern was for my father. I coughed and spat black mucus into a bowl. I wiped my face with my palms and saw the blackness there too. I remarked to Charlotte that I appeared not to have breathed in too much smoke or to have otherwise suffered, and I saw that she resisted the urge to say something harsh to me. She knew that I had not returned home until long after midnight, and that I had not been entirely sober when I had crawled up the stairs. I had a vague memory of her appearing above me and holding up a lamp to see what was making so much noise in the darkness. I still wore half my clothes; the remainder lay where I had either thrown or dropped them.

I went downstairs and into the parlour. My father sat by the dead fire in his nightclothes. Emily was still beside him, pulling his arms into a coat and folding a blanket over his legs. Here, too, the window had been opened to let the night air into the house.

Anne brought a bowl of water and washed my father's face and hands. The old man took the cloth from her and wiped himself. He asked all three of them how I fared. He insisted he was unharmed and wanted to know only how I had suffered. It pierced me, knowing what I had done – the calamity

I had almost caused – to hear the concern in his voice.

'He is unharmed. A little smoke in his lungs, that's all,' Charlotte told him. She held him where he sat.

I felt the cool draught from the window across my face and started to shiver. Emily brought me a blanket and dropped it in a bundle into my lap. There were others in the house by then, people from the town, all insisting on playing their part.

Several men, led by John Brown, ran upstairs and then returned to us. A man carried out the blackened remains of the burned curtains. He threw these into the garden and then stamped on them. A woman told him to stand back as she poured a pail of water over what little remained.

Charlotte came and knelt beside me. 'See?' she said, the word more mouthed than spoken. *See what a spectacle and unnecessary drama you make of us all.*

I thought to tell her that the small fire had been an accident, no more or less, and though this poor rebuttal formed in my mind, the words did not reach my mouth.

'I'm sorry,' I whispered to her.

'Of course you are. You're always sorry. You're sorry for everything you inflict upon us.' She looked at my father, who now sat with his head bowed while Emily combed his hair. 'Be only thankful that *he* has not

195

suffered,' she said to me.

John Brown came back into the room. He saw how things stood and he too went to sit beside my father and reassure him. He told us Wheelhouse had been sent for. 'No need for the Halifax Volunteers to gallop to our rescue,' he said, grinning at the remark. 'Besides, best time they'd make, they'd be here for tomorrow's dinner to scavenge whatever was left.'

My father started to cough violently and was held forward until this subsided and he was able to clear his throat into the basin at his feet.

'See?' Charlotte said to me again. *Do you see what you have done, the harm you have caused? Do you see how worthless all your apologies and excuses truly are?*

I could only nod my acquiescence to the word. I kept my own head down, unable to face her.

When my father was recovered, John ushered all the townspeople out of the house. A fire was not such an uncommon thing, he told them. Anne waited at the front door and thanked everyone for their concern and help, though in truth she saw as well as I did that most had come just to form an audience for our upset.

The drama was almost over when Wheelhouse finally arrived, accompanied by Greenwood.

'I brought him in my trap,' Greenwood announced to us. Wheelhouse looked as though he had spent an hour dressing and preparing himself. He came into the room, saw me where I sat, and started to come to me.

Charlotte stopped him. 'See to Father,' she told him.

Wheelhouse needed no urging. He apologized to her and went to where my father sat with Emily.

The last to leave, John Brown waited in the doorway. Seeing that there was no disaster in the house, Greenwood suggested to him that the pair of them should wait by his trap in case Wheelhouse deemed my father to require further attention elsewhere.

Overhearing this, Charlotte thanked the two men for coming, but insisted that my father would be going nowhere, and certainly not to a hospital. Both men knew her well enough not to argue with her. John Brown asked her if she knew how the fire had started.

'No one is certain,' she told him. Considering the burned window and curtains, it cannot have been a difficult deduction.

'Besides, all has ended well,' Greenwood said, sparing her further excuses. He himself had had a blaze at his shop less than a year earlier.

Wheelhouse took out his stethoscope and

held it to my father's chest, tilting his head and closing his eyes to listen closely to whatever he heard. All three of my sisters watched him intently, waiting for the smallest sign.

When the man finally withdrew and re-fastened my father's nightshirt, Charlotte said, 'Is there anything?'

'Some congestion,' Wheelhouse said. 'A thickening of the lungs.' As usual, he managed to make his every remark an announcement.

'Caused by the smoke?'

'Very possibly. Or at least greatly exacerbated by it.' He put his stethoscope back into its velvet-lined case, and this into his bag, which sat on the floor like the small altar it was. He took my father's hand and felt his pulse.

We again waited for the seconds to pass. Eventually, Wheelhouse released my father and rubbed his palms together, as though contact with the man had chilled him.

'Well?' Charlotte said, her impatience starting to show.

'He's had an excitement,' Wheelhouse said. 'A fast pulse. Heart palpitations, an increase in nervous compulsion. These are symptoms all to be expected in a man of almost seventy.'

'Seventy-one,' Charlotte corrected him.

'Thank you,' my father said, drawing us all

to him.

'You'll survive,' Wheelhouse said. From anyone else, the remark might have been an affectionate one, made to release the room's tensions, but not from Wheelhouse.

'Of course he shall,' John Brown shouted in to us. 'For how would the rest of us continue without him? It was a bit of smoke, that's all.'

Charlotte shook her head, but said nothing.

'And now for the boy,' Wheelhouse said, meaning me.

There was nothing I could do to stop him. The man leaned down to me, pulled my eyes wide and then told me to open my mouth. I did this and he flinched at my breath.

'He was closer to the fire, the smoke,' Charlotte said to him.

I was almost grateful for the remark.

'He's been closer to a great deal else, too, I should imagine.' Wheelhouse pushed a finger into my mouth, withdrew it and examined it. He pinched my cheek, causing me to exclaim in surprise, and then watched as the pale mark slowly regained its colour. 'He is careless of himself,' he said.

'And others,' Charlotte added.

I wanted to push the man away from me and tell him to spare me his cold concern. There was no doubt anywhere in the room that I was not deserving of even this, let alone what little expertise he might actually possess.

'A greater conflagration has been avoided and we should all thank the Lord and His watchful eye over us for that,' Greenwood said from the doorway. After the fire at his shop, which had destroyed most of his stationery supplies, there had been gossip in the town that he had set the blaze himself to claim money from his insurers. He had sworn to my father that this was not true. He was my friend; I would not have blamed or judged him either way.

'Amen to that,' Wheelhouse added.

My father coughed again and Emily held the bowl back to his lips.

'Our thanks,' Charlotte said to Wheelhouse, meaning that he was now free to leave us.

'Plenty of water and fresh air for a day or two,' the man said. 'For the pair of them, for all of you. No coal gas in the house. And you might expect black spittle for a few days to come. No harm in it. I've seen autopsied miners in the teaching hospitals whose lungs were more coal than flesh.'

Charlotte picked up his bag and gave it to him. 'I shall call for your bill,' she said to him.

'Bill?' Greenwood said. 'Surely ... I mean...'

Wheelhouse left the room without saying

anything further.

When we were once again alone, the five of us, Emily insisted that my father should go to her bed and that she would sleep with Anne. Anne concurred with this. My father started to protest, but saw that resistance was useless in the face of his daughters.

'And me?' I said.

'On the floor beside me?' my father suggested.

'He can sleep in here tonight,' Charlotte said. She added my father's blanket to the one already covering my legs.

Emily and Anne helped my father out of the room and then slowly up the stairs. I heard their shuffling steps across the boards above me. I thought for a moment that Charlotte might help me into my own makeshift bed on the settle, but instead she merely blew out the lamp she held and then waited as its glowing wick died before leaving me in the darkness. I had seldom felt so alone or so abandoned.

30

I did not see my father again till three days later. It seems a strange confession in such a close household. He was standing in the churchyard and studying the ground. As I made up my mind to approach him, he took several strides to one side, and then turned and came back the same distance. I guessed then that he was measuring out the new extension to the burial ground, already proposed to the Church Commissioners.

I had avoided him during those days, sparing us both the excuses and evasions he would feel compelled to make on my behalf. He had spent most of that time in Emily's room, and I had returned to the room blackened by the fire. It was an uneasy time in the house overall.

Usually, I waited until I knew he was otherwise engaged before leaving my room and venturing downstairs – often delaying my appearance until one or other of my sisters had gone in to him, taking him his meals or sitting with him, reading to him and assuring him that all of his duties and commitments were being undertaken by others, themselves included. None of them asked anything of me. Charlotte had suggested to me that the two of us – he and I – might now share a room so that he might keep a closer watch over me. My first impulse was to tell her that she had spoken wrongly and that it was *I* who might now watch over him. I accused her of making a child of me, but she did not deign to answer me.

'You won't avoid him for much longer, surely?'

The voice, so close behind me, made me start. It was Emily, who stood in the doorway, her finger in a book.

'I might have killed us all,' I said, too much of a coward still to turn and face her fully.

'You exceed the truth,' she said.

'It opened my eyes.'

'Then perhaps you're an awakened sinner, the best sort.' She was teasing me.

'Don't,' I said to her.

She came closer to me and looked out at the figure in the churchyard.

'Among his beloved dead,' she said.

'He walked all the way to Roe Head because Charlotte wanted him to visit her there.'

'And fetched her home from Silverdale to save her,' she said.

'Don't,' I said again, not wanting to be reminded of that unhappy time and the close deaths of our sisters.

'He knows they await him,' she said. She herself was as convinced of this as he was.

Neither of us spoke for a moment.

Then I said, 'He was praying over me yesterday. I feigned sleep. He came into the room and knelt beside me.'

'He does it more than you know.'

'He said I had let myself fall from unguided passion into neglect and despair. I almost wept on hearing it.'

'He never hid the truth from anyone.'

'Least of all his wayward son. Charlotte believes I possess no strong will or self-governance. She thinks I seek oblivion and that I destroy everything that is pure or good or strong that comes too close to me.' I waited to hear her denial, or at least something in my favour.

'Only because she wants to protect *him*,' she said, again indicating my father, who was still engrossed in his calculations.

'A father protected from his own son. Am I truly such a monster, such a joke?'

'She believes you have a fixed idea which tyrannizes your spirit.'

'A fixed idea?'

'A notion of something deep inside you that you cannot shake.'

I knew then that she was talking of Thorp Green and Lydia.

'Which tyrannizes something I no longer possess?'

'She fears for your—'

'Sanity?'

'Your well-being. Yes, and your balance of mind. She believes your obsessive nature and disordered existence will one day lead to violence, to harm against yourself.'

'And instead, I disappoint her even in this grand notion by putting a cheap candle to an old curtain.'

She smiled at this. 'She thinks your sorrows bear too heavily on you, that they make even the smallest recovery beyond your grasp.'

'Recovery? To what end?'

She shrugged. 'So that you might continue writing? Extend your translation, perhaps?'

The words, and all the kindness they contained, surprised me. 'And she still believes me capable of such a thing?'

'Of course. We all do,' she said. 'Including Father.'

'I intended going out to him,' I said.

'Then go. He'd be glad of the company.'

'He's marking out where the new graves will fit.'

'The Commissioners are questioning any expansion. Their letter came yesterday; Charlotte hasn't shown it to him yet.'

'Does she fear a relapse?'

'Perhaps. The Commissioners believe old burial plots might be more profitably stacked or reopened.'

'He'd rather bury people under our feet in

here than disturb the dead,' I said.

'I imagine it is what he'll say to them when he learns what they're proposing.'

'They'll deny him,' I said. One more battle for him to fight.

'And he them.' The words hung in the air as she left me, pushing the door wide open so that I might at least fulfil my intention of going out to that old man pacing contentedly among his parishioners.

31

Against all warnings and advice to the contrary – and despite Emily's words of only a week ago – I have again written to Lydia. I sent my note care of Allison at the coach house. I trusted the man during my time there, and I know that Lydia trusts him still. I say I know this, but the truth is that I know nothing of how these things stand after two years. I know as I hope, and all I know and hold dear to me is still buoyed beyond reason by that hope.

I spoke of my hopes concerning Lydia and our future together to Emily soon after my return from Thorp Green, and she told me with her usual forthrightness that my hope was like an abandoned and rotted nest,

206

empty and ready to crumble and collapse in the first strong wind.

It was another of our small fractures in those tumultuous days, and one I felt keenly.

I had known all along how Charlotte might respond to these same confessions – and Anne was bound too closely to me where Thorp Green was concerned – but I had expected that Emily, at least – the possessor of so many of her own secret ambitions – might consider me and all I was then enduring with greater understanding and sympathy.

Once, several months after my return, I had gone to Charlotte and showed her a letter and the cheque it contained that had just arrived from Lydia. 'It is not from her,' she had said. 'And nor is it a letter, not truly. A note, that's all. Telling you that here is some money and that your silence is required. She knows you better than you know yourself. She buys you, that's all. She pays you to stay away from her and to keep your mouth shut. And what is worse – you ask her – you *beg* her – for the money. You are complicit in your own undoing, your own deception and betrayal.'

Later, when Edmund Robinson died and my hopes were again raised, and when *still* no word came from Lydia for me to go back to her, Charlotte became merciless in her insistence to me that I was blinder than ever to the woman's intentions. She called me a dog which endlessly returned to its brutal master for another beating, always hopeful, always disabused. And the more disabused I became, she said, the blinder I became.

'She watches her money and her comforts, that's all,' Charlotte had said. 'And you are thrown your scraps so that you do not threaten any of that.' She told me that Robinson's will was pointed at me like a pistol. Why, she asked me, if I was so convinced of Lydia's enduring love for me, had I not once attempted to return to her since her husband's death?

Some days, I look in the mirror and see nothing of the man I have become, only the man I would surely be were Lydia again to offer me even the smallest encouragement. I am a new Philoctetes, a man whose wounds can never heal, and, as Charlotte said, I know only too well that I have betrayed myself far more than I have ever been betrayed by any other. My time of promise – that happy ghost – is long past.

Only yesterday, Emily remarked to me that I carried my anger like a man who carries a gun on a moor, waiting only for the slightest sound or movement to swing and fire, blind to whatever his target might be, or however deserving of his lethal attention. And because I was in no mood for her preaching, *I* told *her* that *she* was like a proud housewife who abhorred everything outside of stultifying routine, and who could not unfasten her own emotions for a single moment for fear of where they might lead her. I told her that everything was put in a box with her, and that however well she *wrote*, she did not *live* well. She shook her head at all of this and told me to believe what I liked.

A few minutes later, after she had gone and I was once again alone for the day, I regretted every word I had said to her. A week ago she had come to me in compassion and kindness, when neither Charlotte nor Anne would even mark my existence, and now I had done this to her.

It has long since occurred to me that, just as the quicksilver falls in the barometer as a storm approaches, so I have something similar in my own nature, something which rises and then falls in accordance with a greater, outward scheme, and over which I am unable to exercise any control whatsoever. Perhaps if I knew when that quicksilver was falling, then I might at least shut myself away from everyone and endure my moods and terrors alone and unremarked, returning to society only when the glass was on the rise again.

Emily says I am like an excitable dog in a fruitless ecstasy of expectation. Is this the same dog, I want to ask her, which forever skulks towards its beatings?

32

I saw John Thompson and Will Geller in the company of Leyland, and for a day and night we socialized as though the recent years had not passed, and as though we were all four of us still young and waiting for our fame and our fortunes to come. After recent events, the day was a great tonic for me. I was my own man again in the company of these others, and I sensed something of the same in all of them, Leyland especially.

Thompson had come to visit Leyland, summoned by him because of his own gathering troubles, and he had called en route for Geller – likely for some support in the encounter – who had then insisted on accompanying him to Halifax on the Bradford coach. From Leyland's studio they had drifted towards our usual haunts and the currents which carried us from one to the other. I joined them in the Old Cock, and all three men rose from their seats and held up their glasses to me the moment I entered.

Thompson declared that providence and not preparation had brought us back together, and I could only agree with him.

From the Cock we walked to Sugden's

Talbot, where Geller's credit was always good.

I had not seen Leyland since our day at Haworth Fair over a month earlier. I had sent him three notes since then, suggesting an outing, but had heard nothing from him. In the Talbot he rose to his feet, bowed to me and then pulled out the linings of his empty pockets. He said he had received only one of my notes, but that the other two probably remained unopened amid the ever growing pile of his bills and demands. He apologized to me for his slackness, and Geller said immediately that he would soon be tight enough.

'Everything I touch these days seems to crumble to dust – quite literally, in some instances,' Leyland said, and he was the first to laugh at the remark.

Thompson and Geller shared their own, lesser troubles, and we all four of us drank to these.

'Out of sight, out of mind,' Thompson said.

I told them of the fire I had started, and not a single one of them condemned me for it. All of them asked after my father and my sisters.

Thompson said he had spent the previous evening in the company of Robert Story, who had recited his latest poems. John James had also been present, and he in turn had entertained the company with news of his latest archaeological labours on the banks of the Ouse. The mention of the river could only stir my own unsettled thoughts, but I concealed these from my friends.

Hearing Thompson talk of all these encounters made me envious of the wider society he still enjoyed, and I saw what a poor alternative I had made for myself in Haworth. When I had lived in Bradford, I had spent more time in the George in the company of these same men than I had at my lodgings. My lively evenings there had seemed never-ending – if not with Thompson, Geller, Story and James, then with Illingworth, Reaney, Anderson and the Cousen brothers. We declared often enough on those nights that we were a company that would never be parted; and vowed too that the first of us to gain our rightful recognition in the world would share that glory with all these others. I doubt if any of us could say with certainty when the sun had finally set on those golden days.

Thompson – perhaps the most successful among us – spoke of the commissions upon which he was currently working, but his fortunes contrasted too sharply with our own – mine and Leyland's, in particular – and so he was reluctant to say too much on the matter, happier instead to add his smaller woes to ours. Geller called us all comrades in adversity.

'I myself have a magnetic power for misfortune,' I told them. 'The harder I exert that power, the harder it drives all fortune away.'

'You'll right yourself soon enough,' Geller insisted to me.

'Aye, like an upturned boat,' Thompson added.

I was the first to raise my glass to the suggestion. I saw how much more encouraged in my efforts I would be were I to live regularly in such like-minded company, rather than in the company of people who saw only the collapse and failure of those same efforts.

Later in the evening, all of us in our cups, and our brains and tongues loosened, Geller said to me, 'I see your sisters cause a stir.' He glanced at both Thompson and Leyland as he said it, and I knew from their averted eyes that they would rather he had not raised the subject in front of me.

'They always did,' I said quickly. 'But whatever they do, they are still only wise virgins wandering in an unbounded wilderness.'

The harshness of my remark embarrassed Geller and he was anxious for one of the others to speak.

'He meant you no insult,' Leyland said to me, his hand on my arm.

Before I could respond, Thompson said,

'They should marry, that's all. Secure something of the years ahead and take themselves beyond all uncertainty.'

And again before I could keep up with this roundabout conversation and its blend of sympathy and diversion, Thompson said, 'My own vile sister has been married three times, widowed twice, and lives well enough on her provision.'

'Some women have far too much juice to quench the thirst of a solitary man,' Geller said, raising his glass to his mouth and sucking loudly at its contents.

Thompson then recounted the tale of his own recent conquest, which was news to us all. He said he had been attracted to a girl by the 'delicious movement' of her body. He savoured the words and then drew a finger across his wet lips when he'd finished speaking. From what little he'd said, I was left uncertain precisely what had happened between himself and this girl and all her delicious movements.

'A stir?' I said to Geller, returning us to our starting point. 'You said my sisters caused a stir.' It was the same word Searle Phillips had used, and I wondered what, if anything, this signified.

Geller was reluctant to explain himself. He took off his spectacles and wiped them.

'Are they all three now back at home?' Leyland asked me, putting himself between

214

Geller and myself. 'They have plans, surely?' He was ever my defender and my advocate.

'A wealthy husband would come in useful,' I said, remembering what my father had said to me about the precarious nature of all our lives. 'Besides, I have my own comforts to consider.'

'Of course you do,' Thompson said, laughing loudly, but without conviction.

Upon his asking, I told Geller that Anne had recently been unwell, but that I was no longer her confidante, and that a great deal was kept from me by them all.

Thompson asked after my father, not because he knew the man well, but because he too longed for these safer topics. Our intoxication increased with every passing minute; who knew what uncontrollable passions lay ahead of us.

Geller remarked that I must be proud of all my father had achieved on behalf of his parishioners.

Perhaps, but at what cost to his own children, I wanted to say to him, but kept silent, knowing what an insult this would prove to us all.

Then Leyland talked again of his diminishing commissions, and Thompson and Geller of their own labours. I spoke of the poems I had published a year earlier – longer – as though they were fresh from my pen.

Geller said that John James was working on a study of the Apocryphal Book of Esdras, banned from the Bible because of its promotion of the superior strength of women over men, and I wondered if this, too, was somehow in connection with my sisters and the 'stir' they were supposedly causing in the world.

'Ah, the speech of Zorobabel,' Thompson said, raising his glass.

Then Leyland put his arm round my shoulders and asked me if I remembered our walks together over Warley and Wadsworth moors. I told him that I did, that I remembered them in the closest detail and with the greatest fondness. More – I confessed to him that I sometimes dreamed of those times together, and that they now seemed more real to me than any of the days and weeks through which I currently wandered.

He promised me that we would visit the same places again when he felt stronger and better able to undertake the journeys. It surprised me to hear him say this, and especially with such sadness and resignation in his voice. A walk of a full morning or afternoon – a full day, even – and in all weathers had never been a problem to the man, to any of us.

Sensing this sudden slump in our conviviality, Thompson proposed a toast to all our sisters – vile and otherwise – and to wives and mothers and daughters, and we ended the subject in a rattle of glasses and a splash of froth.

Geller tried to rise from where he sat, but could not, and so he sank immediately back down. 'We should all thank the Lord for the lives we lead and have made for ourselves,' he said, fumbling with almost every word.

'Of course we should,' Leyland told him.

'And for all our friends and companions,' Thompson added.

'Them, too,' Leyland said.

'For I am bold to tell you...' Geller went on, but then faltered in his drunkenness.

'To tell us what?' I prompted him.

'That there are too many people in this world forever asking why they were brought into it only to struggle and to suffer and then to die.'

'Hear, hear,' I said. I imagined he was going to rise on to his box and expand on the subject. It was how he usually finished his evenings, and we were all familiar with the speech, and we all indulged him in it.

But instead, losing track of himself and where he was headed, he said, 'A dog's nose?' and then called to the watching landlord for more ale and a bottle of rum.

Leyland alone declined the offer. 'Not after the last time,' he said. 'Besides, we must all of us suffer to some degree or other.'

'And every single one of us must die,' Thompson added.

I told Leyland that I would spare him his excuses and would drink his share of the mixture for him.

'You often do – did – do,' he said, his own power of speech and reasoning starting to fail him.

The ale and rum arrived at the table. I uncorked the bottle and sniffed it. The landlord waited for Geller to scribble his mark against his growing debt to the man. Thompson pulled a handful of coins from his pocket, but succeeded only in dropping most of these. I tipped an unequal measure of spirit into each of the glasses and distributed them.

Geller was the first to raise his. 'To men who must struggle and suffer, but who remain their own masters,' he said.

We all did our best to repeat the toast.

The rum was lost in the ale, hardly there, and so to taste it I took a long swallow from the bottle, handing it on to Geller, who did the same and then passed it to Thompson.

Leyland again refused and said he felt sick. His cheeks and forehead were already shining with sweat.

'None of us know the half of it,' Geller said.

'Half of what?' Leyland asked him, a hand

to his mouth.

'*It*,' Geller said. '*It*,' and he winked and tapped his nose. And, as all so often on those long nights, it made both perfect sense and absolutely no sense at all.

33

I was last in the church to hear my Father speak at Aunt B's funeral, but never to worship there. I am uncertain what I prove to my father by my absence, but I know that the gesture – however futile or hurtful in the eyes of others – is real enough to me.

The high pulpit stood before me.

I DETERMINED NOT TO KNOW ANYTHING AMONG YOU SAVE JESUS CHRIST AND HIM CRUCIFIED.

Whenever there is restlessness or noise in the congregation beneath him, my father falls silent and holds a finger to the board. His audience invariably quietens at this, and he continues speaking as though there had been neither interruption nor command.

I remember as a boy watching people walk on the inscribed flagstones in the aisle, and how I always wanted to tell them not to, to watch where they trod. I could have been little older than five or six when I first did this, my cheeks flushed with indignation, and I remember too the humour and quiet concern with which my father consoled me. He explained to me about that which lay beneath and that which had long since risen above. It was a reassurance, of sorts.

I asked him why those who had risen above never came back down below to inform and reassure the living – and, presumably, the ever-hopeful future ascenders – what it was truly like in God's Kingdom. He answered this particular concern by assuring me that there was no need for this – that any man, woman or child secure in the knowledge of God's love, grace and protection knew exactly what awaited them upon their own arrival there. Besides, he added, it was all part of God's plan that none of us – himself included – should ever know these things for certain, thus diminishing our sense of awe and wonder upon attaining the place ourselves and that we should accept without doubt or reservation that whatever *did* await us would far exceed all our earthly expectations. Anyone who doubted this, my father said, was not yet secure in God's love.

Belief, he told me – *true* belief – was shaped as easily as clay, and we were all

God's clay. He shaped us, and part of Him resided within us ever afterwards. I considered all this, but knew, even then, in my child's heart, that I would never accustom myself to those people walking where they walked. Neither Maria nor Elizabeth were yet dead and buried when he told me all this, so they cannot have been the cause of my anxiety. I myself have never once set foot on the slabs without a fleeting sense of guilt, and both Emily and Anne have confided the same to me.

34

I dreamed last night of my visit to Hartley Coleridge at Grasmere, and the dream came to me so clearly in its close details and essentials that I woke from it with a start to find myself shaking and close to tears, my heart beating hard in my chest. And even as I woke from it, I immediately wished myself back within it, so perfect and so sustaining was it to me, even after all these years. I might still swear with my hand on that same heart that it was the happiest day of my entire life.

I lay in my bed for a few moments, listening to my father's laboured breathing.

221

It is no surprise to me that this one solitary day should return so vividly to me, or that even now, and despite all that has happened to me since, I should still seek to embrace it and cleave to it for all it once signified to me.

I always harboured a bitterness at being an inferior employee to men who possessed nothing of my intellect and learning. Money always made its mark in the world, and I was always in thrall to what it offered and signified. Postlethwaite at Broughton was no exception to this.

How many of these same dead ends must I run up against? After all my unanswered letters to Blackwood's and others, all those poems and essays scattered to the winds, here, finally, in Hartley Coleridge, was a man I might meet as an equal. What was Charlotte's cruel dismissal from Southey compared to this?

Coleridge answered me in Broughton and said he could think of no better way to spend a day than in the company of another 'striving' man of letters. He said we were both 'sons of men', by which I understood him to mean that we lived in the shadows – however benign – of others. I could not entirely agree with this – our fathers were beyond comparison – and besides, unlike him, I was still at the start of the struggle to make my place in the world.

Come at 'punctual midday', he wrote to me, and I allowed myself twice the time necessary for the journey from Broughton. He warned me that I should meet no 'sophistical' company in the place where he dwelled, merely himself and the labouring people upon whom he depended. I wondered for every moment of my journey towards him what he expected to see approaching him in that place so filled with the memories and associations of others.

I arrived an hour before the designated time, tired after my final approach on foot over the low fells. I had told Postlethwaite that I was owed a day's liberty, but what did he care?

At midday I approached Coleridge's home, and as I entered the front gate, he came out to greet me. He shook my hand and looked all around us as he spoke. I had heard it said of him that he was more of a nervous boy than a man, and that he had become reclusive, withdrawn from the world and afraid of all its incursions.

His hair was vividly white, and though I knew him to be in his fifth decade, he seemed considerably older to me, and nothing like the child I had anticipated. He was short, no taller than any of my sisters, and with a stooped back and shuffling gait which gave him the appearance of even greater age.

He asked me if he surprised me, and I told him that he did this only by his kindness and his sacrifice to me. He asked me what I meant by this latter, but as I began to explain, his mind wandered to something else and he asked my opinion of something he had recently published in the *Westminster Gazette,* which I had not read. He told me that a week earlier he had argued with a local man, and that this man had called him 'pathetic' and accused him of inhabiting a fantasy world at the expense of those few people who still cared for him and his sanity. All this was pressed upon me within moments of our encounter.

It was not an unduly cold day, but he declared himself perishing and insisted we go inside to his fire. We did this and afterwards sat close together for those few happy hours. We talked of our respective work, and he praised again the poems I had already sent to him. He asked to see the pieces of translation I had carried to him in my satchel. He frequently asked me my age, and when I reminded him that I was twenty-two, he said 'remarkable' every time. He offered me both wine and ale, but said he would not partake himself on account of having recently turned into a 'milk and water man'. Everything he said was a grain of gold to me.

I told him of my own undersized childhood and we compared our experiences. He told me that he had long endured seizures of his own. He asked me about my father, but was reluctant to talk at length about his own. He said that too many people were now turning their recollections to profit, and that these accounts were altered and shaded and caused him great anguish to read.

When I asked him for advice in dealing with editors, he told me of his acquaintance with the men; he spoke of many of these as though they were his friends or members of his family, which I supposed had a great deal to do with his father; I cannot say my own experience of those same figures has been so encouraging.

He told me he was flattered to be quizzed like this. When I asked him how many others sought him out – assuming these pilgrims to be plentiful – he bowed his head and said that he was happier for them not to come and to be left to his own purposes. He told me that it was his ambition to live as the Chaldean shepherds had lived, and I told him of my father's sermons among his own sheep-rearing congregation. This amused him and he said he had not laughed so much in the year just passed. He told me I was a boon to him.

Perhaps I imagined then that there would be many such visits, and that this encounter was only the first of these. Perhaps I imagined that with his sponsorship and recommendations I might at last gain a hearing from all those men who had so far conspired to ignore and deny me.

When I asked him why he had chosen to lead such an isolated existence, he said that he could not reasonably complain of it. Besides, he added, it was the perfect life for the creation of poetry. His mind was narrowed, he said, forever pointed towards its goal. He said he spent days in a dull stupor, and that he would then suddenly emerge from this to compose rapidly. He told me his lonely days were like the soil in which things grew. He told me to beware of the Philistine demands of others and to shun the incubus of debt.

When I told him of my circumstances in Haworth, he said it sounded a perfect place for a man of my disposition and appetites.

I wanted to ask him outright if he would write to those editors he knew on my behalf, but when I started on the subject he held up his hand to me and said that he valued my company and conversation far too much – even after so short an acquaintance – to waste our time in that direction. I told him I agreed with him and pretended to share his laughter.

He asked me – being the son of a parson – if it was true that a man who believed he was possessed by the Devil dare not cross himself for fear of the inner agony this would provoke. I told him that it was what Grimshaw had believed, and that he always watched his congregation closely to catch those who avoided the gesture. He asked me more about the man and said he sounded like the perfect subject for a poem. I could not have disagreed more with this – the fanatic parson was the everyday stuff of my life – but again I feigned agreement.

He said that his own father had told him that a man staring into a mirror long enough would almost certainly see the Devil there. I had heard the same thing said at a hundred barn-gatherings and roadside pulpits.

It was May Day and I wished we could have walked together, along the shores of Rydal, say, or up the slope behind his home – his cottage seemed shut in to me, its air stale – but he dismissed the suggestion with a wave of his hand, as though I had been making another joke. He told me that his father had been a great walker. As was mine, I said. Ah, no, he said – a walker for the purposes of imaginative contemplation, not a man forced to walk for want of transport. He asked me if we owned a carriage, and when I said not, he said, horses, then?

His mind was again elsewhere before I

could frame my answer, and he recited to me from memory a dozen lines of the hundreds I had sent to him in advance of my arrival. He assured me that he knew the rest, and insisted that poor verse did not allow itself to be committed to memory like this. He urged me to complete my translation of Horace's Odes, certain that my own poetic leaning would continue to do justice to the work.

Towards the end of the afternoon – he seemed unaware that the fire was dying on us for want of fuel – he asked me what places such as Leeds or Bradford or Halifax were truly like – I had mentioned all three to him – but before I could answer him, he said they must be a sort of lesser Hell on Earth. The judgement surprised me, and dismayed me a little, but he would hear no contradiction. He spoke of the mills and factories, the pits and furnaces, of fire and turmoil and striving, and of the degraded lives of the people living and working there, asking over and over how any of those places could *not* be a kind of lesser Hell.

He asked me how often I visited London and met with the rest of 'our' society there, and for a moment I wondered if he had taken even the slightest notice of me and all I had just told him. And then he clasped me by the shoulders and said that of course I didn't pander to such men, that I was wise enough, and secure enough in my talent, to have nothing whatsoever to do with them.

The falling sun cast a shadow across one wall and he saw this and said immediately that he imagined I would need to begin my journey home. I had told him all about Postlethwaite and his family, and that I would be expected to show myself before them first thing in the morning. I swear even now that if he had asked me to stay, to spend a single night or day longer with him, then I would have left Postlethwaite and his stupid children to rot. But he made no such offer. On the contrary, he seemed now eager to be rid of all company and to be left alone.

He had a drawer filled with coach and ferry timetables, and he showed these to me in case I was uncertain. I reassured him that I had already planned my journey and paid for the tickets in advance, and he responded to this as though it were the most remarkable accomplishment imaginable – planning a journey, changing coaches, calculating times, and all without the help of others. And all of this happening as darkness fell. He said it was something he himself could never attempt – that others now made every such arrangement for him, and that he envied me my spirit of independence. It was something else to be added to my stock of virtues.

We parted where we had met, at his gate. He had given me back my manuscript, saying that if it remained on his desk he might mistake it for one of his own and begin his unwarranted alterations to it. It was another of his great kindnesses to me, but his last.

35

I have missed Luddenden Fair, another of my summer markers. I promised Leyland and Geller when last we met that I would join them there, and now I have forgotten our arrangement completely and have missed it. One bright day amid this gathering dark and it has passed me by. Others might confound and deny me, but I confound and deny myself most and worst of all. There can be no doubt whatsoever now that I have become a far greater loss in my own life than I have become in the lives of others.

I have not yet attempted to contact either Leyland or Geller, and likewise I have received no word from either of them.

Three days after the event, I told Anne what had happened, what I had missed, what pleasure I had forfeited.

She told me I ought first to contain my anger and to lower my voice, and then she asked me if I was blaming *her* for what had happened.

'*Someone* might have reminded me,' I told her.

Keeper was at her feet, and he snapped at my shins at hearing my raised voice. It was late in the forenoon, and the two of them had just returned from a walk.

'I was taking him back to Emily,' she said.

I stamped my foot at the small dog and he growled and bared his teeth to me.

'You make an enemy of yourself,' Anne said. 'Besides, if you'd wanted to go to the fair as badly as you say, then you would have made a reminder to yourself.'

'I never needed reminding in the past,' I said, knowing that I was yet again making the argument against myself.

'To enjoy and to intoxicate yourself, no,' she said. 'And to many, that will be the only wonder now that you missed the thing.'

I asked her if either Leyland or Geller had sent word to the house.

She shook her head. 'And I doubt they will,' she said. 'The day is long over.'

The dog climbed the stairs and sat whimpering at Emily's door.

'That dog has more common sense and notion of allegiance and duty than you do,' Anne said.

231

'He has the instinct of an animal, that's all.'

'Perhaps, but those instincts guide, correct and satisfy him every waking minute of his being.'

'And mine do not? I still know right from wrong,' I said, knowing that this too was no valid argument in her eyes.

She pulled off her thin gloves. 'You look everywhere for blame or fault except where you know it truly lies,' she said, and then she walked past me into the kitchen.

At the top of the stairs, Keeper started to scrape softly at Emily's door.

I followed Anne into the kitchen and told her I was sorry for how I'd spoken to her, and that she was right, that I had only myself to blame for my loss.

She fastened a white Holland pinafore to her waist.

'I'm angry only at myself,' I said. 'It would have revived me, that's all. I miss the company of my friends.' I tried to remember how long had passed since our night together in the Cock.

'Even those who forever lead you into temptation?'

'*Especially* those who forever lead me into temptation.'

'It sometimes seems they are the only kind you have left to you,' she said. She slapped my arm, but gently. Then she called up to silence Keeper, and the dog immediately obeyed her. A moment later, he reappeared at her feet.

'He's swapping his affections,' I said.

'Don't,' she said quickly. 'Emily is getting stronger every day.'

Two months earlier, we had been saying precisely the same of her.

'Of course she is,' I said. 'I only meant–'

'I know what you meant,' she said.

I left her and walked out into the garden. The dog walked with me, but only as far as the open door, whereupon he turned and went back in to Anne.

36

I was with John Brown at the corner of Changegate when we were forced to leave the road by the arrival there of a carter who was having difficulty driving his horse and its overloaded cart up that steep hill. For every step the animal took, it stood for a moment and panted, bracing itself against the backward drag of the cart. As often happened, the carter carried lengths of timber to push beneath his wheels. Few brakes were equal to their task on that slope.

The cart carried a load of cases, along

with two large barrels marked with the name of William Thomas. Both John and I knew our brandy merchant well, and we speculated on one of the precious kegs falling from the cart and rolling down the hill.

As the carter drew closer towards us, he attempted to turn the horse so that the cart wheels did not face down the slope, but he was unsuccessful in this, and the animal seemed suddenly anxious and uncertain of what was being demanded of it. The man beat the creature on its neck and head with a switch. He held the reins and walked alongside the horse, having climbed down from his seat at the bottom of the hill.

'Let the beast rest and gather its strength,' John called to him. He approached the man, making soothing noises to the horse.

'None of your concern, mister,' the carter shouted back at him. He looked from John to me, studying me as though he and I were already acquainted.

John went to the horse and put his hand against its cheek. 'He's burning,' he said to the man.

'Of course he is – and so am I.' He pointed his switch at John's chest, causing him to return to me.

'Leave him,' I said. I had seen a thousand horses and their loads struggle up that street.

But, as I expected, John would not be so quickly persuaded.

'Rest him a minute or two longer,' he called to the carter.

And even though this was a sensible argument, the man, unhappy at being told what to do, and displeased too by the attention of the small crowd gathering across the street, came back to the horse and coiled its reins around his forearm. He began to strike the creature again on its ribs, cursing it and shouting at it to move. Another twenty yards and it would be on a gentler gradient, where it might at least stand without fear of the cart rolling.

The animal strained in its harness and the cart moved up from its timbers. This time the horse managed half a dozen strenuous steps before stopping halfway to its goal.

'See?' the carter called to us. He turned to the crowd and said the same to them. A few of them answered him back and so he scowled at them as he had scowled at John. He raised his switch to them and several of the woman and children among these onlookers left and went about their business. 'You want a show?' the man shouted triumphantly. 'Then throw me some money.'

John nudged my arm and indicated to me the cart's load, which trembled at the horse's exertions. 'Not safe,' he said. He called out the same to the carter, who shook his head at the warning and told us again to mind our own business.

Convinced that the horse would soon reach the turn in the road, he went back to his beating. But this time the animal had no strength left to move.

It was late afternoon, and warm, and the horse had most likely been pulling one load or another all day. It was why many deliveries came early to the place, or came to it over the tops, avoiding these steeper gradients.

'We ought to move,' John said to me, and he took my arm and we walked a further few paces from the cart, whose load was now rocking from side to side. And even as we did this, and as we turned to look again at the exhausted animal, a rope flew loose and several crates fell from beneath their cover to the ground. In response to this, the carter shouted more loudly at the horse and quickly unfastened himself from its reins.

Unbalanced by the loss of part of its load, the cart slewed at an angle to the animal and then tipped slowly on to its side, raising its shafts, pulling the horse off its feet, and then dragging it in its harness to the ground, where it whinnied in fear and pain and struggled to right itself.

More cases fell to the ground, shattered and spread their contents on the cobbles, and both of Thomas's brandy barrels also fell. Neither of these broke, however, and likewise neither of them rolled further than the kerb, where men from the crowd secured them and stood them upright.

The horse, meanwhile, continued its struggles, filling the air with its noise. The carter retrieved its lead rope and tried to raise its head from the ground. A man approached him with a knife and told him to cut the harness and let the creature attempt to stand unconstrained. But the carter was adamant that this should not happen. It was a new harness, he insisted, an expensive one, Spanish leather, fetched all the way from Northampton.

John laughed at hearing this. It was a worn and much mended harness, thin and frayed with wear. 'Besides...' he said to me, and indicated one of the horse's forelegs, which the animal held at an angle to its chest, and then at the bloody gash across its ribs. 'It won't stand again,' he said matter-of-factly.

'Or be worth the saving?' I said.

He shook his head and then called for the carter to listen to the man who was offering his knife.

The fallen horse continued with its snorting, and a bloody froth now flew in a spray from its mouth.

Eventually, still in its uncut harness, the

animal fell quiet, its eyes wide. Blood and lather ran in lines from its neck, and its long mane lay wet to its flesh.

Several terriers appeared and darted snapping and growling at the animal, adding to its torture. The carter kicked ineffectually at these and then went to check the secured barrels. The men he had sworn at earlier said they had a good mind to push the barrels over and let them continue down the hill. Where was the profit to any of them in that? the carter said, and the men could only agree with him.

After this, the man with the knife cut the horse's chest strap and its spar tethers, allowing it at least to lie clear of the toppled cart.

Then someone in the crowd shouted out, 'Tozer,' and John and I turned to see the town's fell-monger approaching, carrying his bolt and wearing the heavy, blood-stained apron he invariably wore. He was smoking a pipe and singing loudly as he came.

The carter recognized him immediately and went to him with his palms out. He called for Tozer to stay away.

'Beast's as good as dead already,' Tozer said. He ignored the man's pleas and looked only at the animal as he spoke. He goaded the man by waving his bolt in his face. The crowd, warming to the confrontation, cheered him on.

Tozer would have begun making his calculations of work and profit the instant he saw the horse on the ground. A month earlier it had been his boast in the Lion that he had dispatched and butchered a hundred hefted wethers in less than an hour. A military contract. The sergeant pay-master, he bragged, had calculated four hours for the work, and had paid Tozer accordingly in advance.

'He needs rest, that's all,' the carter insisted, his voice now lacking all conviction.

'And if I have to go away and then come back again later, you'll pay double for the same work,' Tozer said, grinning. 'What, you're going to leave the creature blocking the street and wait for one of the worthies on the Parish Council to send you a second bill?' He looked at John and me as he said this, drawing hard on his pipe and then grinning again as he blew out the smoke. It was said of Tozer that he was able to smoke in his sleep, more often than not in his chapel pew. The monger said he smoked to keep his lungs clear of the stench amid which he worked.

He stopped waving his bolt and showed the carter the tube with which he would position it on the horse's forehead, and then the heavy iron mallet hanging at his waist with which he would drive the spike home.

'You haven't got a pistol?' the carter said, the words an abrupt end to his argument.

'A pistol?' Tozer said, feigning incredulity. 'Bullets cost money. Where you been living, then? Leeds?'

The crowd laughed at this and Tozer turned to receive their applause. Then he took out his mallet and dropped to his knees close by the horse's head.

37

Several days after this incident, I woke to find myself on the slope above Skirden Clough, the sky above me filled with birds. For a moment I could not recall how I had come to be there, but then I gathered my thoughts and remembered that I had walked out before dawn following another sleepless night beside my father.

I had encountered Charlotte in the garden – she, too, had been unable to sleep; she told me she was concerned now for the health of Emily *and* Anne, as well as with my father's diminishing energies – and I had told her that I was going for a walk so there would be no alarm later at the discovery of my absence. I asked her if she wanted to accompany me, but she declined. Besides, she said, she was already more asleep than awake. She breathed in deeply the night's scents.

'Look,' she said, pointing vaguely to the sky in the south, and when I asked her what she was showing me, she said simply, 'Lucifer's Lantern.'

'The Star of Morning.'

'I remember your celestial panoramas,' she said.

I had made them as a boy with a pin scratched through black wax dripped on to glass.

It was a rare intimacy between us. In the distance, I could hear frogs croaking and chirping in the dykes.

'What else do you see?' I asked her, wanting to prolong our encounter.

She lowered her pointing finger to the glow of the horizon. 'Only the world,' she said.

I told her not to worry about the world, that the world would stay where it was – where it belonged – and that it would not bother to come any closer to us and add its particular burdens to our own small part of it. This amused her, and she told me that I seemed very certain of myself. And despite all I knew of her own recent broader horizons and the world's incursions, I told her I was.

She kissed me and told me not to wander far.

I left her and walked towards Hollin Hill, over the brow of the slope and beyond all view of the town.

I walked for a further hour until I came to Skirden Woods, and then I climbed the slope above them. I lay at the edge of the trees. The night was far from cold, and the air calm. It was my intention to await the sunrise there.

I woke to find that the sun was already high above the eastern hills, and that it was dimmed by thin cloud. The birds were all around me – in the trees and on the slope above – and I identified as many of their calls as I could manage. The ground beneath me was hard, and wet with dew which had not yet burned off so close to the trees. My arm was numb with cramp as I pulled it from beneath me.

Sitting upright, I felt suddenly weak and was forced to rest propped on my elbow until my senses calmed. There was grass on my face, and when I brushed it away I felt something on my lips. I touched this and saw dry blood on my finger. My first thought was that I had rubbed against a stone, but then I understood that I had suffered another of my seizures as I'd slept.

Ten weeks had passed since my collapse in the house. I felt rested and peaceful; at other times, my whole body felt exerted and sore.

I let myself slip back to the ground and lay

listening to the birds again. The cramp went swiftly from my arm. My satchel lay beside me and I made a pillow for my head.

A small hawk hovered above me, perhaps alerted by my movements, and for a moment I was his distant prey. Then the bird came lower, saw that I was a man and veered off into the rising wind, following the land towards Halifax.

I heard dogs barking in the distance, and after that, gunshots. The shooters were out on Warley Moor, and I remembered the time Willy Weightman, John Brown and I had camped out overnight in the place to catch the dawn incomers flying low across the brows towards us.

This small, sudden fragment of memory made me sad for the loss of my friend. I had loved and admired William better than I might have loved my own brother, and it had been the greatest insult to me, only a month after his death, for Anne to shout at me that the man was everything I was not, but which I might so easily have been. She had clearly intended the remark to pierce me – perhaps to stir me from my lethargy following the loss – and though it did strike me hard, the blow was softened by the realization that it was precisely what I might have said of myself. I *could* have been William Weightman – I *could* have worked harder and applied myself better; I *could* have formed myself in the image of that man. But by then, of course, and pursuing my usual path, it was far too late to attempt the transformation. Besides, just as Anne's words to me were an insult, any half-hearted efforts on my behalf to imitate even the smallest part of the man would have been an even greater insult to him and to his memory.

When Willy had been with us, John and I had persecuted him with notions of romance. We told him he might have his pick of my sisters, all three of whom were more than fond of him. He had quickly refuted this in the case of Charlotte, and she too had joined in our game. Only my father had been against these shenanigans, declaring that it was not proper behaviour in his curate, however short his tenure or sincere his feelings.

And then the man was gone from us – first back over the hills, and soon after that from this world. It was not a single blow to us, but many, and we all in our own way bore our loss of the man. Why, I goaded my father, had his Loving God not spared a man so good as Willy? Why did rogues and scoundrels and profiteers thrive and live their easy lives, while men such as William Weightman died so young and so painfully and at so great a loss to all around him? But this, of course, was no argument to him, merely another of our slackening bonds finally severed.

The guns and barking dogs grew more distant. I searched the horizon for tell-tale puffs of smoke, but saw nothing. I felt happy to hear the noise. I might easily settle back into my rough bed and imagine myself among the hunters. I might even imagine Willy Weightman back beside me, sharing a flask and pointing out to me the approaching birds flying low towards us across the heather and bracken and calling as they came so close to their roosts.

I identified the calling of a skylark somewhere high above me, and invisible, and I closed my eyes to listen to its rising song.

38

The very next day, the Halifax Sheriff's Officer came to the house, ordered by Thomas Nicholson at the Old Cock. The man has been threatening this much for the past year, happily serving me – serving *all* of us – during that time, and yet always, it now seems, carefully tallying up. The appearance of the Officer was a great blow to me, my final calamity. I owed money at a dozen places – the Talbot, the Swan, the George, the New

Inn, the Bowling Green, the White Swan, the Bull's Head; I even owed Jackson and Haig up at the White Horse and the Craig Vale Inn. Everywhere I had ever been, it seemed, I was now a debtor.

I was not alone in any of this – I daresay Leyland's debts far outweighed my own in all those same places. Hard times have made for all this hard reckoning. I daresay, too, that there were other, lesser creditors who, alerted to this first assault, might now drag themselves to the same sorry feast to pick at my corpse.

Pay up, I am told, immediately and in full, or I will be served with a court summons and be taken off to prison in irons, most likely Leeds or Wakefield, to await my fate there. Everything is charged with this drama.

The same thing happened two years ago with the Officer from York. My debt then was smaller, and quickly repaid by others. I was spared my prison cell and my shame. It was difficult for me to see how the same thing – the same escape – might be achieved now.

Anne opened the door to the Officer and was quickly backed up by both Charlotte and Emily. Charlotte, as usual, and as any desperate man might hope, did most of the talking and pushing-out; but even she was quickly made to understand the seriousness of the situation, of the pending summons, and was driven to desperate measures.

My father was sleeping upstairs during this commotion – they always come early, these men – and I knew that everything Charlotte and my sisters did, they did more for his sake than for my own.

I went to Charlotte at the door and she held me away from it.

The Officer was a man I did not recognize, but with him stood another, a short, corpulent man called Todd, whom I knew to be a common debt collector. My first thought was that he had led this official to me like a dog pointing to a stricken bird.

'That's him,' Todd shouted upon seeing me behind my sister.

'Mister Brontë,' the Officer called to me. He waved a sheet of paper above his head and started to shout its details at me.

Charlotte snatched this from him, and the instant she took it, the man fell silent.

'How much does he owe?' she asked him.

'It's all there,' he said. 'Though I imagine it's only a part of his overall debt, and a small part at that.' He tried to take the paper back from her, but she was too quick for him.

'He always hid behind their skirts,' Todd said with a sneer.

I could tell by the Officer's response to this that he thought little of the man or his position, and perhaps even regretted his presence there now that his own official business was underway.

'Either them or his preacher father,' Todd went on. 'The man's a drunkard and a coward, running from one dark corner to another these past years, and living on unpaid credit everywhere he goes.'

'Be silent,' Charlotte told him, holding the man's gaze until he, too, fell silent.

Beside me, Emily and Anne shared a grin. Both had come from their beds at the disturbance, and both wore coats over their nightdresses.

'He brings disgrace to everyone around him,' Todd said, but by then no one was listening to him except me. He might as well have burned the words on to my forehead with an iron.

'How soon?' Charlotte said to the Officer.

'How soon what?'

'How soon must' – she read from the sheet – 'this Nicholson be paid?'

'By rights, it's within my power to demand the full amount here and now,' he said. 'And by rights, it should have been demanded a lot sooner. Nicholson only held off taking this course because your brother gave him his word that he would pay him.'

'Meaning the man was content to go on extending credit to him and his cronies while at the same time crying debt and poverty?'

Charlotte said firmly.

'That's none of my concern,' the Officer said. 'And you'd do well to make it none of yours. An unpaid debt is an unpaid debt. I think you'll find the Law is very clear on that.'

'The man's a dead weight,' Todd added quickly. 'And he'll tie himself to all and any of you if it means saving his own worthless neck.'

Charlotte was about to answer this when there was a noise on the stairs behind us, and my father called down to ask what was happening.

'Nothing,' Charlotte called back up to him. 'Tradesmen.' She motioned for Emily to go up to my father and reassure him.

'This *will* be settled, one way or another,' the Officer said, raising his voice to take advantage of the situation while my father might hear him.

'I have five pounds,' Charlotte said. She took several paces towards the two men, causing both to back away from her.

'He owes much more. It's all there.'

'Considerably more,' Todd added.

'I am asking you if five pounds paid immediately will satisfy this Nicholson for now,' Charlotte said to the Officer, ignoring the man beside him.

I wanted to be brave and ask her what sum the man was demanding of me, but I had no true idea what I owed him – five pounds seemed the least of it. My debts these days came and went like leaves in a strong wind and I had long since lost all track of them in the rising storm.

'I can take it to him,' the Officer said unhappily. 'But if I am to come straight back, then you'll be charged for my trouble.' Todd pulled at his sleeve. 'And him.'

'A guinea,' Todd said. 'Finder's commission, all legal and above board.'

Charlotte told them to wait where they stood and then closed the door on them. She turned to me and pointed to the kitchen, and I followed her there. She took several bills from the dresser drawer. 'These have all arrived recently,' she said.

'I don't–' I began to say.

'More of your creditors.' She recited their names to me, and I couldn't deny a single one of them, not with any certainty. 'Spare me your lies and excuses. The wolves are again at the door. This is hardly the time.' She shook the pieces of paper in my face and I felt their cold draught.

I could think of nothing to say to her.

'Most of them are settled,' she said. 'At least in part. And especially the ones threatening further proceedings.'

'I never knew,' I said eventually.

She laughed at this. 'Of course you never knew. You would have hidden them or destroyed them and then continued along your ignorant path to the prison. Father knows. He paid most of them himself.' She looked me up and down and then briefly closed her eyes. 'Even Nicholson sent in his earlier demands and then took what he was given.'

'He said nothing to me.'

She laughed again at the remark.

'May I see?' I asked her, holding out my hand for the bills, which she gave me.

'Most say in one devious way or another that they have not already had recourse to the courts solely on account of Father's position and standing here.'

'So I—'

'So you are again in his debt, yes. They use him as leverage against you, and with every demand they send, you threaten and compromise us all further.'

I handed her back the bills, unable to read them.

'John Brown went to see Nicholson on your behalf.'

'I wish—'

'I asked him to go. To see Nicholson and to placate him, and to find out how many others you owed.'

'And did he tell you?'

'He told John that your creditors would make a longer list than the new Mayor's subscriptions.'

251

'John said nothing to me,' I said feebly.

'To what end? What would *your* knowing have achieved?'

'I might have–'

'You might have what? Written another begging letter to your beloved and oh-so-generous Lydia?'

'Don't,' I shouted at her.

She pushed the bills back into the drawer and took out her purse. Then she left me before I could say anything else.

I heard her in the hallway talking to Emily, asking about my father. It seemed these conspiracies were now the air I breathed.

I waited a minute and then followed her back to the door.

The Sheriff's Officer and Todd were both still there, both still waiting for their money, the latter still deriving great amusement from my predicament. News of what was happening would be the talk of every public house in Halifax by noon.

Charlotte counted out what money she possessed and gave it to them – notes to the Officer, a handful of coins to Todd.

I avoided the gentle restraint of Anne and went to stand beside Charlotte as she did this. 'Tell Nicholson that he waters his spirits and inflates his prices,' I said to Todd.

'*Now* he's brave,' Todd said. The man studied what Charlotte had given him. I almost expected him to put the coins in his mouth and bite on them.

'I shall still have to return,' the Officer told Charlotte. 'To collect the debt outstanding.'

'Of course,' Charlotte said, then added, 'And tell Nicholson to send a full account of his tallying-up.'

I could hear the relief in her voice now that she had averted disaster and gained some control over the situation. Telling Nicholson to send the details of my debt was her victory note.

'How long do you think he will allow?' she asked.

'Nicholson? He chases a dozen others. A month is usual.'

'He might not have a month left in him,' Todd said, pointing to me over my sister's shoulder. 'Besides, I could pick up a docket on the man in any of a dozen other places and be back here tomorrow and the day after that and the day after that until Kingdom Come.'

Charlotte smiled at the empty threat. 'I daresay, but you may find yourself otherwise engaged on *that* particular day,' she said.

I had heard it said of Todd that he was a Sadducee, a denier of the Resurrection, and I wondered if this had any bearing on his chosen occupation or his manner.

'Every day is a day of reckoning for the

likes of us,' Todd said. 'Running round after the likes of him so that honest, decent folk can clothe and feed their children.'

'You have your fee,' Charlotte told him. 'I shall not be so forthcoming in future without proved accounts. I daresay a properly issued summons is harder work for you than simply banging on a door with your fist and making your demands.'

'It is,' the Officer told her. 'Everything done according to the Law is a thorough and complicated business.'

Todd finally put the coins into his pocket, leaving his thumb to keep guard over them.

'You need to sign this,' the Officer told Charlotte. 'I'll amend the amount once I've spoken to Mister Nicholson and my clerk, and then I'll come back to you.'

'Your clerk?'

'Everything these days is paperwork,' he said.

'Will Nicholson settle privately, without further recourse to the Law, do you think?'

'Will your brother avoid gaol, do you mean? On that score, perhaps. But there are others who might not be so accommodating. Once his other creditors learn that he's either paid up or defaulted on the present summons, there'll be a rush to take out their own papers on him.'

'First come, first served?'

'There are better ways of putting it.'

'So it's best all round for Nicholson if this *is* kept private.'

'Perhaps,' the man admitted. 'But these things have a habit of getting out. It's Halifax, after all. People talk to each other. Money's tight. The Poor Rate's running at seven shillings in the pound, and folk don't like to see others spending *their* money so recklessly.'

'And especially not spending it like *he* spends it,' Todd said. He looked back and forth along the parsonage front. 'And if he hadn't been forever bolting back here, then all this would have landed at his feet much sooner.'

'I know all that,' Charlotte said.

'Full of blabber-mouths and tittle-tattle, Halifax is,' Todd went on. 'It's that kind of place. Can't trust nobody.'

'*All* my brother's genuine and proven debts shall be paid in full,' Charlotte said firmly to the Officer. 'If they come directly to me and are not made public.'

'Who are *you* to be telling others what they can and can't do?' Todd said.

'The landlords will want their money,' Charlotte said. 'And knowing the breed, most will take the easiest route to it.'

'Just like *he* did to their doors,' Todd said, disappointed when no one laughed with him.

Emily came to me in the hallway and put her arm through mine. I thought she was going to say something to console me, but all she whispered to me was, 'You fell, that's all.' The words surprised me and I could think of no answer.

Eventually, I said, 'I'm thirty-one,' though without any real understanding of what I truly meant by this. 'Praise and blame are nothing to me now,' I added, equally uncertain why.

'You are weak and without resolve,' she told me quietly. 'And you veer from self-pity to hysteria and back again. You have no true comforts or guide.' Then she released my arm and left me, climbing the stairs to go back to my father. Anne stood a short distance from us and watched her go.

Beside me, Charlotte closed the door on the two men and then stood with her back to it, braced, her eyes closed and breathing heavily.

'Will you tell Father?' I asked her.

'And tell him something he already surely knows or can easily guess at? I think silence on both sides would be best.'

I followed her back into the kitchen, where she put away her purse. 'I need a list of all your creditors beyond the ones who have already announced their intentions. There can be no more secrets waiting to burst in on us like this.'

I bowed my head. It was an impossible task.

'Are they here, too?' she said. 'In Haworth, already at our doorstep?'

I nodded.

'I'll talk to John,' she said. 'Will he know?'

I nodded again.

After that, the three of them left me.

I could hardly stand, and so I sat beside the range to stop myself from falling to the ground.

39

The day after all this, Charlotte informed me she wished neither to speak to me nor even to see me in the company of the others in the house until we knew the outcome of her offer to Nicholson, and until at least some of my other, more pressing debts had been discharged. She said she would act swiftly, that any delay would work against us all. I wanted to ask her by what right she made me an exile in my own home, but the fight was not in me. She assured me there was money for these payments, but that it was not in limitless supply.

Her every word to me was an agony for us both, and I saw that it was all she could do to refrain from striking me as she laid out these demands.

Emily stood beside her during all this, and she half raised her own hand to restrain her sister. In her turn, Emily now treats me like one of her strays, or like one of the abandoned birds she tended as a girl. She asked me last night how much time had passed since I was last in the church to hear my father preach. I guessed and told her six months, but we both knew it was considerably longer. She told me bluntly that the loss of my belief had become unbearable for him. She told me that she believed I had taken a wrong turning in my life and that I had never properly recovered myself. I responded cruelly to this and told her not to concern herself on my behalf – that if public opinion was to be believed, then I was bound for Hell faster and sooner than any of them. She covered her ears at the words.

In the days following all this upset, I tried to resume my work – to show resolve and willingness, remorse even – but I achieved little. I spent most of my time gathering together as many of my scattered papers as I could find. There was finally a great pile of these. I am uncertain what I hoped to achieve by this labour, except perhaps to display the true extent of all my failed enterprises. I know only that the task had little to do with either regret or contrition.

I read aloud to an empty room my poem

'Azrael, The Eve of Destruction' – a poem Leyland, Phillips, Collinson and Dearden had all once praised as the greatest of my accomplishments. A mockery now. The Jewish Angel of Death. Good enough for the *Bradford Herald,* but never even worthy of consideration by Blackwood's.

I wrote to Leyland and told him of the Sheriff's Officer and of Nicholson calling in his debts. In all likelihood, Nicholson had set the same men on to him, casting a wide net in the hope of catching at least something. I told him I had been instructed to stay clear of Halifax until a good outcome was guaranteed. I saw where this left him – his studio was only a short walk from most of our haunts – and what privacy I enjoyed in Haworth.

And having recited to no one my collection of published poems, I sought out everything I had written as a boy, read parts of this, and then wept at its innocence and unfettered exuberance. I wept, too, at the sight of all those interwoven lives and imaginations, the freedoms and perfections we all four of us had once enjoyed and practised without doubt or expectation.

Later, I spoke with John Brown, and he confirmed what I already knew – that Charlotte was working hard to save me from the world's censure. My sister's every absence from the house made me wonder where she might be and what she might be attempting on my behalf.

To change the subject, John told me that a wig-maker had lately been in Haworth, and that for the past two days the Bull had been filled with girls arriving to sell their hair. It was something I would have liked to have seen. He said that Sugden had been paid to clear the back room while the buyer worked. In all, John said, eleven sacks of hair had been collected, ranging from the palest blonde to the deepest black. The buyer, apparently, said he had never seen the like of the black hair and had encouraged the girls from whom he'd bought it to grow him more for his visit in a year's time.

In the days since the Sheriff's Officer's visit, I have spent several hours of each day with John and his family. They continue to embrace me even as my own family make me a beggar at my own door. The girls in particular are affection and kindness to me. I am offered no regular drink there, and on the few occasions when John has suggested a solitary glass, I have refused him, knowing that this, too, will find its way back to Charlotte. I made a joke of the matter and told John that the drink was like rain to all the seeds of trouble and discord lying dormant within me. The whole family laughed at this – both at the humour of the remark and at the bitter truth of it.

I never once left that household – especially recently, and certainly during those few days – without wishing that someone would hold me back and insist on my staying longer. Was I once such good and welcome company everywhere, I wonder.

40

The day after – and like an even greater *elemental* judgement on me – a pall of smoke hung over the town, blowing and gathering from the giant pyres made of the newly felled timber towards Stanbury and Lumb Foot. As foretold, men have been working there for several weeks, stripping out the last of the copses and unmanaged woodland. There is as much soil, root and deadwood as good timber thrown on to the fires and this is what has blackened and thickened the smoke. Anyone attempting to take fuel for their own hearth is driven away. Lumber merchants have come from Leeds and Bradford to bid for what can be salvaged, but there is still great waste.

I stood with Greenwood by Sladen Beck and watched the men at work. Every door and window in the parsonage was closed and stuffed with rags, but the smoke and soot still found its way in to us. The church, too, smelled heavily of the drifting smoke. A finger traced along any surface turned black.

'I asked the man in charge to wait until the wind changed,' Greenwood said to me as I joined him.

'I can imagine his answer.'

'He said the wind never changed. Whichever way it blew, someone would suffer. It might be summer, but it's rained almost every day since they started. He told me they'd had trouble keeping some of the fires alight.'

Mounds of charred wood and pale ash lay like spoil heaps across Stanbury Side. I was reminded of the fires made by the lime-burners beyond Skipton, the dense white smoke turning black and then white again as the kilns blazed and then cooled over days.

We watched as an ancient oak succumbed to the fellers and toppled to the ground, its branches smashing as they dropped, a cloud of leaves and birds rising from it as it settled.

'At least there will be no nests,' Greenwood said. It seemed a small consolation for all else that was lost. 'These are unsettling times for us,' he added, watching as a group of men rushed to the fallen tree and began sawing at its limbs. A dozen carts stood near by. Horses dragged sawn trunks back and forth.

'What's it all in aid of?' I asked him.

'Someone said a new factory was to be built.'

'Up here?' It seemed unlikely.

He shrugged. 'Nothing stops things once the land is in private ownership. Whatever comes, it can hardly be *less* profitable than what is there now. I saw your father earlier, and when I told him that I intended coming up here, he said it was best not to interfere.'

'Five years ago, he would have led our protest,' I said.

'He would certainly have made our feelings clear,' Greenwood said sadly.

Everywhere I looked around us, it seemed that all strength and vigour was being wrung from the land – from its farms and industries, from its hills and rivers, its fields and woodlands – and wrung, too, from the men and women who lived and worked there, and who now struggled against rising odds to keep their places in that exhausted world.

After a moment of silence, I said, 'A photographer came to us.'

'Oh? To make your father's likeness?'

'To stand at the gate with his equipment on its tripod and photograph the parsonage. Charlotte instructed us all to stay inside.'

'Is she at last speaking to you, then?'

'Of necessity more than want,' I said.

'Still…'

'The man was there for two hours while we hid behind the curtains, waiting, half the time hunched beneath his black cloth as though it were his shroud.'

'Didn't even your father go out to him?'

'Charlotte persuaded him not to. She said she knew why the man was there. She said there would be no peace for any of them if they agreed to even his smallest request. I volunteered to go out and chase him off, but she told me, too, to stay inside. She said he would grow tired of the smoke and leave soon enough. Others gathered around him, inspecting his camera and asking him questions. My father said to Charlotte that perhaps *she* might go out to the man.'

'And did she?'

'That particular suggestion alarmed her most of all.'

'I see,' he said. He avoided my eyes while all this was said, and I knew that he, too, understood their secret, and that – along with all those others – he and I were now bound and yet kept apart by our complicity. I also sensed that he understood something of the guilty pleasure I now felt at Charlotte's discomfort in the face of the photographer, and especially in the light of her behaviour towards me these past days.

'That tree will be sorely missed,' he said, indicating the high and noisy blaze that had been swiftly made of the fallen oak.

On the slope beyond the fires and the felling, the shadow of the rising smoke flowed like a shallow flood across the land.

'Old Zillah Seward came to see me and said it was a portent,' he said.

'Of what?'

'Oh, the usual.'

'Judgement Day?'

'Among other things. She said we had let everything of worth fall carelessly from our hands and that because of this we deserved whatever punishment now befell us.'

'She's been saying exactly the same for as long as I can remember.'

'I know. And I said as much to her. Whereupon she announced proudly that everything that had happened to us in all that time had only proved her right. She said we might as well throw ourselves on to the fires and let that be an end to everything.'

'Did she volunteer to lead us by her example?'

He smiled and shook his head. 'I told her the trees were always owned by someone, and that the owners had every right to clear the land, but she only accused me of being ridiculous and on their side.'

'It's how most of her ranting ends,' I said.

It made me happy to be indulging myself in such an inconsequential conversation.

'I know, but I could well understand the point she was making to me,' he said. He started coughing and took a moment to compose himself. 'Has the photographer gone now?'

'An hour ago. After which, Charlotte went out to stamp triumphantly around where her defeated enemy had once stood.'

'Do you think he took his picture?'

'He would hardly have wasted so much of his time otherwise.'

'No, I suppose not.'

The smoke around us thickened, and we both covered our faces until it cleared. It stung our eyes and left us with its smell.

After this, and seeing that there would be little respite from the stuff, we left the slope and walked home together.

Returning to the parsonage, I saw that there was still a small crowd gathered at the front of the house, and that the curtains at the windows remained drawn.

I parted from Greenwood, who said he was going to the Bull. He asked me to join him, and when I declined, he feigned surprise and told me I was a reformed character. Hardly, I told him, just on probation, forever watched and prodded and sniffed at for the first returning sign of my weakness and fallibility.

I looked back in the direction I had come. High on the moor, that same dark shadow continued to flow, steady and unstoppable, to the edge of the world. In places above this, the sun shone through in vivid shafts of light, made brighter still by the darkness they pierced and illuminated.

I waited where I stood, deciding whether or not to return inside. It had been my first true outing in almost a week. And then a movement at an upper window attracted my attention, and I looked up to see a curtain pulled back and Emily's face there. She watched me where I stood for a moment, and then looked beyond me to that same dark smoke rising and gathering across the horizon.

41

Late the next morning, Anne came to me in a panic, shook me awake and told me that they could not find Emily. At first I didn't understand her. We had all been with Emily earlier, standing around her bed as my father had said his usual household prayers, after which I had returned to my own makeshift bed.

'Her bed is empty,' Anne said. 'And

Keeper is not with her.'

I was still uncertain as to the cause of this urgency. Emily was unwell, but she had seemed better of late. She came and went, as Aunt B used to say. She had certainly seemed well enough two days earlier, when she and I had walked close round the church with the dogs. Her bed may have been empty, but it was news to me that she was now confined to it. They were none of them late risers.

'Charlotte and Father are already out searching,' Anne told me.

'Searching?' I rose from where I lay. 'I'll come out,' I said. My effort would be another part of my rehabilitation.

'Charlotte said you were to look Middle Moor way.'

'As far as that? Surely she'll be much closer to home.' I tried to remember when Emily had last walked that far.

Anne didn't answer me. She tied on her bonnet and shawl and left the house ahead of me. I wanted to shout after her that I myself was not well, and that I certainly didn't relish so long and futile a journey. Emily – even if she *had* gone so far – would surely soon return of her own accord. She knew the hills and all their paths better than any of us. I wanted to shout that perhaps it was a good – perhaps even a *propitious* – sign that she now felt strong enough to go outside, but by then Anne was far beyond my hearing, and the air of alarm still filled the house. I certainly knew what I would forfeit by *not* rushing outside and joining in their efforts.

I paused in the doorway. It was another cold late-summer day. The sky was overcast and threatening rain. I heard my father in the churchyard, calling for his child. There was something both desperate and pitiful in his voice, as though he was already resigned to having lost her. He reminded me of nothing more than a moorland ewe bleating for its dead lamb.

Men and women stood at the parsonage gate, and it embarrassed me for them to see him like this.

I left by the side entrance and followed the path towards the Low Moor, and not until I was clear of all these onlookers did I start my own calling.

It was a path Emily frequently took. The land on either side was clear of obstruction, and I searched all around me as I went. I called her name, trying to sound a note of urgency but also to avoid the desperation my father could not disguise. I shouted for her as though she were hiding from me. As children we had often played along the same path, and I knew how easy it would have been for her to conceal herself from anyone if that was her intention. The heather was thick and the peat riven with fissures and pitted with holes. With no true vantage point, and especially if she *had* chosen to hide, it would be impossible for anyone to see her from even a short distance away.

My calling put up a few birds and I mimed shooting at them, drawing a line along their course and shouting bang at them. I searched for birds she too might put up.

I came to a standing stone and climbed it. I gained a little height, but still I saw nothing. A few ponies grazed in the distance ahead of me; men worked in the fields along Leeshaw Bottom.

Climbing down, I continued towards Wadsworth. It was my opinion after a further half an hour of fruitless searching that I was on a fool's errand, and that Emily had either been found already or had returned of her own accord to discover and then dismiss the alarm she had caused. Soon, I guessed, I would hear others calling for *me* to tell me that she was safe and well. And then I would return home wet and exhausted, but redeemed. Emily, no doubt, would insist to everyone around her that she had never once been lost in her entire life and that our panic on her behalf had some other cause.

I walked to the Stoop Hill cross-path and sat down there on an ancient trunk. When we were children, it had been the limit of our travels. Haworth had been long out of sight beneath us, and ahead of us was only the rising emptiness of the north and the west, each the direction of a foreign land.

I lit a pipe and brushed the dirt from my trousers. I called again, but my voice now was lower. Curlews sounded close beside me. I wondered if the birds were still rearing late broods. The cloud thinned briefly and I felt the warmth of the sun on my face. I closed my eyes and leaned back where I sat.

It was then that I heard a voice, broken and indistinct, but clearly a woman's voice, both amplified and then muted in the breeze. I opened my eyes and sat upright. I rose to my feet and looked all around me. I waited to hear the voice again, but nothing came, only the same close calling of the birds and the rustling of the sedge along the path. My next thought was that I had not heard a voice at all, merely some combination of these other sounds, and that they had come to me as a woman's voice because that was what I had so desperately wanted to hear.

And then I heard it again. A woman's voice, the words still indecipherable, but definitely a voice, and definitely shouting. I knew that in a strong wind on that path two people walking side by side would not be able to make themselves heard to each other.

I rose on to the fallen trunk and searched around me. I called Emily's name at the top of my lungs, and the instant I did this, the unseen woman abruptly ceased her own shouting.

The next time I called, there was nothing to distinguish the silence which preceded my shout from that which swiftly followed it.

I continued to scan the rising land, at first seeing nothing but the movement of the heather and the grass; but then, catching a sudden flash of blue far ahead of me, I saw a figure standing halfway to the horizon. I guessed the blue to be a cap or a bonnet and I tried hard to remember what Emily wore.

I called her name again. The distant figure stopped moving, and though I could not see anything for certain, I imagined that whoever it was was now watching my approach as intently as I was keeping my own eye fixed on them.

I left the path and moved in the direction of the figure.

After several minutes walking – during which time the figure remained fixed in its spot – I became more convinced than ever that it was indeed my sister ahead of me, and that she now watched me come and awaited my arrival. I even convinced myself that she would be as happy to see me and to have my company in that empty place as I would be to take her home with me and then warm myself in the praise of the others.

As I approached her, I said her name over and over, as though this were a charm and I might fix her where she stood, and not spur her into flight like another of those birds.

Eventually I arrived close enough to see that the woman standing ahead of me was indeed my sister, and knowing that she must now recognize me too, I was confident enough to call to her again.

She raised her hand at this, shielding her eyes to watch me approach. Then she walked both to the left and right of where she had stood, her hands raised above her. She seemed agitated in her movements, anxious – though whether this was caused by my approach, I couldn't tell.

'Emily Jane,' I called to her. 'It's me – Patrick Branwell. They sent me out to walk home with you.' I paused for a moment, gauging the effect of my words.

Gradually, her pacing stopped and she lowered her hands. She called to me and I continued towards her more quickly. Where she stood, the heather grew mixed with low thorn and bracken, and because she was on no true path, I had difficulty getting beside her. Had she crouched down on her heels, I would have seen nothing whatsoever of her from only twenty feet away.

I called for her to come to me, and she walked towards me in a straight line, seemingly oblivious to the snags which pulled at her skirt. I told her to be careful where she walked, but she ignored me and continued directly towards me.

Finally, after a short detour to cross a drain, I was able to reach her and put my arms around her.

She was surprised by the gesture.

'Everyone says you are lost,' I said to her.

'Lost?' she said. She looked beyond me as she spoke. 'How could I be lost in this place?'

'My exact argument,' I said. I thought she might laugh at the suggestion, but she did not. Instead, she continued to look all around us. She seemed confused by something, perplexed; or if not this, then at least distracted.

I took her hand and led her back to the main path.

'My skirt is torn,' she said, looking down.

'No wonder,' I told her.

The remark puzzled her.

'You were a long way from the path.'

'Not so far, surely?'

Arriving back at the fallen trunk, I told her to rest for a while.

'Why?' she said.

'Three hours ago, you were reckoned to be

unwell. Father prayed for you while you slept.'

'I remember,' she said. 'You were with them.'

'With my eyes half open. Charlotte woke me and commanded me to attend. Perhaps my own contribution is what made you suddenly so strong again.'

She smiled at this. 'Am I reckoned too weak to wander up here, then?'

'Everyone else would say so.'

'And yet here I am.'

'As am I,' I said, sitting beside her to catch my breath.

'And *you* the one lacking vigour.'

'Perhaps I was weakened by all that praying,' I said.

She smiled at this, too, and we sat together in silence for several minutes, listening to the wind and the birds and the movement of the grass.

Eventually, Emily rose and tugged me up beside her, and we walked side by side back towards Haworth.

'I was searching,' she said unexpectedly, moving a short distance ahead of me, her face hidden to me as she spoke.

'For what?'

She faltered in her step, but kept walking. I asked her again.

She stopped and turned back to face me. 'This,' she said. 'All this.' She raised her arms again and cast them wide.

I looked in every direction she pointed.

'Did you imagine it might be altered or lost in some way?' I asked her. I remembered her face at the window, looking out at the distant smoke.

'Everything *is* lost,' she said. She came back to me, seized my arm and looked into my eyes. 'Surely *you* can see that? You of all people?'

'I know we live in a world where nothing is allowed to remain as it once was,' I said. 'I know that success outbids failure every time, and that discord trumps calm everywhere you look.' I paused, and then I said, 'And I certainly know that *you* have changed, all three of you.'

She understood my meaning perfectly.

'And do you envy us that change – our achievement, our – what? – our notoriety?'

I flinched from her gaze and all she was suggesting to me. 'Would you have it for yourself?' she asked me.

'Some part of it, perhaps,' I confessed.

'Then if it were mine to bestow, I would give it to you. And certainly that whole part of it attached to me.'

I told her I believed her. 'Charlotte–' I began to say.

'Charlotte inhabits a different world entirely – one still mapped and measured by her ambition.'

'And you do not?'

She closed her eyes.

'Anne?'

'She at least seems better suited to it than I am.'

I wanted to ask her if it was true about her not having written anything in the past year, but this was beyond me.

We stood together without speaking for several minutes, surrounded by only that wind-filled emptiness.

'We thought only to spare your feelings,' she said eventually. It was the most any of them had said to me on the subject.

'I know that,' I said. 'At least, *now* I know it.'

'Good,' she said simply. She released her grip on my arm and took several paces from the path. Then, without warning, she threw up her arms again and shouted, 'Answer me, answer me, answer me,' at the top of her voice.

I was about to tell her that I already had, but then saw that her demand was not directed at me.

She fell silent after that, and her arms dropped back to her sides. A moment later, she returned to me and held me tightly again.

'You can tell them I've lost my mind,' she said, grinning.

'Is that what you were shouting before you

saw me?' I asked her.

She nodded once.

'And were you answered?'

'Only by the wind,' she said. 'And the birds.'

I clasped my hand over hers. 'What were you hoping for?'

'Oh...' she said.

I told her I understood her perfectly.

'We saw the mummers up here, remember?' She pointed along the path towards Stairs. 'When we were children. Dressed in their animal skins and antlers, carrying their torches and blowing their horns and banging their drums. They fastened up their slaughtered wrens on every gate. Anne and Charlotte were both terrified, but you and I, we stood our ground and watched them come. I wonder if we are so brave today.'

'Not I,' I said.

'Me neither.'

We continued walking, and after a further long silence she said, 'What will you tell them?'

'That I found you walking on the path, taking the air, that's all.'

'I *was* lost once,' she said. 'One Easter. At the Pace Egg play.'

'I remember,' I told her. 'And it was I who found you then.'

'Only because I hid from all the others.' She pressed her cheek into my arm. 'You

278

look out for me,' she said.

'A pity I can't do the same for myself,' I said.

She was about to answer me when a voice called her name and we both looked along the pale line of the path ahead of us to see Charlotte waving frantically in our direction.

'Mother Hen,' I said. 'This will mean even more prayers to give thanks for your safe return.'

'And you will still be kneeling with your hands loose and your eyes half open.'

'Possibly,' I said. I held her more tightly for a moment, feeling her return the embrace and then lock her small hands behind my back.

Finally separating – prised apart, it seemed to me, by Charlotte's distant calling – she pulled my face down to her and kissed me on my cheek.

'My dearest brother,' she said to me.

'My dearest sister,' I said to her.

Along the path, Charlotte called to us again.

42

When I was a boy, I was bitten by a dog that was said to be mad, and the wound it inflicted on me was never cauterized. Some said it was the cause of my nervous disorders; others that it had led directly to my fits and seizures.

The same thing happened to Emily a few years later, but she was afflicted by none of these things.

John Brown told me that any dog which attacked a man was always called mad. Otherwise why would it have shown such savagery in the first place? Killing the dog afterwards was thus more easily justified.

There is little to protect any dog in this world. As a boy I once watched a dog stoned to death in a field at Colne Fair. It had savaged several sheep and was brought to the fair by the farmer, tethered to a stake, and killed there by anyone passing by who cared to pick up a stone and throw it at the animal. My father had been with me at the time and he had brought me quickly away from the spectacle. When I asked him if he believed that what was happening was cruel and against God's will, he said only that the behaviour of his fellow man never failed to surprise and disappoint him.

I cannot remember if this was before or after I was bitten.

When Emily was bitten, Wheelhouse was immediately sent for and her wound was cleaned and wrapped.

Aunt B said that salt water would clean flesh best, and that sea water would be the most effective of all. We all knew by then, of course, that what she really meant was that *Cornish* sea water would be the most efficacious cure of all. It usually fell to me – her favourite – to make the proposition to her. Cornish sea water, she said, was a proven cure to a long list of complaints, and it was a well-known fact that every Cornish seafarer, wherever he sailed on the world's oceans, carried a bottle drawn from his own home port for just such emergencies.

I doubted if there was a place in the whole of England that was further from the sea than Haworth was. Places in the Midlands, perhaps, but not many. Occasionally, flocks of gulls would arrive in the town and people would speculate on where they had come from or why they had arrived here. I daresay all the reservoir building might have accounted for their appearance. Whatever the reason, the birds seldom stayed.

When they did come, and however brief their stay, Aunt B sent me in search of their eggs. A gull's egg, she said, was like eating an egg and a small fish at the same time. I could think of nothing I would want to eat less. The yolk of a gull's egg would seal and protect an open wound. A gull's egg, she said, would both settle a disturbed stomach and loosen a hard bowel. Perhaps her own long agony of dying might have been eased by the things – if not by actual remedy, then by fond association and memory instead.

It was Wheelhouse's unasked opinion that her love of ordinary, lesser eggs had led to her frequent and painful constipation, which in turn had caused her cancer.

When she was finally confined to her bed, I had sat with Aunt B and read to her. I told her repeatedly that if it had been within my power, I would have sent to Cornwall and had a thousand of those eggs and those bottles of water delivered to her.

When she died we were all dispatched to stop the clocks in the house, and Emily was sent to John Brown's to inform him of our loss, but only after she had first gone to his hives and told the waiting bees our unhappy news.

It was Aunt B who had always insisted that my carroty hair was a sure sign of the genius beneath.

It was Aunt B who, making up the numbers at a funeral, had whispered to the boy close beside her that if the poor could somehow die for the wealthy, then what a living the poor would start to make for themselves, and who had then given the boy her handkerchief to help suppress his untimely laughter.

While she still lived, and when the day was mild, she insisted on me opening her window so that she might at least hear whatever birds were in the garden or churchyard. I told her that if she waited longer, then the gulls would undoubtedly reappear and remind her of her one true home. She smiled at this and told me kindly that it was the last thing she wanted to hear. Only long afterwards did I understand her true meaning.

43

I woke to find my father kneeling beside my bed and mumbling in prayer. As often before, I feigned sleep to avoid confronting him, though what I was truly avoiding confronting I cannot say. He doled out his prayers to us all as another father might dole out sweets or medicines to his children.

Yesterday, following my joyful return with Emily, I had heard him praying aloud with Charlotte and Anne to give thanks for that safe homecoming, after which Charlotte had read from the Bible.

I was reminded then of sitting with Elizabeth and Maria and listening to my mother sing her beloved Wesley's hymns. We all knew what my father thought of singing in the house, but he could do nothing except stand in awe of his wife and her voice. It was a far thing from his hushed pleading now beside my bed.

When he had finished with me, he prayed again for Emily, who had gone to her own bed upon our return, though not before telling her sisters that they must no longer ostracize me.

Listening to him like this, I wanted to open my eyes and confront him and tell him to devote all his energies to her instead, that he wasted his time with me. I wanted to tell him how mortally sick I had grown of all the lies and fantasies and subterfuges that have gripped me these past months. Also, listening to him like this, each of us only inches from the other, and both of us with our eyes closed, I felt like a man laid flat upon his own tomb watching his gathering mourners.

When I was a boy – *when I was a boy, when I was a boy, when I was a boy* – I would take great delight in lying in my warm bed and listening to all those sounds of the house below rising up around me – the voices of my parents and sisters, the noise of the fires, the barking of dogs, the creak of the boards and the doors throughout the place, the opening and closing of cupboards and closets, the cracking of the range as it heated and cooled, and the clatter of crockery being set out or cleared away.

And with all these sounds would also come the scents and aromas of the house – the smell of cooking and bread-making, the smell of the fires and lamps and candles, and of the flowers and herbs forever being brought in. It sometimes seems a different place completely to me these days.

When I was ten I went with my father to a cleansing at Oxenhope Church where, after the rushes had been scattered and lit, brimstone was crushed and strewn amid the embers. I was warned not to stand too close to the acrid smoke, but being the inquisitive child I was, I disobeyed and breathed some in. I wept and choked for a day afterwards, much to the anguish of some and the amusement of others, my father included. I was disinfected, he said, as clean inside as the church now was. He told me that if I ever believed my soul to be destined for Hell, then I had better get used to the sting of that brimstone. I promised him that it was a course upon which I would never embark. He was my one true God, then, and I his most devoted follower.

When I first saw my father climb up into his new pulpit it truly did seem to me that he had *become* God, or that at the very least he was the embodiment here on Earth of both God's grace and His wrath. I was told twenty times a week that true sinners were forever beyond the reach of redemption and were destined for eternal torment. I knew and accepted this, as I knew and accepted the rising and the setting of the sun.

I once heard my father preach that on the Day of Judgement, the sun would turn to darkness and the moon to blood, that the stars would fall from their orbits and that both Heaven and Earth would dissolve into raging flames and pass quickly away. It was a thing I believed throughout my boyhood.

I was once alone with Charlotte high on the side of Sladen Beck when a bolt of lightning struck the hillside above us, followed an instant later by a clap of thunder as loud as an explosion. The ground seemed to shake at our feet. I screamed at all this and Charlotte held and comforted me. I can have been no more than six or seven, she a year older. When I stopped screaming, I asked her if the Earth was dissolving in flames and the moon above us turning to blood. She held me at arm's length from her, her hands on my shoulders. 'Not yet,' she told me. 'Not yet.'

A few years afterwards, I had been walking on Jackson's Ridge with Emily when a small storm had appeared in the distance. We two were still in sunshine and beneath blue skies, but ahead of us the sky in that one small part was black and filled with the fury of the coming weather. Emily had asked me what it signified – a storm so isolated and distinct when the rest of the world was so calm and warm – and I had told her that the storm was put above a hamlet by God because the people who lived there no longer believed in His almighty power. This cheered Emily instantly and she started to speculate on the nature of the inhabitants' punishment and suffering.

Beside me now, my father fell silent, and unable to continue my deceit, I opened my eyes and looked at him. When his own eyes opened, he said, 'Did I wake you?'

'No,' I told him.

He showed me his watch. 'You must surely be hungry? Especially after all you did on our behalf yesterday.'

'Perhaps,' I said. I felt no hunger whatsoever.

On our behalf.

'Emily was able to eat earlier,' he said. He took his spectacles from their case and fitted them to his eyes, blinking at the sudden sight they gave him. 'Charlotte says I ought not to read so much,' he said.

'She knows what's best for everyone,' I said, wishing the words did not sound so harsh.

287

'We all give her plenty of reason to worry,' he said.

'And especially me,' I said, again wishing I had said something different, that the words did not sound so self-serving. He pushed himself up from beside my low bed, groaning at the effort and then rubbing his side.

'Are you in pain?' I asked him.

He smiled. 'I suffer no more or less than my allocation.'

'More, I think,' I said, causing him to smile at me.

'Perhaps. Sometimes. But I only have to look around me to see that my blessings far outnumber my woes and that there are men and women suffering much more than I.'

'They are always with us,' I said. 'The poor and the suffering.' Now it sounded as though I was making a joke at his expense.

'You speak true there,' he said. He pressed a fist into his side. 'Will you come down?'

'I'm truly sorry,' I said. 'About the Sheriff's Officer.'

He considered the words and then nodded. 'Charlotte told me everything. Besides…'

'I shall do all I can to discharge my debts,' I said.

'I know that.'

'And then to pay you all back.'

'I would never ask it,' he said.

288

'I feel...' I said, uncertain of what I might say.

'You feel as though–'

'I feel broken,' I said, unable to stand another of his kind excuses for me.

'Broken?' he said absently, and then, 'There is nothing that is broken which cannot be mended, which cannot be made whole again, surely?'

Neither of us spoke for a moment, and then he said, 'Do you believe me?'

I struggled with my answer to him, but before I could speak, Anne arrived at the doorway and looked in at us.

'He's awake,' she said. 'Hallelujah.'

'He's exhausted,' my father told her. 'Yesterday was a great trial for him.'

Anne came to me and wiped my face with the sheet. 'I'm sure it was,' she said, adding in a whisper that only I heard, 'Not too many inns where *you* were sent looking.' Then she rose and said, 'Charlotte says we should believe one word in ten of what he says, and believe exactly the opposite of half of the remaining.' She laughed as she said it.

'As much as that?' I said.

She wiped the hair from my forehead and then traced a finger around my jaw. 'He needs a shave,' she said. 'He needs to be made respectable again.'

'Then I need another miracle,' I said.

My father closed his eyes at the remark. 'Did you come on an errand?' he asked Anne.

'Charlotte wants to know when the man last came to wash the windows. She says looking out of them is like looking through a mist.'

'Your sister would find fault with the view down from Heaven,' he said. He took Anne's arm and the pair of them left me where I lay. I heard Anne's laughter as they went down the stairs, and then the long midday chiming of the clock in the parlour, each note rising and then reverberating in the empty room.

I was ever swathed in such tolerance and kindness, and I felt the warmth of the tears in my eyes where I lay.

44

I have rowed with Leyland, my truest friend. And worse still, we have rowed over money – the money I asked to borrow from him, and which he, for the first time in all my years of asking, did not possess to lend to me. As I surely knew, his own life is hard and his troubles and responsibilities far greater than my own – his mother is suffering again – and yet still I asked him.

Having written to him and told him of my need – as ever, I called it a 'loan' – I received no immediate reply, and so I went to Halifax to see him. I had still not heard from him since our missed appointment, and so I knew he perhaps nursed another grievance against me.

I found him in his studio, surrounded by the mess and disarray of his failed business. When I told him I had written to him, he merely pointed to a pile of unopened correspondence, mostly bills and demands, and told me bluntly that my own unopened letter would be somewhere amid them. He told me he had been too cowardly to open anything sent to him for the past month.

At first, he seemed almost pleased to see me, though I could tell that this was an effort for him.

'You?' he had said upon my appearance at his door. Perhaps he had been expecting another of his own angry creditors, and this was the reason for his surprise.

'I am a stranger to you,' I confessed to him, uncertain which of us was the most saddened by this. Almost three months had passed since the happy day we had spent together at the fair in the company of Roman Sharp and his attentive daughters.

'No – you are still my friend,' he insisted.

His clothes were stained white with dust and plaster, and one of his hands was bandaged with a dirty cloth. There were dark rings of sleeplessness around his eyes. He wore no collar or jacket. 'I am somewhat unwell,' he said, after which he was racked with a seizure of coughing which forced him first to bend himself double and then to sit upon a crate.

I went to him and rubbed his back. The whites of his eyes were yellow, and his flesh was pale. He loosened his bandage and showed me where he had torn off a fingernail pulling at a wire frame.

'Six weeks,' he said absently.

'What?'

'Since we last sat in the Talbot, with Thompson and Geller.'

'I remember it well,' I told him, though in truth it seemed much longer ago. We both spoke of it as though it was a history now beyond all retrieval, however hard we might try.

Neither of us spoke for several minutes. The disarray of the room and its enterprise mirrored the disarray of our lives.

'Why have you come?' he said eventually.

'To see *you,*' I told him. I spread out the unopened letters and slid my own from the pack.

Seeing this, he said, 'Did you write to me again?'

'I told you.'

'Have I missed an appointment with you, then?' He cleared his throat and spat heavily into the rubble at our feet.

'No, not at all. Besides, I can see how you stand, what confusion reigns here.'

He smiled at this. Then he gestured at the letters. 'Final notices and threats of proceedings, mostly.' He picked up several of the envelopes and screwed them into balls. It was an empty, futile gesture, and it, too, was a mirror to our lives.

'Have you no work, no commissions?' I asked him. I pushed my own letter deep into my pocket.

He shook his head at the enquiry. 'Gateposts and mantelpieces. Philistines shouting their wealth and taste to the world.'

'You should have returned to London,' I said.

'So you keep telling me – so *everyone* keeps telling me – as though the place itself were a panacea for all ills. Well, it certainly never did *you* any favours. Besides, *I* have others to consider.'

'Me, too,' I said, stung more by what he said about London than his sideways remark concerning my present responsibilities.

He laughed coldly at this. 'Who?' he said. 'Who do *you* have that is dependent upon you? Who do *you* have to feed and clothe and care for? Who depends on *you* for food or succour? Who? Go on, tell me, give me their names. In fact, no, don't speak, you will only shame yourself. It would be easier to ask you what you yourself do *not* now possess that is not wholly provided by the labour and charity of others.'

I was frozen in shock at hearing the words.

He picked up a bottle, shook it and then threw it back down. He sat with his head bowed, breathing heavily.

'Forgive me,' he said eventually. 'I meant to say none of that. My anger and my own despair get the better of me.'

'I understand *that* well enough,' I said.

'I suppose so.' And thus our vague apologies were both indirectly given and accepted.

'Is there nothing coming in at all?' I asked him, steering us back into calmer waters.

'Mason's fees,' he said. 'You have very little idea. Even men with money spend sparingly and shave every small margin. The concord of opinion is that I should abandon all artistic endeavour completely until every one of my debts is settled. I owe for six months' rent on this place alone. I'm starting to forget which promises and excuses I am beginning to repeat.' He reached to the table for a second bottle, and this proved more fruitful than the first. He bit out its cork and drank from it before offering it to me.

I tasted its stale contents and took several swallows.

'Show me your letter,' he said to me.

I told him I would prefer it if he left it unread, but he insisted and dug his hand into my pocket to take it.

'Ha,' he said. 'Old man Nicholson got to you first. The rest of us just received his warnings that the Sheriff's Officer was about to be engaged.'

'He's one among many,' I said.

'I know *that* well enough. I heard from Ely Bates at the Pear Tree, telling me I owed him money from five years ago. Five years. I'm afraid the scent is up and all we can do now is run. Have you settled anything with Nicholson?'

'Something,' I said, unwilling to admit to him that my father and sisters had taken charge of me.

'And you thought *I'd* be an easy touch for some of the rest?'

'I would never consider you anything so...' I stopped speaking. Whatever I told him, the facts would stay the same and I could only do us both more harm.

'Look around you, Paddy, look around you. And look hard and long at everything you see here. It is an ending, the ruin of a life – a classically proportioned ruin, I grant you, a statue in every corner, but a ruin all the same. I live the life of Job. Listen hard enough and you'll hear the approach of every single one of those creditors gathering to squeeze my bones, who will then delight in hanging me out to dry and watching me twist in the wind.'

It cheered me a little to hear him talking like this; he seemed, however fleetingly, his old and careless self.

'What chance do you imagine you, my old friend, stand against that same army?' he said. He fell silent after this and seemed to sag where he sat.

I passed the bottle back to him.

'We make a sorry pair, you and I,' he said. The drink dribbled down his chin. 'We both saw our paths bright and well-made and stretching far into the future ahead of us, but those paths were an illusion, that's all. We were deceived. We have wandered from day into night, and we never for a single moment believed that this would – that this *could* – ever happen to us, not *us*, not men such as you and I.' After a pause, he said, 'Do you know how much you owe?'

I told him the figure Charlotte had calculated and then driven into me like a spike.

'Then we should both thank God,' he said, 'that we are not already broken and buried under the weight of our debt.'

I wondered if this was a joke and I was meant to laugh. 'My father and my sisters do their best by me,' I finally admitted.

'Of course they do. As they have always done.'

Then I admitted to him that I had again written to Grundy enquiring about the likelihood of work.

'You have too much faith in the man,' he said. 'I daresay he knows to a farthing his own incomings and outgoings.'

'No doubt whatsoever.'

'Besides, the man looks after Number One. He always has done and he always will. It has a bearing on every decision he makes.'

'Meaning he will suffer by association with me, that I will contaminate his reputation?' It was something I had long since understood.

His answer lay in his glance away from me. Then he put his hand on my shoulder and said, 'The man achieves nothing in his own right, but only at the instruction and bidding of others. You and I are cut from a different cloth entirely. *We* feed our spirits and our appetites; he feeds only his stomach and his coffers.'

This time, I did my best to laugh at the remark.

He gave me back my letter. He had once told me that I sent out all my communications as though they were distress flares.

'I truly wish I were in a position to help

you,' he said.

'I know,' I said. 'But I ask too much of you. I always did. Besides, I doubt if I have ever been so low in the estimation of others as I now stand.'

'Not mine,' he said. 'If you believe nothing else, then believe that.'

His hand was still on my shoulder and he tightened his grip on me.

'I believe it,' I told him honestly. 'I believed I had nowhere else to turn. I am smothered at home, and beyond those walls I am only pitied and mocked. I sat for an hour yesterday with my father's pistol in my hand. It wasn't even loaded. Melodrama *and* cowardice. The click click click of the trigger and the tap tap tap of the hammer in the pan. What did I think I was doing? What did I imagine I might achieve by even that empty gesture? Imagine the outrage if any of my sisters had come in to me.'

'We have all of us spent an hour with a gun to our temples,' he said. 'One way or another.' He brushed the dust from his legs and chest and then resumed his coughing as this enveloped him in a cloud. He took back the bottle.

'When were you last at home?' I asked him.

'Five days ago. My creditors arrive there daily and are repulsed by others while I cower in here out of all harm's way. How

298

long, I wonder, before my landlord tells them all where I am?'

'And loses his own last chance of payment?'

'I suppose so. You should consider yourself doubly fortunate that your father's name and reputation stand guard and guarantee over you. Besides, who would fight with Charlotte? Or Emily, come to that?'

We laughed at this. I refrained from telling him of Emily's wandering or of her worsening health.

'It's true,' he said. 'You are a fortunate man and your home is a fortress and a sanctuary compared to my own.'

'I suppose so,' I said.

He examined his injured finger and then retied the dirty cloth.

'Will Nicholson persist with the Law, do you think?' he said.

'Who knows?' In truth, my guess was that Nicholson – followed by all the others – would soon receive their payments sent by Charlotte and would then turn their greedy attention elsewhere, and considerably closer to home; and I knew he understood this every bit as clearly as I now did.

We were like two men lost in a maze, wandering separately through its puzzle of paths, neither of us any true help to the other, and both of us without the faintest notion of where our confused wandering might lead us or when it would end.

We sat together in silence for several minutes, both of us lost in our thoughts. The bottle was finally emptied.

Then I suggested going outside into the fresh air and sun for a while.

'Has it finished raining, then?' he asked me. He pointed to a large pool of water beneath a skylight at the far side of the room.

'When did you last eat?' I asked him.

He looked up, surprised by the question. 'The same time as you, by the look of things,' he said eventually.

45

Following my return home the next day, Charlotte saw in an instant that something had befallen me. She asked me where I'd been. In my absence another of my creditors – Walton of Ovenden Cross – had sent word that he was about to pursue me through the Law.

'He says that you lodged with him, and that in addition to your bills for drink, you owe him rent.' She waved the note in my face.

'We had some arrangement or other,' I said, unable to remember. It had been at least four years ago.

'Father gave something to the man who came, and promised him the rest soon.'

I saw how tightly she restrained her true feelings, and how hard that was for her. I saw, too, how far and wide, and how far beyond my recollection my debts had now spread.

'Where were you?' she asked me.

I told her about my visit to Leyland. I said that he had fallen on the same hard ground.

The remark – and all the excuses it contained – angered her. 'And what?' she said. 'The pair of you now lie together on that hard ground side by side with your hands held up in the air for passing alms? If he has indeed fallen, then he has fallen for precisely the same reasons you have fallen.' Then something occurred to her. 'Please do not tell me that you went to him for the money.'

'Of course not,' I said.

She did not believe me. 'You always expect too much of others,' she said.

And receive too little, I thought.

'Why must you always presume upon friendship?'

'Mary Walton was my friend.'

The remark confused her. 'Who?'

'Walton's daughter. At Ovenden Cross. She admired and encouraged my writing. It was the reason I stayed there. She and I–'

'Don't,' she said firmly, immediately lowering her voice and glancing at the ceiling above us.

'I honestly thought she had come to an arrangement with her father for me to lodge there without payment,' I said, knowing this for the lie it was. I had taken advantage of the girl, and through her, her father.

'Meaning what? That you led her to believe she might have expectations of you?'

I almost laughed at the clumsy remark. 'Who are *you* to talk of expectations?' I said to her, knowing even as I spoke that I had far overstepped a line.

She considered the remark, calmed herself and then touched a finger to my chest. 'You understand me perfectly,' she said. 'Mock all those others – mock *me*, if you must – but the people in this house are now all that you have left to you.'

'I know that,' I said. 'I apologize.' I asked her if my father was at home.

'Charity Merrall died,' she said. 'He has gone to her laying-in.'

'I saw her only three days ago,' I said, remembering a brief encounter with the woman at Bessy Hardacre's. 'She seemed well enough then.'

'So? You saw her, she seemed well, and now she is dead. She took to her bed on Tuesday and woke on Wednesday with a fever that delivered her to her Maker on

302

Thursday.' She made it sound like a child's rhyme. 'Father says the family showed him great kindness when he first came here.'

'And Emily?' I said. I had looked in on my sleeping sister before my departure for Halifax.

'She ate something last evening, and again this morning. Morsels, but something. Anne is with her now. We are hopeful.'

'We are ever that,' I said.

Her eyes narrowed and she looked at me slowly from my head to my feet.

'Did you fight?' she said. 'With Leyland?' She saw right through me and heard all the things I left unsaid to her. I bowed my head.

'You and he shall endure,' she said. 'A scoundrel will always love another scoundrel.'

'Is that what I am?'

'What would you have? A "lovable rogue"...? You are too old and too persistent in your ways for that.' There was a small note of affection in her voice and I was grateful for that.

I took off my coat and felt its dampness as I hung it on a peg.

Leyland and I had finally parted in the middle of the evening, in the Clarendon, never one of our usual haunts, but where what few coins we gathered between us were still good.

I had left Halifax with the intention of walking home, but had been thwarted in this by bad weather and the weakness in my legs. I had taken refuge for the night in a ruined and leaking barn on the road beyond Delph.

I had woken in a shallow pool. Several cattle had wandered into the shelter after me and stood at the far side, watching me as I woke and then rose. The floor between us was more liquid than solid. They shuffled nervously as I pushed myself upright and confronted them. I was a moment or two remembering how I had come to be in the place, and a moment or two longer recalling all that had passed between myself and Leyland the previous day.

It was still raining, and countless drips found their way through the roof and pitted the ground around me. The broad door rattled loosely on its hinges in the wind. My remaining journey to Haworth was four miles, and the whole of Nab Hill and Clough Head was lost to me in the rain.

Upon my eventual return – where my hope had been to go in unobserved and to take off my wet clothes and retreat to my bed – Charlotte had seen me and come to me in the hallway.

'Is Leyland not in good health?' she asked me now.

'He blames the torpidity of life itself,' I said.

'No – he develops your facility for excuses,' she said. 'A man can fight against torpidity, just as he can fight against most things.'

Despite the remark, I heard in her voice her true concern for Leyland, whose earlier work she admired as much as I did, and whom she still held in high regard, whatever his recent failings. Or perhaps she imagined these were all *my* fault, and therefore deserving of a greater forgiveness than she was now prepared to show to me.

'He says we share a single path through life,' I said.

She shook her head. 'You forever pull each other back to the same bad path, that's all.' She took my damp coat down from the peg, surprised by its weight. Then she pressed her palm against my chest. 'You're soaked to the flesh,' she said.

I told her how I had spent the night.

She had started to unbutton my jacket when the door opened and my father came into the house.

'He was caught in the rain,' Charlotte said to him.

By then my coat had dripped a puddle on the floor.

My father took off his hat and skimmed the water from its brim with his finger.

'The Merralls?' Charlotte prompted him.

'Abraham fears his youngest will follow his mother in the next few days. I told him to send for me.' He looked at the water beneath my coat. 'And the lass they employ has refused to go back into the house while Death is waiting to pay a call on the place.'

'She was always too showy for her own good, that one,' Charlotte said.

'Abraham says he regrets having left the Church for so long. He imagines they are being in some way punished. I told him he was wrong, that the Lord welcomed all into His House, however steadfast or faltering in their belief. He said he didn't believe me. He said that *I* might be a wonder of kindness and forgiveness, but that the God *he* worshipped was not so accommodating of late.' Stamping the water from his boots, he turned to me. 'Are you home to stay?' he said.

'Until I resemble less a drowned rat and more a fit lop,' I said. It was what Aunt B had often said to me as a sprouting youth, and he remembered this and smiled. Then he told us he had a sermon to prepare and left us.

Charlotte watched him go, squinting at him as he climbed the stairs.

'It's him you should be looking after,' I said. 'Not me.'

'I know what I *should* be doing,' she told me.

306

My vest was as wet as my jacket and my shirt, and so she told me to remove this too, pulling it roughly over my head when I was slow to obey her.

She looked at me and put her hand to my chest. 'You've lost weight,' she said. It was not a thing said lightly in that house.

'My appetite...'

'And your skin is so pale. It seems blood-less.'

I wondered what there was left that I might say to her.

She took away her palm, and then turned and left me half-dressed and shivering in the hallway. I watched the outline of her hand fade and then gain colour where she had pressed it to me.

46

Two days afterwards, a boy came from the Bull to tell me breathlessly that a man was waiting there for me. Come from York, he said, by which I immediately understood him to mean from Thorp Green. The man wished to see me straight away and in private. Be-lieving this could only be a communication from Lydia, I left the house at once, careless of my clothing, and unconcerned, too, as to

307

whether or not I was observed, or even followed.

Entering the Bull, the boy indicated the door to the back parlour. I paid him with the solitary coin I possessed, straightened myself, knocked once and went in.

Gooch stood at the small window. In all my frantic reckoning, I had expected coachman Allison, but here instead was Gooch, Lydia's doctor.

'She has finally answered me?' I said to him.

The man looked from side to side, anywhere in the empty room but at my face.

This response made me even more wary. 'I expected Allison,' I told him, as though I still possessed some say in the matter.

'You had no right to expect *anyone*,' he said loudly. His distaste for me was evident in his every word and gesture. 'However, this time, *I* am the chosen emissary. And be under no illusion, Brontë, I am under firm instruction to make myself plain to you.'

He sat at a table and I called through the hatch to the girl serving drink.

'Not for me,' Gooch said. 'I was asked to come, to deliver my – *her* – message to you, to ensure you understood me, and then to return as soon as practical.'

The girl brought in two tankards and set them down. She stood beside us, and eventually Gooch paid her.

'Is that all?' she said to him, counting the money.

'There is more than sufficient,' he told her. The man was renowned in Thorp Green for the meticulous keeping of all his patients' accounts.

'Not for what *he* owes,' she said. She was hard-faced and had no shame in pointing at me. Debt was now the air I breathed, the blood in my veins, the ground upon which I walked.

'I can well imagine,' Gooch said, smiling. He took out his purse and gave her more, telling her as she again counted the coins that it was all she was getting.

'You need not have done that,' I said when she had gone. 'I shall settle my own debts.'

He considered his response to this, then left it unspoken.

'I didn't ask you to pay,' I said.

'No – not like you ask others,' he said.

I slapped my hand on the table. 'Are you instructed to behave so badly towards me?'

He sighed and shook his head. He picked up his unwanted drink, looked at it and then set it back down.

I took up my own and saw the tremors of my shaking hand unsettle its surface, causing the ale to spill over its rim on to my fingers.

Gooch saw this too and made no effort to

hide the fact.

'I've been unwell,' I told him.

He hesitated before continuing. 'Lydia – Mrs Robinson – showed me your application,' he said.

'Application? It was no such thing. It was a letter between old friends.'

'You asked her for money to keep yourself beyond the Law. Your name was printed in the weekly lists of all those served.'

'Empty threats,' I said dismissively. 'It would have come to nothing.'

'Perhaps so – but only because others now stand guarantee for you.'

'You seem very certain of that,' I said.

'She showed me your other ... letters.' He gave the word a deliberate edge. 'All of them, one way or another, asking her for money.'

'Which she then sent on account of her continuing affection for me,' I shouted at him.

He smiled at my outburst. 'She warned me you continued to delude yourself,' he said.

'She once felt–'

'Whatever she might have *once* felt for you – and I daresay even then it was not the same thing in her mind as in your own – she feels it no longer. Everything in her life has changed, and you have not. It is clear to her – clear to us all – that you *cannot* change.'

'I never asked for her pity,' I said.

'Who speaks of pity? Besides, you crave it with every word you write to her. You do nothing other than play on old affections as though it were your right to do so.'

'*She* would never say as much to me.'

'Those are *her* words. Why do you imagine she asked me to come here, and not her coachman?' He tapped his pocket as he said all this.

'Give it to me,' I told him.

'I was asked to make her intention clear to you before doing so.'

'You were *instructed*, you mean. She employs you, nothing more.'

He waited a moment and then said, 'Believe what you will. It seems forever your course.'

'Meaning what?' I said. 'And besides, you do not know me – not truly – not how *she* once knew me – and you know even less of my life here.'

He looked at the squalid room around us, and then at the alleyway outside. 'Perhaps,' he said. 'But I can easily enough imagine.'

I held out my hand to him.

'When she asked me to come here, I asked her if it was intended that I cushion the blow to you or if–'

'Blow? What blow?'

'Or if I was to act purely as her enforcer.'

I laughed at the word. 'For a messenger

311

boy, you give yourself airs and graces.'

'Perhaps I do,' he said, 'but she made plain to me that I was to make myself just as plain to you.'

'Oh, you make yourself plain enough,' I said. 'In fact, I doubt you have sufficient understanding of the matter to be anything *but* plain.' I emptied my drink and slammed the tankard on the table. Then I took up his and drank half of it.

He finally reached into his pocket and took out an envelope.

I snatched it from him and opened it. It was a banker's order for thirty guineas, drawn on a Bradford bank. There was no letter, no note even.

'Is that all there is?' I said. 'Give me the rest.'

'There is no more.' He held his jacket open. 'I doubt it will settle *all* your debts, but it may settle the most pressing, and keep you out of gaol.' He paused. 'Besides, I imagine your clever sisters will soon be able to provide whatever else is demanded of you.' He took a sly pleasure in saying this to me.

'*Them?*' I said.

'Yes,' he said. '*Them.*'

I finished the drink and called for the girl.

He went on. 'I am also told to impress upon you that this will be Lydia Robinson's final communication with you. You cannot continue to threaten her or her position with your ill-considered demands on her. She can tolerate it no longer.'

'Her damn husband,' I said. 'Even in death he controls her and forces her to lie and to deny her true feelings.'

'Such dramas you create. He does no such thing. She loves the man's memory as much as she loved him in life.'

'And now she protects that memory and her children's inheritance alike,' I said.

'Perhaps. But what loving mother would not do the same? Besides, that has nothing to do with what is happening here today. As I say, her feelings towards you are clear to everyone who still knows her.' He looked from my face to my trembling hands. 'Look at yourself,' he said. 'Look at what you have allowed yourself to become. How old are you?'

'Thirty-one,' I said.

'Precisely. And still as dependent and un-caring and as spiteful of others as a spoilt child.'

'She would never–'

'Never what? They, too, were *her* words.'

I felt this like a blow and could think of nothing to say to him.

The girl came back in to us at that moment and put down more drink, hesitating before leaving.

'You were paid enough before,' Gooch told

her sharply. 'Is this entire place filled with fleecers, shavers and sharpers?' She scowled at him and left us.

'Threaten?' I said.

'What?'

'You – she – said I threatened her with my demands.' He waited.

'I would never threaten that woman,' I said.

He saw my sincerity and seemed to soften a little. 'She says your head is filled with exaggerated expectations,' he said. 'She says you dwell only in the past.'

'"Where once all hope rose daily like the sun".'

He again waited, and then said, 'Whatever your belief, there must be no further communication to her.'

'She's said the same before, and yet afterwards–'

'She has *asked* it of you before. She has depended – unwisely, in my opinion – on your feelings for her. Now she *demands* it of you. She has no feeling for you. None whatsoever. You have exhausted her every sympathy. Another word from you, and she will approach the Sheriff's Officer herself. She still has a great many friends in York, and I promise you, they all side with her and against you. She has kept every note you have ever written to her as evidence.'

I felt cold at hearing him say this. I folded

up the money order and put it in my pocket.

'Allison reported after his last visit here that he left you in a state of considerable anguish. He told her he was glad to get away from the place, that you threatened him with violence.'

'He was above himself,' I said.

And again he looked at me and shook his head. 'She is serious,' he said. '*I* am serious. I would not have come all this way as a favour to her otherwise. I told her that she had no obligation whatsoever to send you the money. I daresay she does it partly out of her fondness for Anne. Elizabeth and Mary asked me to remember them to her.'

A full minute passed, and then he said, 'I have to tell you that my advice to her was to go directly to the Sheriff.'

'But I have no debt with her.'

'Perhaps. But it seems to me that you have foundered completely and that you strike out at all around you without knowing why, and without any true idea of the trouble you cause.'

'I cause ten times more trouble to myself than to anyone else,' I said.

'Another delusion.' He rose from the table and went to stand in the doorway.

'When Allison last came...' I said.

'What?'

'Nothing.'

When Allison last came I had collapsed in the street outside and my father had been sent for. He and John Brown had carried me home. I had fitted on and off for three days afterwards and had been kept to my bed for a week.

'What now?' I asked him, seeing that he was intent on leaving me.

'I shall tell her all that happened here,' he said. 'Nothing more, nothing less.'

'And will you tell her that I still have feelings for her?'

He considered this and then said, 'I shall not.'

'It's the truth,' I said.

'I don't doubt it's what you *believe*, but I must tell you that I consider this belief to be a morbid sickness of the brain.'

'And is that what you'll tell her?'

'I already have,' he said. 'And she seemed relieved to hear it.'

I saw how completely my argument was lost.

'Then tell her I will honour her request,' I told him.

He could have made another cruel response, but instead, and considering me at the table beneath him, he said only, 'I shall tell her.'

I closed my eyes for a moment, and when I opened them he was gone, and I was alone in the room with my full pocket and my empty tankard and my even emptier heart.

47

Maria came to me, stood before me and smiled affectionately at me. *My brother,* she said. She pointed her hand at me, closed at first, but then with a solitary finger directed straight at my eyes. Her smile remained. *My brother,* she said again.

'Maria,' I answered her.

Why were we ever parted, you and I?

I could only shake my head at the unanswerable question.

I stood in the church doorway, looking in. There was little to choose between the cold of the wind behind me and the cold of the stone inside. I trembled at hearing her.

'Why have you come to me?' I asked her.

Because you called to me. She looked beyond me to the open door. *I can smell the lilac,* she said. *In the garden.*

I breathed deep, but nothing came to me. My breath clouded briefly in the church air.

'I'm suffering,' I said to her. 'I feel myself an empty man in an empty world.'

I know, she said.

'Then are you here to help me?' I asked her.

You must help yourself. She seemed disappointed by what I'd said, and I regretted this.

I took a step towards her and she beckoned me even closer. But I was reluctant to go, knowing what might ensue.

'I dream of you all the time,' I told her. 'Of you, and of Mother and Elizabeth.'

God's Kingdom is a place of ease and comforts, she said. The smile was back on her lips.

'I cannot believe in it,' I told her. I bowed my head.

Now you cannot, she said. *But soon you might know it for the place it truly is.* From the open doorway, she looked at the church around us, at the freshly varnished pews and the new plaster work. Then she sniffed the air again. *Is it Monday?* she said.

'Monday?' It was.

I can smell baking, she said. *And the proving bread. Do you remember how it was once my job to guard the resting dough when it was set outside?*

'To attract the wild yeast,' I said.

You often sat with me and told me tales to pass the time. You were watching over me just as I was watching over the bread.

Neither of us spoke for a moment.

I wondered what to say to her next.

'Emily is unwell,' I said eventually.

I know.

'She hardly ever goes out and has no strength left in her.'

I know, she said again, and it was a kind of comfort to me.

Her reluctance to say more made me wary, and so I said, 'And I, as usual, continue to play the Eternal Disappointment. Charlotte despairs of me – worse – and Father's affection is stretched ever thinner.'

Charlotte subdues her nature to her life, she said. *That's all. You must cleave to her. She has strength enough for you all.*

And only then did it occur to me that I was talking to a young woman and not a girl.

The call of a distant curlew came into the place and seemed to echo there. She heard it too and turned to look around her, as though the bird might have flown into the church itself.

Did you hear it? she asked me.

'A curlew. Up on the moor.'

Is that what you think?

'Perhaps a child,' I said.

She waited with her head cocked for a further call, but none came.

Eventually, she turned back to me. *You have lost your joy in the world,* she said. *It is the saddest loss of all, the hardest to bear.*

'My spirits have deserted me.'

And you seek all the wrong remedies.

'Nothing will put right what *I* have lost,' I said.

319

We all suffer, but some of us make more of that suffering than it deserves.

'I love you,' I said to her, unable to bear her admonition.

I know you do. We were once so close, I could never imagine being parted from you. We spent days hand in hand. Elizabeth vied for her brother's attention, but I was always your favourite and you never hid the fact. We made enough plans together to fill our whole lives.

'And then–' I stopped abruptly, unable to continue.

Yes, and then… she echoed in a whisper.

The call of the curlew returned, but this time she did not remark on it. And in truth I could not be certain now that it was not the cry of a nearby child.

She pointed to the ground at our feet. *The willow is down,* she said. She stared mesmerized where she pointed.

On Palm Sunday, for want of fronds, my father's parishioners filled the church with willow and rushes. I looked, but saw only the cold flags and tomb plates.

We used to burn the flattened rushes beside the wall outside, she said, her gaze still fixed at her feet. *And sweep the church clean of a whole winter's dirt.*

'Good honest dirt,' I said, mimicking my father.

In the Everlasting Kingdom, the grass is always green and the corn forever ripe and ready for harvest.

'Don't,' I said to her.

You and I might walk there together, all our plans brought into being.

'I have a good deal to repent of first,' I said.

She shook her head at this.

'Is that why you came?' I asked her. 'To persuade me to repentance? To prepare me?'

Prepare you for what? She raised both her hands, palms upwards, so that they framed her face.

'I cried for a week when you were taken from me,' I said. 'The same for Elizabeth and Mama.'

She made no reply.

'And I believed then, and with all my heart, everything Father said about the door you had passed through into that other room. I was joyous at the thought that I would one day join you all there. But since that time...'

She grew pale at the stumbling words.

'...since that time...'

She closed her eyes and lowered her hands. The smile fell from her lips and her mouth grew tight, and I knew that I had upset her.

After the last willow-strewing, John Brown had approached my father to suggest that the habit of carpeting the church in this way be abandoned. Some in the place said it was unhygienic. My father had insisted other-wise, but the weight of the argument was against him. Heavy matting for the entrance was suggested. Parishioners would be asked to scrape their boots before entering. Much of that good, honest dirt might be left outside. My father, true to his nature and his congregation, considered it a genuine loss.

I wondered why Maria saw the willow now, so long after the ceremony.

Do the alders still grow along Bridgehouse Beck? she said, distracting me from my thoughts.

'Mostly gone for spools and bobbins,' I told her, surprised that she should have turned to something so ordinary.

I'm cold, she said then, as though following a different conversation completely.

I looked her up and down and saw that she was shaking from head to foot, the tremor most severe in her chest and arms. She seemed suddenly much younger, almost a girl again, not a woman at all.

'Even in a good summer, the place never warmed,' I said.

I'm cold, she repeated. Now the tremor was fiercest in her legs and she looked hardly able to support herself where she stood.

My instinct was to go to her and to hold her, to take off my jacket and to wrap it around her, and then to embrace her in my arms so that she might share my own living warmth. But something kept me from doing any of this; something held me at arm's length from her.

She looked back to me briefly and then her eyes closed, and after that her head fell forward so that she was lost to me. Her hair fell over her face and fanned across her chest.

'My sister,' I said softly to her, but she made no response. I strained to hear her words, but there was nothing.

I closed my eyes, held them tight for a moment, and then opened them.

I was alone in the place, and it was colder than ever around me. The same distant bird cried out on the far moor and the same sly wind pressed at my back.

48

The next day I watched John Brown at work in his small stoneyard. He laboured without cease, that man, always ready to swap one job for another.

I stood at the gate and looked in at him. Mary sat close by on a block of grit. She saw me and raised a hand to me. John saw this, paused in his work and did the same.

'A new lintel,' he said, brushing his hand over the piece of stone on which he was working. He took off his gauntlets and held out his hand to me. Mary came to us, held her husband's hand and kissed me on both my cheeks.

The yard around us was stacked with pieces of cut stone and finished work. It was a fortnight since my last visit to them.

'The men in Bradford are asking for hundred-year guarantees,' John said to me.

'And you give them?'

'Naturally. They are old men, creating everlasting shrines to themselves.' It was the same thing Leyland had told me.

'Then shame on them,' Mary said, but good-naturedly.

'He works under divine guidance,' I told her.

'I work mostly under instruction from your father,' John said, and all three of us laughed at the old joke.

'People will always want stone for building,' I said.

'Or for their graves.'

'Or that.'

I asked after their many daughters.

'All well, thank God,' John said. 'All healthy and well.'

The girls were the couple's treasure, and they shared them with others like some men shared their trophies in a cabinet.

'Hannah found a snake,' John said.

'Oh?'

'Here, in this very yard.' He pointed a few feet from where we stood. 'Basking in the sun on one of the millstone blocks.'

'Was it an adder, or something harmless?'

'An adder. She knew to leave it well alone.'

'The child is fearless,' Mary said, unable to hide completely the note of concern in her voice.

After a moment of silence, John said, 'And you? You've been unwell of late.'

'Mostly recovered,' I said. I slapped my palm against my chest as though in proof of this, though convincing neither of them.

'It's good to hear,' Mary said. 'We value you. The girls, especially. You are their uncle.'

I caught my breath at hearing her say this.

'And *I* treasure *them*,' I said. 'I only stay away on account of being unwell.'

'Then come back to us soon,' Mary told me.

John put a hand on my arm. 'Soon,' he repeated.

A call from a passing woman distracted Mary and she left us to go and talk to her.

'Old Mother Redman,' John said. 'Joseph's mother. All gossip and malice.'

Joseph Redman was the Parish Clerk and Lodge Secretary. We both raised our hands

325

to the woman.

'*Are* you well?' he asked me when we were alone.

I bowed my head. 'I sometimes feel that I lack all purpose,' I said. I wanted to tell him that I had seen my dead sister, but knew what a barrier this would put between us.

'Some men settle early to their lives,' he said, 'whereas others go right to the end undecided one way or the other.'

'Then I am most likely one of the latter, goal-less wanderers. I was certainly never a go-ahead sort of man in the eyes of others.'

He laughed at this. 'Not like the men who commission me,' he said.

'My father says they confuse their wealth with their true fortunes,' I said.

'So he does.' He glanced back at the block of stone being shaped chip by chip into a lintel.

'I'm keeping you from your work,' I said.

'Never.'

Then I remembered the purpose of my visit. 'I've been sent on an errand by Charlotte. She wants oil for the oak settle.' I rattled the coins in my pocket, the exact amount, pointedly counted out one at a time by her and placed in the centre of my palm.

John fetched me this, refusing to accept the small change in return.

I called to Mary and told her I was leaving, and as I turned from John he gently clasped my arm and said, 'I heard of your visit to see Leyland. I hear he has no work.'

'He has a mountain of debt that would swallow up any work he acquired. Did you also hear that I made a fool of myself to him, my truest friend?'

He pursed his lips.

'My life was changed – truly changed – upon first seeing his Spartacus,' I said. 'And then changed again when I first set my eyes on his bust of Lucifer.'

'I imagine many felt the same,' he said.

'And now he is reduced to cheap ornamental pieces and chiffoniers.'

'Just as I grow calluses in the service of men demanding glory.'

'Who shall all, one way or another, find their way into the hard, cold ground.'

'Go back to Leyland,' he said. 'Rescue your friendship. Make *that* your purpose and your goal.'

I promised him I would.

'Good,' he said, and then he drew on his gauntlets, picked up his mallet and turned back to his work.

49

Again unexpectedly summoned, I arrived at the Bull to find Grundy waiting for me in the same back parlour in which I had encountered Gooch only twelve days earlier. He immediately indicated the drink which also awaited me, and told me as I picked it up that he had seen Geller, who had seen Leyland, who had told him of my visit.

'And so you came to see the pitiful and ungrateful supplicant for yourself,' I said to him angrily, weary by then of all his empty promises to me, and sick of the tales of his own good fortune. I wanted to ask him – *him* of all people – what gave him the right to interfere in this way.

'I came to tell you that Leyland – Joseph – himself is greatly suffering, that he can scarcely bear his own debts, let alone–'

'Let alone give his money to someone as undeserving as me – to a man who has only ever squandered his own opportunities and never paid back half of what he owes? I know all this. He made that much clear to me himself. Why is it that everybody speaks only of *him* and shows such scant regard for me?'

'For pity's sake. His mother is unwell. What little he does possess, he devotes to her.'

'I know that, too,' I said.

'Then do you also know that he *did* afterwards send what he could spare – and, believe me, it was not much – to help settle your own debts and keep you out of the cells? He sent it to Charlotte, and she returned it to him. She promised him that you were far from the gaol. Geller warned him against doing it – as did Dearden and Thompson – but, as always where *you* are concerned, Leyland insisted. Like you, he hopes against hope that the world will soon turn in his favour.'

It had been my intention following my promise to John Brown to return to Halifax and make my peace with Leyland.

'No – I see that you had no idea,' Grundy said. 'And why should you? Every time you make your demands of the man, he does his utmost to oblige you. Sit down – you make me uncomfortable standing there.' He was at the end of his patience with me.

I sat in front of him and finished my drink.

He considered me closely for a moment. 'You've been unwell,' he said.

I laughed at the remark and all the work it did on my behalf these days. 'So everyone delights in telling me,' I said. 'Though I imagine their reasons for doing so vary.'

He called to the barman for hot brandies

and these were brought to us.

'Your father was here earlier,' he said hesitantly. 'He came to warn me of your state of mind. I told him I wouldn't mention this intervention, but he insisted it would make no difference to you either way. He said you were beyond their warnings and entreaties now. They are all worried for you.'

'They fetter and bind me with their worries and cold concern,' I said, and then, 'The railway will not come to Haworth.'

It was long since common news.

'I'm afraid not, at least not for some considerable time. A speculator panic, apparently. You grow accustomed to such excitements and disappointments.'

'But if the railway were to come, I should breathe again,' I said. 'I should travel again, away from this tight shut room of a place. Perhaps Leyland and I might even return together to London.'

'Ah, that old story,' he said. 'If that was your intention, then there are plenty of other stations close enough.'

I drank the warm drink and Grundy told the man at the hatch to bring in the food he had ordered upon his arrival.

'I'm not hungry,' I told him. 'The smell of cooking meat makes me sick to my stomach. They keep sending that quack Wheelhouse up to prod and poke at me.'

'Can he not even–?'

'Why did Joseph himself not come if he is so concerned for me?' I asked him. 'If he is so great a friend and benefactor to me, why did *he* not come?'

The question – and the spite in which it was wreathed – surprised him, and he looked at me with suspicion and disbelief for a moment before attempting his answer.

'Who knows? Perhaps his own creditors have finally found him in his studio and driven him from it. Perhaps his every possession and piece of work has already been seized or dunned by the bailiffs.'

'They'll not fetch much,' I said, and again the remark angered him.

'Joseph has nothing but fondness and sympathy for you,' he shouted at me. 'And you talk of him as though–'

'Pity,' I said. 'You mean pity. He has nothing but pity for me.' I rattled my empty glass on the table top and waited for him to order more drink, which he reluctantly did.

'And your sisters?' he said to me as the drink came.

'What of them?'

'I ask after them, that's all.' He looked away from me and then back.

'Perhaps you should call on them,' I said. 'God knows, they get enough other unwelcome gawpers these days, gathering at the gate like lost sheep.'

'I don't understand you,' he said, but without conviction.

'Charlotte and Anne went to London,' I said. 'Did you know that? Shortly after you and I last met, and when you again insisted to me that my reappointment to the railways was imminent.'

It was a confusion of events, but I doubted if he would remember the specifics of the occasion; he made his promises to me like other men gave their greetings.

'You were your old self then,' he said.

'And now I am my new self. Besides, I no longer have need of the railways. Searle Phillips has been to see me.'

'To what end?'

'I should have thought that was obvious, even to a Philistine such as yourself. He was here to enquire if I had any further poems ready for publication. He insisted it was now my *duty* to present them to the world. He said an imbalance needed righting.'

'What did he mean by that?'

I saw that he already knew what he now expected me to confess or confirm to him. But again I disappointed him, and said, 'I don't know. I told him my manuscripts were scattered and disordered, but that with sufficient effort and clarity of mind, I might gather them up and present them in good order to the world. He is a good judge, Phillips, a good judge.'

'I see,' he said, angry at my evasion.

Then I reached across the table to his own untouched glass and something attracted his attention.

'What is that?' he said.

I feigned ignorance.

'Up your sleeve,' he said.

'A knife,' I told him. It was a bone-handled carving knife which I had taken from the kitchen as I had left the house.

'But why? You knew it was *I* who awaited you.'

'Perhaps I imagined it was a trick and I was about to be confronted by another of my creditors who needed fending off,' I said.

'But not with violence, surely? And certainly not with–'

'Or perhaps I thought it was Beelzebub himself who had finally come to fetch me. Is that who you are – Satan in disguise?'

He grew even more alarmed at the suggestion. 'Satan?'

'I've seen him in here before,' I said. 'Besides, why not? Everyone else has forsaken me. All except Emily, and she is too unwell to care for me.'

'No one has forsaken you,' he said. He tried to take the knife from me, but I held it firmly in both my hands.

'Well, as you can see, I am most definitely *not* Satan,' he said. 'I am your old friend Francis Grundy.' He held up his tankard to

333

me and waited for me to do the same with my glass.

Eventually, I laid down the knife and he turned its blade away from us.

'I wish I were able to help you more,' he said. 'We all do.'

'Wasted effort,' I said, looking hard into his eyes. 'Charlotte informs me almost daily that I am beyond all salvation or redemption.'

'Surely not. Beyond redemption? Surely not.'

'She takes a great interest in my wayward existence. I daresay Leyland's mother is the same with him.'

'Perhaps,' he said, but only because he did not want another argument.

'Or perhaps he is not so far down the same road,' I said. 'Perhaps the places *he* now wanders alone and uncertain are not so empty or so hostile towards him as my own haunts.'

'You might soon–'

'Soon? Soon? *Soon* it will be autumn proper, and after that, winter. And then the spring might be long in coming, and then the summer after that might be every bit as wet and cold and profitless as the one that has just passed. Soon? Soon?'

Whatever he had been about to say, he decided against it.

'Golgotha,' I said suddenly.

'Now what?'

'One of my haunts. Where I wander alone. The Place of Skulls.'

'I know what Golgotha is, man. I merely wonder what exaggerated fancies feed your disordered imagination.'

'Why? Because hearing me say these things makes you uncomfortable?'

'Of course it makes me uncomfortable. All this talk of Satan and Golgotha. I don't even know if you are serious, or if you are simply entertaining yourself with this constant condemnation and mockery of me, of us all. I thought you and I were friends. God knows, I have tried hard enough on your behalf in the past. Surely I deserve better than this?' He folded his arms and awaited my contrition, which did not come. He was further deflated by the return of the man with our food, which he set before us. Then he laid down cutlery and two cloths. He stood beside us for a moment, waiting for us to start eating.

'You may go,' Grundy told him.

'Oh?' the man said. *May* I?'

'I mean, thank you,' Grundy said.

'Or perhaps you want to run and blab to my father,' I said to him. I laid my hand on the handle of the carving knife.

'What?' the man said.

'Ignore him,' Grundy said.

'Most people hereabouts do,' the man said.

335

He looked again at the plates of steaming food and then left us.

'Must you antagonize everyone?' Grundy said in a loud whisper. 'I daresay if Satan *did* come to see you here, you'd treat him in exactly the same way.' He started eating.

I pushed my own plate away from me.

'What do I care?' he said. 'And if you're waiting for–'

'Waiting for what? Another of your promises?'

'Please, not that again,' he said. 'How many times must I explain to you that–'

I rose suddenly from where I sat.

'Now what?' he said.

'I have to leave.'

'*You* have to leave? Why? To be elsewhere? You don't even know what time it is, what day even. Leave for where? Where must you be so urgently?'

'That's right,' I said. 'To be elsewhere.' I picked up the knife and slid it back into my sleeve.

'But where? Tell me.'

'Where what?' I said.

'Where do you have to be so urgently that you cannot stay a while longer and eat a free dinner? And for pity's sake, please put down that knife. You'll only do yourself harm with it while you're in this state.'

'Perhaps I shall,' I told him. 'Perhaps I shall do myself harm and then everyone will be proved right about me. Imagine the re-joicing then.'

He shook his head. 'No one wants this,' he said. 'No one.'

'How do you know *I* don't want it?'

'More ridiculous riddles. You do yourself no favours, you know, with all this pushing-away of people.'

'I would certainly be doing *myself* a con-siderable favour in being rid of you and all your worthless promises and guarantees,' I said.

He threw down his knife and fork and rose from the table. 'So be it,' he said. He picked up his coat.

'Are you leaving?' I asked him. 'Do you, too, have urgent business elsewhere?'

He struggled to pull on his coat in his haste to get away from me.

'I came here out of–'

'You came here because you're no differ-ent from the rest of them,' I shouted at him. I felt the blade of the knife across my palm, uncertain of whether or not I had cut my-self.

'There is no reasoning with you,' he said, and he pushed aside his chair and left me, slamming the door behind him.

Outside, he stopped at the window and looked in at me, shaking his head at what-ever he saw standing there.

'*Satan,*' I shouted at him, pointing at him

with my knife. '*Satan.*'

The name had the desired effect and he walked swiftly away from me, still struggling with his coat as he went.

I laughed at his defeat, and went on laughing until the man who had served us returned to the room and stood looking at me where I sat.

50

During the following days I wandered in an agony and a confusion of mind far greater than anything I had before experienced. All rational thought and calm reason now seemed lost to me, and I lived in a storm of turmoil and anguish. I avoided everyone who approached me; I spoke to no one. I scarcely slept, and certainly not at night or in my bed. I neither properly dressed nor undressed, and even the scant sleep I did obtain was quickly invaded with nightmares as terrible as my waking fears.

I dreamed that Lydia and her daughters were dancing around me, laughing at my plight, pointing their fingers at me and mocking me with their laughter. Lydia shouted at me that I had been less than nothing to her, that she had only ever played at loving me.

The dancing girls repeated everything she said in a chorus of the same malicious amusement.

When I woke from this dream I screamed back at them that they were all liars, that not a single word they spoke was honest or true. But all they did then was stand and stare at me, amused more than ever by my charges.

When I stopped shouting I saw Anne and the girl who helped with the laundry standing side by side in the doorway, watching me. The girl clutched Anne's arm and asked her what they should do.

'Nothing,' Anne told her. 'He woke from a nightmare, that's all.'

I made no attempt to either answer them or compose myself. I struggled to my feet and then pushed past them and ran out of the house.

I ran across the graveyard and into the empty church, where my shouting was amplified, and where my words fractured and then returned to me as gibberish, making a clapping and swishing noise all around me like the sudden flight of panicked birds.

I ran from the door to the altar and slapped my hands hard against the wooden box until the air was filled with my drumming.

And after that I must have fainted and collapsed, for I remembered nothing until

339

someone spoke my name and tugged at my arm and I opened my eyes and saw the stone floor wide around me and felt its coldness on my cheek. My shattered spectacles lay a short distance away.

John Brown helped me to my feet and then sat with me on a pew while I composed what little remained of my senses.

'I thought a madman had come into the church,' he said. It was meant as both a reassurance and a consolation to me.

'Perhaps he did,' I told him.

'You fell,' he said. 'Anne said she thought you'd gone out on to the hills.'

'I'm tired,' I told him. I doubt if I heard half of what he was saying to me.

'No,' he said. 'You're ill. Let me help you home and to your bed, where you can be properly cared for.'

'Cared for?' I shouted at him. 'They would rather I was committed so they might be rid of me for ever. And not just them. You would *all* benefit from my removal.'

He turned away at this, and even in my agitated state I knew the great insult I had caused him, and I clasped his arm and begged for his forgiveness.

'Of course I forgive you,' he said. 'You're not in your right mind. But all this will pass. You need peace and quiet and rest, that's all. You must submit yourself to the care of others.'

I saw that he watched the door as he said all this.

'Has my father been sent for?' I asked him.

'He's waiting for Wheelhouse to come.'

'The man has never brought me a moment's ease or comfort,' I said. 'Not me, not any of us.'

'Perhaps,' he said. He took out a clean white handkerchief and wiped my mouth and forehead with it.

After that we sat together in silence, his arm around my shoulders, until the door opened and my father entered the church alone. He saw us where we sat and came to us.

'He fell,' John told him. 'That's all.'

It was the least of what had happened to me, and my father saw this, but said nothing.

He, too, sat beside me and put his arm around me as John withdrew his own.

'Is Wheelhouse not with you?' John asked him.

'He has been called elsewhere.'

John rose and stood before me. He held out his hand to me and I took it in both my own. 'He calls himself a madman,' he said to my father.

'I daresay many would concur,' my father said, and both he and I smiled at the remark and all the kindness it contained. 'But his mind is only disturbed,' he said. 'Not lost.'

'I told him as much myself,' John said. He let go of my hand, rested his own briefly on my father's shoulder, and then left us and walked slowly out of the church.

After a moment of silence, my father said, 'Anne said you were calling out in your sleep.' She would have told him much more. 'She says you frightened the girl.'

'I'm lost,' I told him. 'Everything is lost to me, everything now is beyond my reach and my understanding.'

He drew me closer to him. There was little strength in his embrace, but I felt instead the strength of his love and his concern for me; and I felt, too, his own anguish and helplessness in the face of all that now confronted him. However enfeebled he might have become by age and infirmity, his one true and lasting strength was his conviction, and it was *this* that bound him to me now and which kept the pair of us upright where we sat.

'Everything I touch I harm badly or destroy completely,' I said.

He shook his head at this. 'I shall never forsake you,' he said. 'And nor shall your sisters. And chief of all, the Lord Himself shall never for one instant forsake you or let you be hidden from His sight or His mercy. Your *true* friends will never abandon you.'

'The few that I have left,' I said. 'The few that I haven't already driven away from me.'

'Life is full of trials and tribulations,' he said. He looked at the floor ahead of us. 'Your spectacles,' he said. Neither of us made the effort to retrieve them.

'I fear I shall never recover myself,' I said to him, the words drying in my mouth. 'I fear I shall never again stand fully upright, let alone return to the path once ahead of me.'

'Oh, but you shall,' he said firmly. 'You shall. Of course you shall. Your mind has not been properly at ease these past months, but with more time everything will come right, everything will right itself, you'll see. It must. You are still a young man. You'll see.'

We sat for a further silent minute, after which he turned his face to the windows and said, 'Listen.'

I heard the screeching of the circling swifts, late to depart this year. I saw their fleeting forms where they came close to the glass against the brightness of the sky.

'People are saying they won't return next spring on account of all the felling and burning hereabouts,' my father said. 'If that's true, then I shall miss their gathering at evening.'

The swifts flew in circles around the church and the parsonage, their noise more like that of animals in distress than the birds they were. Many in the town called them the Devil's birds on account of this noise, and because their gathering like this was said to presage death, but my father refused to believe any of this. I had often seen him pause during his summer evening sermons to watch the birds on their circling flight and to listen to their calling.

'If God can waste His time watching over me,' I said, 'then He can surely guarantee the safe return of the swifts.'

'Of course He can,' he said.

He stroked my arm. I felt his head pressed harder to my cheek. With his free hand he clasped my own and made it fit into his. I felt the dryness of his skin, the fragility and weightlessness of his fingers, and I saw again what a frail vessel now contained the power and the burning, restless glory of his spirit.

He kissed my head. '*I* shall help you stand again,' he said to me. '*I* shall help you back on to your proper path.'

I felt the tears in my eyes, the sudden cold tracks over my cheeks, the salt at the corners of my mouth.

'I know,' I said to him. 'But why? Why, after all the shame and disgrace and disappointment I have brought to you?'

He did not answer me immediately. Instead, he caressed my head and held me even closer to him. All around us, the church echoed my sobbing breath, and beyond that there was only the calling of the birds.

Eventually, releasing me slightly and bringing his mouth closer to my ear, he said, 'Because you are my son and because I cherish you. Because I cherish you above all others and above all else.' And the instant the words were spoken, he raised a finger to my forehead and drew a cross there, lowering his hand to gently cover my trembling mouth and to prevent me from saying anything in reply to this.

Patrick Branwell Brontë died nine days later, on the morning of Sunday, 24 September 1848.

The previous day, bedridden and distressed, he had seized John Brown and said, 'Oh, John, I am dying. In all my past life I have done nothing either great or good.'

Branwell died in his father's arms. He was thirty-one.

Emily Brontë died on 19 December of the same year. She was thirty. Following Branwell's funeral service, she never again left Haworth Parsonage. It was widely repeated locally that she had died of grief for her lost brother.

Anne Brontë died on 28 May 1849. She was twenty-nine.

Charlotte Brontë died six years later, on 31 March 1855. She was thirty-eight.

Patrick Brontë, having survived the deaths of his wife, sister-in-law and all six of his children, died, aged eighty-four, on 7 June 1861. He had worked for forty-one years in the service of the people of Haworth.

A week after her brother's death, Charlotte wrote to her publisher, 'There is such a bitterness of pity for his life and death – such a yearning for the emptiness of his whole existence as I cannot describe – I trust time will allay these feelings.'

The publishers hope that this book has given you enjoyable reading. Large Print Books are especially designed to be as easy to see and hold as possible. If you wish a complete list of our books please ask at your local library or write directly to:

Magna Large Print Books
Magna House, Long Preston,
Skipton, North Yorkshire.
BD23 4ND

This Large Print Book, for people
who cannot read normal print,
is published under the auspices of

THE ULVERSCROFT FOUNDATION